THE ITALIAN VILLAGE IN THE HILLS

VICTORIA SPRINGFIELD

Boldwood

First published in Great Britain in 2026 by Boldwood Books Ltd.

Copyright © Victoria Springfield, 2026

Cover Design by JD Smith Design Ltd

Cover Images: Shutterstock

A CIP catalogue record for this book is available from the British Library.

Paperback ISBN 978-1-83633-652-5

Large Print ISBN 978-1-83633-653-2

Hardback ISBN 978-1-83633-651-8

Trade Paperback ISBN 978-1-80656-176-6

Ebook ISBN 978-1-83633-654-9

Kindle ISBN 978-1-83633-655-6

Audio CD ISBN 978-1-83633-646-4

MP3 CD ISBN 978-1-83633-647-1

Digital audio download ISBN 978-1-83633-648-8

This book is printed on certified sustainable paper. Boldwood Books is dedicated to putting sustainability at the heart of our business. For more information please visit https://www.boldwoodbooks.com/about-us/sustainability/

Boldwood Books Ltd, 23 Bowerdean Street, London, SW6 3TN

www.boldwoodbooks.com

To all my readers. I would not achieve anything without you.

Stella's napkin fluttered to the floor. She twisted around as far as her new dress would allow but a smiling waiter had got there first. He spread the fine linen back across her lap.

'Thank you.' She took a spoonful of her sorbet, the deep raspberry red dangerously dark against the pristine white cloth.

'Palate cleansing,' Joe said, his voice filled with a forced bonhomie. Perhaps he was regretting booking them both in for the nine-course tasting menu. Though as a self-professed gourmet he had treated her to several similarly extravagant dinners.

It wasn't the quantity of food that shocked Stella – each dish a mere tiny island marooned in a puddle of jus or stacked in a quivering tower that threatened to collapse at the first touch of a fork – it was the odd juxtaposition of ingredients that surely shouldn't be combined together. Maybe it was old-fashioned to prefer the simple fresh ingredients and bold flavours of the Ligurian dishes she'd learnt to cook at her mother's knee. She felt old-fashioned, old in fact, in here. The black lace-trimmed dress she'd thought so sophisticated and suited to her olive skin and short dark brown hair looked positively funereal against the hummingbird wallpaper and turquoise upholstery.

The two waiters hovering near the fashionable open kitchen kept looking over at her, adding to the feeling she was acting in a play. Act three: the last supper.

'Perhaps we should have booked one of those booths tucked in the corner,' Joe said.

'I'm happy here.' She smiled; it wasn't his fault their table was stuck slap bang in the middle of the room. It didn't matter anyway. She wasn't likely to see him again. Eighteen months of dating apps had taught her the signs. Tonight, something had shifted between them. Perhaps their three-month relationship had been too good to last. She'd never really imagined she'd find a life partner at the age of fifty-nine and was amazed she'd met Joe online, a man who ticked all the boxes: handsome, well mannered, own teeth and more importantly considerate and kind.

The sound of violins, something she recognised from a perfume advertisement, drifted towards her. The music was a pleasant distraction from Joe, who was now shifting awkwardly in his chair. Heads were turning towards the entrance; the other diners had lowered their voices. Joe looked to be on the verge of saying something: kindly expressed wishes for the future, a well-intentioned, never-to-be-kept promise to remain friends. The seven courses she'd sampled – she couldn't help counting down – swirled in her stomach. The modern habit of vanishing without trace – ghosting, didn't they call it? – suddenly seemed preferable to this very public goodbye.

Perhaps she should jump in first and call it a day before Joe said, 'It's not you, it's me.' But the four musicians dressed in black tie were heading straight across the travertine floor towards Stella and Joe's table, grins wide as clowns'. One stood at each corner, bows flying. Oh dear. She wished it was a single squawky accordion player who could be swiftly dispatched by the purchase of a single red rose.

The musicians withdrew to a smattering of applause. Strangely they headed back the way they'd come in, instead of making their way from table to table. Stella was about to comment on this when a waiter appeared holding two sundaes, one with a sparkler aflame. Course eight. No doubt cheese would follow.

'Madame.' The waiter set the boat-shaped dish in front of her. The squidgy pink dessert was decorated with swirly chocolate piping. It looked like writing. Merry something? She hadn't been able to fit her reading glasses in her ludicrously small evening bag. She felt Joe's eyes on her.

'Stella?' How strange his voice was. Beads of sweat bubbled on his forehead despite the near-glacial air conditioning.

'Joe, are you okay?'

For a moment she thought he was going to stand up but he sank to the floor. Stella gasped, alarmed. The restaurant chatter ceased abruptly.

Then she realised one of Joe's flannel-clad knees was resting on the hard shiny tiles. He rummaged in his jacket pocket, producing a small square box. He held it out to her.

'Stella, will you do me a great honour? Will you be my wife?'

He flicked open the box. A square-cut diamond ring flashed in the velvet cushioning.

Stella gasped. Applause rippled across the dining room.

'You do like it, don't you?'

'Yes, yes, it's beautiful, perfect.' It was rather large, but what sort of person complained that a diamond was too big?

He wiped his brow. 'Thank goodness. I'm glad I can stand up now, my knee's killing me.'

He sat back down, took her hand and slipped the ring onto her finger.

She turned her hand this way and that. It really was a huge stone.

'It fits perfectly! I can't believe you've proposed! I thought... oh, never mind. I'm just bowled over.'

'I wanted to make it special, different from the last time.'

'Yes.' She rather regretted sharing the story about Ricky's proposal with Joe. She'd been just nineteen when Ricky had pulled into a motorway service station, screeched his motorbike to a halt, ordered them a couple of plates of egg and chips and slipped the ring pull of his can of cider onto her finger. 'Fancy getting married?' he'd said with a smirk. Stella had screamed out 'Yes' and 'Yes' again! And it felt as though she'd leapt onto the back of a galloping horse – out of control, but what an adrenaline rush!

Joe was right. This proposal was different. She couldn't expect to feel that heady excitement now. Not at her age. She was different too. She wanted different things from the girl who'd married Ricky. Joe was a grownup, someone who understood the seriousness of a lifetime's commitment. This marriage was going to last.

Joe seemed to be waiting for something.

'It really is beautiful.' She smiled, looking at the ring again.

'You haven't said "yes" yet,' Joe said.

'Of course,' she said quickly. 'Of course I'll marry you.'

2

Amy secured three gold helium balloons to Grandpa Lance's wheelchair: one, zero, two. Outside the sky was pale. The wind whistled, a branch of Mum's wisteria knocked against the patio doors.

'It's a good job we're not sitting outside, I might take off.' He chortled. 'Mind you, that would be some way to go – whee-hee, up, up in the air!'

Dad laughed. Mum frowned. 'You're not going anywhere, Dad, not for a long time.'

'Doctors only gave me six months, didn't they? Thought I'd never reach a hundred never mind a hundred and two.'

'You've only reached this age 'cos you're a stubborn old so-and-so,' Mum said.

'That's true enough.' Grandpa chuckled. He twisted his neck towards the mantelpiece. 'Such a lot of cards – marvellous! And that cake, what a treat! I'm looking forward to having a slice, if I may.'

'And some tea?' Amy asked. She made to get up but Mum was already halfway to the kitchen.

'Stay here with me.' Grandpa patted the arm of the sofa. He glanced towards Mum's retreating backside and lowered his voice. 'Shall we watch that video clip again before your mum comes back?'

'I thought you'd say that.' Amy picked up the phone Lance had treated himself to on his ninety-ninth birthday. 'Come and have a look, Dad.'

'Will you press the buttons for me, love? It's a bit fiddly with the old arthritis.'

Amy quickly found the footage. A close-up of her younger brother's face, flushed and happy, flashed briefly across the camera before it cut away to show an expanse of ocean. The picture went fuzzy for a moment then back into focus. Jack was strapped into some sort of seat high up in the air, suspended beneath a red and yellow parachute. He stretched out his arm. The streamer he was unfurling flapped and twisted but there was no mistaking the message printed on it.

Happy 102nd Grandpa Lance!

Grandpa whistled. 'Parasailing, isn't that great! His best post yet. I don't know why your mother wouldn't take a look.'

'She can't stand watching Jack doing anything dangerous,' Dad said. 'And she's still a bit cross with him for not being here. She doesn't think it's right he should miss your birthday, gallivanting off round the world.'

'Nonsense! I told Jack I'd be furious if he arranged his gap-year trip around me. What my daughter doesn't understand is that our Jack is giving me one last great adventure. I'd never make it back to Vietnam or India now. It's a struggle to get down the road to the Raj Tandoori. But with Jack's videos, I almost feel like I'm there myself.' He tapped his phone screen. 'Now, let's put a pin in my map.'

Amy walked over to the bureau. She fished a red drawing pin out from the little box next to the letter rack. Grandpa gestured at the cork noticeboard on the wall behind it with a shaky hand.

'About here?' She hovered the pin just above the board.

'Hmm... Up a bit... right on the coast... perfect,' Dad said.

'We've got a lot of pins in that wallchart now, makes this lounge look like Churchill's operations room.' Grandpa chuckled.

'Churchill indeed!' Mum tutted, closing the door behind her with a push of her elbow and putting down the tea tray. 'Who's for some cake?'

'You sit down, Mum.' Amy busied herself with the china cups and saucers and proper napkins Grandpa insisted upon. Her mother picked up an envelope.

'You've still got another birthday card here, Dad.'

'Pass it over then, love, I'll take a look whilst this tea cools down a tad.'

He studied the creamy white envelope. 'This is a right old scrawl, must be from an oldie like me. Postmark looks like Fife. I only ever knew one fella from there...' Struggling to open it with his pale fingers, he reached for the cake knife and slid it under the flap. Amy smiled as her mum suppressed a tut.

'Well, I never... Marty McGlenn, how on earth did he get hold of my address?'

'You've never mentioned a Marty,' Dad said.

'He was in my regiment, a bumptious little pipsqueak. We weren't friends, but when you've been through something like that together...' Grandpa quickly turned his head towards the garden.

'He fought in the war with you?' Amy trod carefully. Other people's elderly relatives seemed to thrive on trotting out their old wartime stories. But not Grandpa. He'd been captured in Libya and somehow made it back to England. Mum was sure he'd once muttered something about escaping from a prisoner-of-war camp but Lance never spoke about it.

Grandpa nodded. 'Marty was there in the desert. Saw him on TV at the Cenotaph this year, he didn't look so good, surprised he's still with us. There're fewer and fewer of us every year. Soon no one will remember... Hard to understand for today's young people, isn't it?' He patted Amy's hand.

'I can't imagine it.'

'That's for the best, love. I was your brother's age when I joined up; I'm glad he's having a better time of it but he'll be working hard once he starts that engineering degree.'

'He knows what he wants, our Jack,' Mum said. Amy winced.

'And what about you, Amy?'

Amy stared into her tea. Surely Grandpa wasn't going to join the chorus of people nagging at her, expecting her to know what she wanted to do with the rest of her life? All her friends seemed so sure of themselves but after three years of university, Amy was none the wiser. And she suspected a degree in History of Art wasn't going to help widen her options.

'With your grades you could apply for an MA,' Mum said, as if she hadn't raised the subject many times before.

'I wasn't thinking about Amy's career, I was thinking about this summer,' Grandpa said. 'No plans to go gadding off abroad, love?'

'I thought we could throw some pots, like we did before.'

'I'm getting a bit old for that. My hands shake when I'm

trying to shape the clay,' Lance said. 'But if you want to work in my old shed, I'd like to come and help.'

'Sit and chat, you mean.' Mum grinned.

'Amy won't have too much time to play about with pottery, she needs to start looking for a proper job,' Dad said, cutting himself a second slice of cake.

'I'll have to sign up at the temp agency, I suppose.'

'Not for the summer you won't,' Lance said. 'I'd like to employ you myself.'

Amy spluttered on a mouthful of tea. 'Doing what?'

'Typing – you can do that, can't you? You're tapping on that phone of yours often enough.'

'Touché, Grandpa. What do you want me to type up?'

'My memoirs. I've made up a couple of small memory boxes. One for you, Amy, and one for Jack, mementoes to leave you when I'm gone. But recently I got to thinking, I'd rather like you to have them whilst I'm still alive. And I need you to understand the stories behind them. Otherwise, well, they're just clutter, and we've all got enough of that.'

'You can put secretarial work on your CV, no need to tell anyone you worked for your grandpa.' Mum winked.

'When can we start?'

'Tomorrow afternoon any good? When a man gets to my age he can't afford to waste time.'

Making pots in Grandpa's shed and typing up his memoirs. It was going to be a good summer. Jack could travel the world. Amy wasn't going anywhere.

3

The football slammed against the wall of the Chiesa di Sant' Agata, ricocheting back into the village square. Fernanda shook her broom angrily.

'Sinners! Kicking a ball at a church, you'll go straight to hell!'

The three young boys ran off laughing, one tossing the ball as high as he could. He jumped up to catch it, his T-shirt riding up, exposing his bare midriff. Fernanda knew the boys wouldn't dare come back until she'd gone. Although they'd smirked and giggled, she knew she scared them. Yes, she with her tiny frame who could barely reach to polish the eagle on Sant' Agata's lectern. She who was so frail her eighty-seven-year-old body creaked and groaned as she bent over her broom.

She smoothed down her shock of white hair and focused once more on the doorstep. The entrance of the church couldn't possibly get any cleaner but still she worked on, wielding the stiff bristles again and again. Back and forth, back and forth. *Father forgive me, Father forgive us all.* The tall apartment buildings, the restaurants opposite, the people enjoying their morning coffees all faded away. Nothing but Fernanda sweeping away her sins, praying for herself and her dear departed sister.

'Fernanda!' Father Filippo's voice jolted her back to reality. He peered at her through round metal-rimmed glasses, smiling kindly.

'*Buongiorno*, Father.' He was a young man, this new priest, full of fashionable ideas, peppering his sermons with modern soundbites. Words like integration and diversity. She wasn't sure she'd ever heard him mention the fires of hell without looking embarrassed. But she wasn't going to knock him, whatever brought people closer to God and turned them away from their wicked ways was a good thing.

'*Brava*, Fernanda! The step is spotless, *grazie*! But now you have done enough, lay down your broom.' He raised a hand to silence her protest. 'Even the good Lord knew the importance of rest. Please, join me for a coffee. I have something I want to talk to you about.'

'Of course.' She knew he had a penchant for the village bar's *cavolini*. Fernanda rarely allowed herself one of the fresh cream buns, but perhaps she would today. And it would be nice to sit at one of the bar's shady tables knowing that thanks to her companion, she would receive only kindly looks.

Father Filippo led the way, down the passageway beside the church. He had to slow his steps right down to match hers, giving him the effect of having geisha's shoes under his black cassock. A table on the pavement outside the bar was free. He pulled out a chair, making sure Fernanda was comfortable before he sat down.

'Nice to see you, Father,' the woman who ran the bar greeted him. She often left Fernanda sitting there for ages before she bothered to wander out, but this time she appeared almost at once and returned with their coffees and *cavolini* in record time, flashing Fernanda a half-smile and a slightly shamefaced look. The woman was only in her thirties. Her family hadn't even moved to the village until after the war, but Fernanda knew that she knew. Knew that she judged her.

Father Filippo shifted in his seat. He steadied his tiny espresso cup with the forefinger of his left hand as he brought it to his lips.

'How are the preparations for the return of the bones of the unknown soldier, Father?' Fernanda spared him the small talk.

'Not so unknown.' The priest smiled. 'The lab results are finally back.'

'It is Pietro Parodi?' Pietro had fled the village the day the German soldiers came searching for partisans and deserters. His mother and sister had always hoped he'd got away. Months and years had gone by with no letter, no contact. But the hope never went away.

'Yes, it is Pietro, poor fellow.' The priest closed his eyes for a moment, his hands clasped in silent prayer. Fernanda joined him, thinking of the young man she'd once known, reduced to bones, a bullet hole in the back of his skull. Pietro had got less than ten kilometres up the old mule tracks through the woods, his body unearthed on some farmland, buried in a shallow grave.

'Will his sister come back here for the ceremony?'

'Yes, she is the only one of the family left. And of course she will stay for the unveiling.'

'Of the new memorial? My grandson has been working ever so hard.'

'I called into Leo's workshop a few days ago. God has given him a wonderful talent.'

It was the argument that had sealed the village committee's decision, that had quietened the voices that muttered that employing a relative of Fernanda's wasn't right.

They talked of parish business for a while.

Father Filippo's hands twisted together; his Adam's apple rose up and down above his white priest's collar. She knew he was churning over how best to broach the subject of the celebrations. She'd put him out of his misery.

'I will come to the memorial service to see Pietro receive a proper Christian burial and I will make my special focaccia bread for the *festa*. But I will sit at the back of the church and slip away before the unveiling and the dancing. I cannot cope with too many people. At my age I prefer to pay my respects and admire the memorial the next day without the noise and the bother.'

The priest's face gave a peculiar twitch as he tried not to show how relieved he was. He swallowed the last bite of his *cavolino*, wiping a blob of cream from his nose.

She used the edge of the table to help lever herself up. 'Thank you for the coffee, Father. Much appreciated. *Buona giornata.*'

'*Buona giornata*, Fernanda.'

She walked home slowly, greeting everyone she passed, even the ones who replied with nothing but a curt nod. There were fewer of them nowadays; those who'd lived through the war slowly dying away. Fernanda kept her head up, meeting everyone's eyes whether they were friendly or not.

4

Joe had told Stella to come and go as she pleased but even though they'd now been engaged for three whole weeks and she was officially moving in at the end of the month, she still felt awkward just waltzing through his front door without loudly announcing her arrival.

'Hi, I'm here!' she called, dropping her bag on the hall table and walking into the kitchen. The aroma of frying onions made her stomach rumble despite the substantial prawn and avocado salad she and her best friend Carol had eaten just a few hours earlier.

Joe turned away from the range cooker.

'Hello, darling.' He kissed her gently on the lips. 'Wine? I'm cooking my signature spaghetti so I've opened some red. Here you are, you go and sit down and relax.'

She kicked off her shoes and sat on the leather couch at the far end of the kitchen-diner, arranging the overstuffed cushions behind her. A wine merchant's brochure lay on the coffee table. She'd left Joe to choose the drinks for the wedding.

Everything else for the big day was beginning to come

together. Thanks to Carol's gentle bullying, Stella had already sorted out a venue, a menu and a photographer. She'd even found her wedding outfit thanks to her daughter, Lauren, taking an unheard of day off and dragging Stella around the local boutiques. Lauren hadn't exactly been over the moon about what she considered to be her mother's all-too-hasty engagement but when it came to practical matters she was laser-focused.

The dress Stella had chosen was pale oyster, it seemed more appropriate at her age than traditional white and Lauren had promptly declared it 'The One' in a tone of voice that brooked no argument. Stella had worn a white dress to marry Ricky – a short satin number she'd plucked from a rack at the back of a second-hand shop. Ricky had worn his leathers. They'd had a quick registry office ceremony then all gone down to the local pub for sausages and mash. It hadn't been the wedding she'd imagined, growing up. She'd dreamt of the church of Sant' Agata, floor-length white lace, a bouquet of flowers gathered from the Ligurian hillside, her mother's wedding veil. And Gino. She'd even imagined the suit he would wear. Her family and his would put aside their long-held hostility. The whole village would be there, even Fernanda.

'Stella!' Joe's voice cut in. 'Our food's ready. I thought you were dropping off! Your eyes were closed.'

'Oh, sorry!' She scrambled to her feet and took a seat at the kitchen table. The pasta, as she'd suspected, was limp but Joe had tried and that was what counted. Once they were married, she'd gently take over the cooking. She'd make *mesciua* with chickpeas and grains, veal belly stuffed with vegetables and cheese and she'd chop great green bunches of basil to make bright fresh pesto the way she'd learnt back in the village. Back in the days when her mother's kitchen was still a place of energetic endeavour, warmth, joy and love.

She realised he was looking at her expectantly.

'Delicious,' she said.

'I'm glad I decided to cook tonight. I hope this wedding planning isn't tiring you out.'

She bit back a yawn. 'No, I'm glad of something to do.'

'More fun than working in a supermarket.'

Stella smiled weakly. She could hardly believe it when they'd called everyone in to announce the redundancies. They hadn't even wanted her to work her notice, that was how little they valued her.

'It's a blessing in disguise, you know.' He patted her hand. The weighty diamond ring glittered under the kitchen spotlights. It *had* looked a little out of place with her nylon uniform, but she'd enjoyed working on the till at Save Mart, a fact that mystified Joe, who'd been dropping heavy hints for weeks about cutting her hours.

'I'll look for another job,' Stella said firmly. 'Just as soon as I've finished this wedding admin. Every time I cross something off the list Carol or Lauren think of something else I need to do.'

'Perhaps I should have whisked you off to Gretna Green.'

'You could whisk me off anywhere.' She took a welcome break from the spaghetti to squeeze his hand.

'Funny you should say that...'

'Why? Have you booked the honeymoon already?' They'd talked about the Maldives, Portugal, even a safari.

'I'll tell you – show you – after we've finished.' He mopped up the remains of his pasta sauce with a small piece of bread. Conscious her bowl was still half full, Stella chomped through the rest, glad she had a couple of Rennies in her handbag.

He swivelled round and took an envelope from the drawer behind him. She recognised the logo of the high street travel agent at once.

'Open it.' He smiled.

She scanned the printed itinerary. So, he had booked their honeymoon.

'Two weeks in the south of France? How lovely.'

'Look more closely.'

'But that's in less than a week!' Her voice came out in a squeak. Had he changed the date of the wedding without even asking her? Carol would be furious; she'd booked the two of them in a for a whole raft of hard-to-get hair and beauty appointments.

'This isn't our honeymoon, you daft thing. It's for your birthday. You didn't really expect us to celebrate your sixtieth down the local Chinese like I said we would? Take a look at the hotel.' He held out his phone.

She expanded the screen: an exclusive-looking yellow villa with bottle-green shutters perched on a cliff; a terracotta tiled roof; vivid pink bougainvillea cascading down one wall; small tables lit by lanterns on a long terrace. An infinity pool. Absolutely dreamy. It certainly beat the shiny wallpaper and slightly limp pot plants at the Yin Court. And a celebratory meal locally hadn't seemed quite so special once Lauren had cried off to go to some super-important conference in the States.

'It looks like Italy.'

'Portofino.'

'Portofino, of course! I recognise the harbour now.' She'd seen pictures of the exclusive Ligurian resort, but never visited. Never been back to Italy, save for Florence and Rome, since she'd left. 'But surely it's easier to fly into Genoa than Nice.'

'It's not a one-destination holiday. We're going somewhere else first.' Joe grasped her hands in his. His eyes were shining.

'Where?' Stella tried to push down the feeling of dread. She extricated her hand and took another, very large, mouthful of wine.

'I told the woman in the travel agent's the name of the little village you came from but she said there weren't any hotels there.'

Stella let out a breath. No Airbnbs either, she hoped.

'She told me San Remo was the nearest big town and when she showed me the pictures of the palm trees on the seafront I couldn't resist booking us in for a few nights. I know you've probably been there a million times but I hope you'll indulge me.'

'But why do you want to go there?'

He didn't seem to notice the tremble in her voice.

'I want to see the area where you grew up. I want to know everything I can about my soon-to-be wonderful wife. I want to share everything with you. Our present, our future and our past.'

Stella swallowed. She knew she should be honest with the man she was marrying. But she couldn't bear to share her shame.

'The past's been and gone,' she said as breezily as she could muster. 'It's our future together that matters.'

5

'Hi, Mum!' Amy dashed up the front steps, almost tripping over the Home Sweet Home doormat. She set down two shopping bags. 'Sorry I was so long, I thought I'd be back at least an hour ago. The Everglades was mobbed and I couldn't get a parking place. Then I bumped into Rhianna from school and we went for a coffee. Where's Grandpa? Is he in his shed? I'll go and get my laptop when I've put this stuff away. I can't wait to get started.'

'Amy...' Mum's voice was strange as though coming from a faraway place.

'What is it? What's happened?'

Tears welled in Mum's eyes. Dad emerged from the door to the garage and came and stood behind Mum, one hand on her shoulder.

'I'm so sorry, Amy. Grandpa's gone.'

'But he can't have. You're wrong, it's not true!' Amy almost shouted.

'Oh, love, I know it's a shock, but you know how ill he's been.' Dad wrapped his arms around her. She buried her face in his shirt, breathing in that familiar Dad scent of ferny after-shave, fabric conditioner and cigarettes.

Amy untangled herself. 'But he was fine last night. He was talking about... about us going in the shed and his memoirs and...'

'The doctors never thought he'd last so long. No one expected him to make it past his hundredth,' Dad said. 'Sorry... that came out a bit blunter than I meant it to.'

'He was determined to hold your cousin Martha's baby. It was almost as though becoming a great-grandfather was the goal he was holding on for after your grandma had gone. And after that...' Mum's voice tailed off.

'When did it happen? Why didn't you call me? I would have come back straight away.'

'I couldn't tell you over the phone and it made no sense knowing you'd be home soon enough,' Mum said. 'Come on in, I'll make some tea. We can't just stand around in the hallway.'

Amy trailed after her. She didn't want tea. She didn't want anything except to go back in time. She should have been here. She should have taken Grandpa his morning coffee in bed. He might still have been alive. She might have heard his voice one last time, spent precious moments with him. Instead, she'd been sitting in some soulless shopping centre café cooing over Rhianna's rainbow-coloured bikinis as she swiped through her school friend's holiday snaps.

Mum switched on the kettle. She took out a carton of milk and gave it a sniff. Dad opened and closed cupboard doors as though he'd forgotten where the mugs lived.

'Can I see him?' Amy started for the stairs without waiting for an answer.

'Are you sure?' Dad called out but he didn't go after her.

Amy pushed open the door. Lance was dressed in his usual

striped pyjamas, his head back against the pillow. She crept in quietly as though he might be disturbed and stood by the head of the bed instead of perching on the quilt as she normally did. The window was open. Down on the patio, clothes were pegged out on the rotating dryer. The sun was out. It wasn't a day for dying. Maybe he was just sleeping, maybe it wasn't true. She reached out to touch him.

'Grandpa?' His cheek was cool. She snatched back her hand.

A floorboard creaked. Dad crossed the room.

'Oh, Amy!' He smoothed down her hair and kissed her on the forehead the way he'd done when she was little.

'He was the best grandpa in the world.' Amy gulped. 'I was going to write up his memoirs, what he did when he was young, what he did in the war. And now it's too late. I wish I'd asked him about it before. Why didn't I?'

'I suppose it was hard to imagine he wouldn't be around forever,' Dad said. 'Did you see that box sitting on the bedside table? Grandpa made it for you himself.'

She traced her finger over the letters AMY carved into the wooden lid. 'This must be what he was talking about yesterday.' She picked it up. It was lighter than she expected.

'Bring it downstairs and open it.'

'Do you think I ought to?'

'Wasn't that what Grandpa wanted to do today?'

'Not like this... Not without him. It's not fair.'

'It's not fair, love, that it isn't... now let's go down and sit with your mum. That tea will be stewed to the colour of gravy if it's left much longer.'

She followed him down the stairs. Mum was in the living room. She'd poured out the tea.

'Grandpa put this tin of Ceylon Blend in my stocking a few

years ago. I never opened it. It seemed such a bother when it's so easy to chuck in a teabag. Stupid, isn't it?' Mum took a sip. 'It's well gone past the use-by date, but it still tastes so much nicer than the supermarket stuff. Wish I could tell him.'

'Amy's brought down that memory box, Eileen.'

'I found it this morning fallen on the floor by his slippers. He must have been looking at it before he nodded off last night. I wonder what he kept for you and your brother.'

'Oh!' Amy clamped her hand to her mouth. 'What about Jack? Have you told him?'

'We haven't got hold of him yet,' Mum said. 'New Zealand's hours ahead of us. He's probably out in some noisy bar somewhere.'

'He'll be gutted. And he'll be so upset he wasn't here yesterday.'

'What's done is done. I don't want him brooding on that.' Dad picked up the box of drawing pins and gave it a rattle. 'Our Jack's trip was Lance's last adventure. I'll remind your brother of that.'

'Sit down, Amy, love. Drink your tea, then you can open that box,' Mum said.

Amy balanced the box on the arm of the sofa and sat on the end sipping her tea. She wanted to open her gift from Grandpa alone, in the shed. The place where he'd taught her how to shape her first pot from wet clay, where she'd daubed their creations with a paintbrush in her six-year-old hands.

Dad's eyes shifted towards where Mum sat staring vacantly at Lance's wallchart.

Amy took the hint. She opened the box's hinged lid. Lying on top of a black and white postcard was a coin she didn't recognise strung on a leather thong. 'This is foreign, but it's not a euro.'

'Let's see.' Dad took it from her. 'A one-lira piece – it's Italian, the currency they used before Italy joined the EU. That's Vittorio Emanuele, their old king, on the back. And on the front, this eagle is a fascist symbol, this must be from Mussolini's day. What else is in the box – a couple of postcards?'

Amy took the coin necklace from her dad and laid it on her lap, one hand playing with the leather cord. She studied the first postcard: a long expanse of beach, a small stone chapel, swifts circling overhead. She passed it to her mum. 'Look, do you recognise it?'

'Oh, yes. This is Alassio, on the Italian Riviera in Liguria; that's the seafarers' chapel at the end of the seafront. It's where Grandpa grew up. His dad, your great-grandfather, was advised by his doctor to move to a warmer climate for the sake of his health. It was quite a fashionable thing for the English to do, back in those days.'

Amy held out the second postcard, cracked with deep fold marks as though someone had kept it in their pocket. 'This one's a little village.' The place looked like something out of a fairytale, all tiled roofs and a clocktower nestled higgledy-piggledy amongst olive groves and dark wooded hills.

Mum frowned. 'I don't recognise this but I suppose this could be Liguria too. I don't think the family travelled around all that much. I expect it says where it is on the back.' She turned it over. 'Oh, there's a message! Something in Italian, I think... it's not your grandpa's writing. I'll need my reading glasses.'

'Let me see.' Dad took the card before Amy could. 'It is in Italian but I know what it means.'

'What?' Amy longed to snatch it back.

'*Baci e abbracci dall' Italia*. It means kisses and hugs from Italy – it's their equivalent of saying "love from Italy".'

'But who's it from?' Mum, now with her glasses on, peered over Dad's shoulder.

'It doesn't say. And the name of the place was printed in the top corner but someone's struck through it with a thick black pen.'

'Must be somewhere Lance visited as a boy.'

'Love from Italy – do you think these things were from a girl? Maybe a teenage sweetheart?' Amy said.

Dad took the necklace back from her. He ran his thumb along the coin's reeded edge. 'There's something etched into the back. Hard to tell what it is. A letter C or J perhaps but it's a love token for sure. I've seen these before made from an old farthing.'

'That's so sweet,' Amy said.

'First love.' Mum sighed.

An odd look passed over Dad's face. He screwed up his eyes to study the coin more closely. 'What year did your dad's family come back to England, Eileen?'

'Sometime before the war. A lot of English families moved back here in the thirties. Must have been 1937. No, I remember, now, he told me it was 1938, he would have been around sixteen. These keepsakes must have been of some girl he'd left behind.'

'I don't think they can be. This coin wasn't minted until 1941. At least two or three years after they left Italy.'

He handed Amy the necklace back; the metal was warm. 'I suppose he could have found that old lira coin in a flea market over here and made this anytime.'

Mum chewed the edge of her finger. 'That doesn't explain that old postcard of the village or why he kept these things for you. But I can tell you one thing: I never saw your grandma wear that coin around her neck.'

6

The train was pulling into an underground station. The sign on the platform spelt out Sanremo, all in one word, the Italian way, but Stella didn't recognise it at all. She remembered the train tracks running along the coast, a station painted pink, a view of the sea.

Joe helped bump her suitcase down onto the platform. They followed a crowd of travellers to the start of a moving walkway.

'This is so strange; it looks so different.'

'They moved the station inland years ago. Didn't you realise?'

'I had no idea.' There was no reason why she'd keep up with the news from Liguria. She hadn't set foot in the place for more than forty years. She hadn't even gone back for Mamma's funeral. She'd only been twenty-one when she'd heard the news. And she knew she wouldn't be welcome. Why would the mother who hadn't wanted to see her in this world want her hanging around like a spectre as she made her way to the next?

And Stella could not face the stares and whispers, the judgement of the villagers. She couldn't bear the accusing looks on her brother and sister's faces and to hear them spell out loud what a terrible thing she had done.

'Watch your feet!' Joe grabbed both suitcases. The travelator was coming to the end and there was another ahead of them. At last, they stepped into the ticket hall. Outside, a line of taxis stood waiting.

'I'd like to walk,' Stella said. She needed the fresh air, the chance to focus on her surroundings, not the thoughts in her head.

'If you're sure... It's not far to the hotel but you seemed a bit tired on the journey.'

'I'm fine. I think I recognise this street.'

'I guess you must have been here a hundred times.'

'Hardly ever.'

'But your family lived just a few miles away. You can't have spent all your time in your village when you were a teenager. There wouldn't have been much to do.'

'I don't know about that. There was always something going on: a visiting theatre company, a dance in the village square. And every village around has its own food festival. The snail festival was one of the best.'

'You're not serious!'

'Deadly. Food is almost a religion here. And of course we had the saints' days, the parades and the village band. Anyway, my parents didn't like me and my brother and sister to get the bus down to the coast. I guess they felt there were too many temptations.'

'Makes it sound like you grew up in the 1950s, not the eighties!'

'That's the way it was.' Sanremo with its nightlife, its tourists and its fancy shops had only been a bus ride away but for her family it was as foreign as Madrid or Berlin. Or the moon. But she knew it would sound ridiculous if she tried to explain.

'No wonder you upped and left. You must have been longing to stretch your wings.'

'Isn't that the Tourist Office over there?' Stella said quickly. 'We could do with a proper map.'

They picked up a few leaflets and a city plan with all the sights numbered and colour coded. She hadn't wanted or needed to soak up any culture when she and Gino had roared into town. They hadn't needed to visit this or that or eat fancy meals. They had been happy just to be together, to escape their families for a while.

Joe wheeled both cases past the great church of Santa Maria degli Angeli, palest green decorated with white stucco trim like icing on a wedding cake. The colour and style were typical of the big churches in this part of Liguria but the wide tree-lined street that led to the hotel felt more like Paris. Couples strolled past hand in hand; waiters attended tables and chairs arranged under glass canopies. Snatches of conversation reached her: English, Italian, German, none of the Ligurian dialect of home. She could breathe more easily.

They entered another wide street, this one pedestrianised, lined with upmarket clothing stores.

'We'll come shopping tomorrow morning. I'll treat you to a couple of outfits,' Joe said.

She was on the verge of protesting; Joe had spent more than enough money on her and she really didn't need any more clothes but the shopping street was a safe place. Within the air-conditioned branches of Marella and Luisa Spagnoli she could pretend she was in Florence or Milan. Anywhere but here.

'Yes, that would be lovely... thank you. It's so kind of you. I really am lucky.'

'It's only what you deserve,' Joe said.

She bit down on her lip. It wasn't true. She didn't deserve to be happy after what she'd done.

* * *

Amy started packing the uneaten sandwiches into a Tupperware box. Jack wasn't much help, hovering around picking things up and putting them down again with one newly tattooed hand, the other still clutching the poem he'd read. He'd shot up in the nine months he'd been away, the hems on his grey suit trousers now hovering around his ankle bones. The little brother who'd once followed her around like a puppy was all grown up. In a few months, he'd be starting university. Grandpa would have been so proud to wave him off but now he'd never see the man Jack would become. He'd never see Jack graduate or what Amy did with her life. All their family celebrations, their milestones, their triumphs and their tears would take place without him. Grandpa would never meet his great-grandchildren; he wouldn't be sitting in the front pew when Amy's dad walked her down the aisle.

Dad closed the last of the church hall's blinds. 'That was a good turnout, considering.'

'I'm glad they've all gone. I couldn't listen to another person making excuses for not coming to see him when he was still alive,' Mum said. She cast a last look around to make sure nothing was left behind.

'Grandpa said it didn't matter that I missed his birthday, we were going to celebrate later on.' Jack's voice cracked. 'But that was just talk. I should have come back.'

'I didn't mean you, love. He was proud of you, saving up and going on your adventures,' Mum said, holding the door open for Dad, who was laden down with the leftovers.

'You all heard the vicar. When Grandpa was about my age he was fighting in the desert. He was captured in Libya, made a prisoner of war. What've I been doing? Backpacking on the gap-year trail with a load of trust-fund kids. I'm supposed to be flying back out on Monday, but it all seems so pointless.'

Amy thought of the wallchart, the half-used box of red drawing pins. 'You've got to finish your trip; Grandpa would want you to.'

'I don't know...'

'Amy's right,' Mum said.

'He left you his Africa Star medal,' Dad said, as if that somehow settled the matter. He locked up the hall, posted the keys back through the letterbox.

'Maybe Amy should take my place. How about flying off to Costa Rica? You could go rafting down the Tarcoles River dodging crocodiles.' Jack grinned.

Amy tried to laugh. She didn't want to think about what she was going to do next. She kicked at a small stone on the church path. It landed on the verge amidst a scattering of damp confetti. Christenings, weddings, funerals: life would go on but it didn't feel right.

'Amy hasn't decided what to do yet,' Mum said.

'I'll be signing up at the temp agency, I suppose.' She touched the coin necklace nestled beneath her dress.

'Why not just go to Italy?' Jack said. 'Grandpa can't tell you stories about where he grew up but that doesn't stop you going there.'

'By myself?'

'The Italian riviera is very safe. Alassio is a seaside resort,' Mum said.

'It could still be dangerous.' Jack smirked. 'Amy might get blinded by a spray of sand in her eyes or choke on a giant ice-cream.'

She gave him a punch on the arm. 'Very funny!'

'So, what about it, Amy?' Dad said, putting down a cool box and pointing his key fob at the car door. 'Your brother's idea isn't so bad. You can take a few weeks out before you come back and look for a job. I know Lance will have left you a little sum of money and Mum and I can sub you the airfare until probate's settled, can't we, Eileen?'

'Of course we will. It will do you good, love. I don't like to think of you stuck in a call centre or some such all day when you're already feeling down.'

'I dunno,' Amy said. She climbed in the back seat. They drove the short route home in silence. Amy studied the Order of Service even though she knew the hymns and readings off by heart. Mum had chosen a beautiful picture of Grandma and Grandpa's wedding for the back page, Grandpa with a tie pin and a carnation in his buttonhole, Grandma in a homemade two-piece. On the front, a smiling Grandpa sat in a striped deckchair on last year's daytrip to Brighton Beach. Grandpa had bought them all ice-creams; Amy had tried paddle-boarding and waved at him from the sea. Photographs and memories – that was all she had left of him.

Mum unlocked the front door. Amy left Dad and Jack unpacking the boot. She walked into the open-plan living-dining room. Beyond the glass sliding doors, the little robin

Grandpa loved to talk to sat expectantly on the branch of the apple tree. The shed stood empty. She and Grandpa would never sit there working on his memoirs. But Jack was right. Amy didn't just have memories and photographs. She still had the story Grandpa had planned to tell. A story that started in Italy.

7

The piazza was surrounded by bars and restaurants, the table where Stella and Joe sat shaded by a great palm tree. To one side stood a fine dove-grey building, its façade enlivened by trompe l'oeil shutters and balconies. Behind Joe's head, swifts circled the old cathedral's campanile. They'd been shopping all morning but now, having dropped their bags at the hotel, Stella was glad to stop for lunch. She breathed in the scent from the pot of basil that helped weigh down the cheerful red and white tablecloth.

Joe looked quizzically at a cube of potato. 'Strange thing to put in pasta.'

'Pesto, potato and green beans – it's the quintessential Ligurian recipe,' Stella said.

She unwrapped the paper napkin from her fork and dug into her trofie, each twisted strand of pasta coated in vivid green pesto, each mouthful a fresh new grassy, tangy hit, making her tastebuds sing with pleasure. For a moment she was transported back in time: her mamma, papà, brother and sister crammed around the table in their tiny kitchen, falling on their food like they hadn't eaten for a week. Lunch back then, even on weekdays, was a long, drawn-out affair. The church bells chiming twelve brought all work in the surrounding vineyards and olive groves to a standstill. The streets stayed silent for hours save for a splash of rain or a mew of a stray cat. Everyone stayed indoors to eat and then to rest during the hottest part of the day. It was so different here. Many of the boutiques closed for a few hours but Sanremo was still buzzing, accommodating its tourists and their eccentric, non-Italian ways.

The couple on the next table were finishing off their lunch with a cappuccino. At half past twelve! If they'd asked for that in the village bar, old Signora Dossetti would have flat-out refused to serve them – and given them a lecture on the dangers of too much milk in the stomach. Stella couldn't help smiling to herself. Not all her memories of the village were bad ones. But she couldn't afford to think that way. She'd cut all ties. She was as much of a tourist now as Joe. She studied his kind, handsome face as he finished off his pasta. He was her future.

The waiter removed the basket of bread and cleared their dishes away. Joe asked for the bill.

'Where shall we go after this?' she asked briskly.

Joe spread the map from the Tourist Information in the space where their bowls had been. 'The old town, if you'd like.'

'It's known as La Pigna, meaning pinecone, because of the layout of the streets.'

Joe paid the bill and stood up, slipping his wallet into his back pocket. He took her by the hand. 'The pinecone it is! I'm looking forward to this.'

'Same here.' It would keep them far away from the seafront

where she and Gino had lain in each other's arms. Before her world ended.

As soon as they left the lively piazza behind, Stella knew she'd made a mistake. The rough stone walls of the passageway that led them away, the lantern above her head, the feel of the cobblestones rolling beneath the thin soles of her sandals – she was back in the world of her childhood, all crumbling archways, narrow *caruggi* and little shrines to the Virgin Mother.

They emerged into the Piazza San Siro. Church bells were tolling; a couple of strutting pigeons flew away at their approach. *Concentrate on the little details, Stella.*

'This is so charming.' She pointed to a donkey flanked by two palm trees carved into the soft stone above the cathedral's latticed wooden doors. Across the piazza, sun glowed on the yellow façade of the Battistero di San Giovanni.

'It feels like we've stepped back in time,' Joe said.

'Mmm,' Stella murmured. She fixed her eyes on the piazza's third, smallest, church, studying the concentric half-circles of yellow, black, green and navy glass on the high window. Below, asymmetrical steps led up to the church door. In front of those, an ancient marble drinking trough stood supported by four stone lions, their faces worn smooth. More water drizzled into the trough from a lion's head spout.

'We could walk up to the Regina Elena park,' she suggested.

Joe consulted the map. 'I think we need to go that way.' He set off down a side street. Stella followed, content to let him take charge, her head too full of memories to concentrate on directions.

He led her across a road to where a sign told them they'd reached the Porta Montà, one of the town's old gates. They set off up the sloping street. She'd forgotten how it felt to be always climbing upwards and downwards, passing through archways, taking narrow passageways, walking on stone steps bowed from the tread of ten thousand feet. Joe was quiet, his face rather red from the unaccustomed exertion.

Post-lunch sounds emanated from behind lace curtains: televisions humming, the clatter of washing up. They walked on past parked mopeds, pots of pink hydrangeas and yellow houses.

Arriving at a small square at the base of the park, Joe stopped to read an information board. Stella didn't usually bother to look at them but this time she waited patiently, glad of a rest before they continued their uphill climb. A black and white photograph on the board showed the view before them as it had once appeared. A large apartment block was quite unchanged, the other building in the photograph was no longer there, it must have been demolished.

'It says that was once the site of the Villa Åberg, used as the headquarters of the Gestapo, but weren't the Italians on the Allies' side by the end of the war?' Joe frowned.

'Mussolini was toppled in July 1943, the armistice with Britain and the Allies was a few weeks later,' Stella remembered from school. 'But the Germans weren't happy about losing their ally. They parachuted in, plucked Mussolini from his prison in the mountains and set up a puppet regime, the Salò Republic on Lake Garda. Northern Italy was basically controlled by the Germans until the end of the war.'

'I didn't know that. I remember learning about Vichy France and the French resistance at school but hardly anything about Italy.'

'In France the story was simpler. Apart from those who collaborated with the Nazis, people were on the same side. But here things were... complicated. Mussolini had been in power since 1922. Many people still supported him, they felt betrayed when the new government surrendered. Some people wanted to keep fighting, others couldn't understand why Italy had gone to war in the first place. Many soldiers hid out in the mountains and countryside to fight the new fascist threat. The North descended into a kind of civil war.'

'Thank goodness that's all in the past,' Joe said.

'But not forgotten.' She thought of the stone obelisk commemorating the villagers shot in cold blood where her mamma and papà laid flowers every year.

'Hey!' Joe chucked her under the chin. 'Don't look so glum. Shall we carry on to the top of the park and up to the Sanctuary?'

'Yes, let's do that.' She'd been there once on a school outing. Even as a typical bored teenager she'd been impressed.

They climbed up and up but it was worth the strain in her legs. The Sanctuary of Madonna della Costa was even more beautiful than she remembered it: a vast pale Wedgwood blue and vanilla church set against the cloudless sky, crowned by a great central dome and a smaller one at each corner turned green with age.

Joe stopped to take a selfie, his arm around her.

'I'll send that to Lauren,' Stella said. Her daughter was probably in some high-powered meeting right now, silencing some chap in a suit with a withering look.

Stella crossed the petal-patterned pebble mosaic paving, past plinths topped with white marble cherubs. After a look inside, gasping at the frescoed ceiling, the twisted marble pillars and sheer sensory overload of colour and statuary, they reversed their climb, resting for a while on a bench by a small glass-fronted shrine to the Virgin Mary set into the rough stone wall. Stella had started to notice the signs of devotion every-where and each time, an image of Fernanda, Gino's mother, came unbidden: a tiny ancient woman wielding a broom on the church steps. Of course, Fernanda couldn't have been all that old back then, no more than mid-forties, but her stern countenance made her seem as old as the stones she swept.

'Are you okay to carry on?' Joe said.

Stella stood up, creaking slightly. Perhaps Carol was right to nag her to join the yoga class at the Leisure Centre. She'd be fit for nothing when they got back to the hotel except for lounging by the pool. She wasn't too sure of the way back but she soon recognised a particularly vibrant display of geraniums by someone's front door. And as long as they kept walking downwards, they'd reach the main town for sure.

Joe strode under an archway, past a small café with tables around a fountain with a bull's head through a small courtyard where washing hung across the balconies and down more steps. Somehow, they ended up on a piazza directly opposite the place where they'd had lunch.

'I don't know how we got here,' Joe admitted.

'But we're here, that's what counts.' Stella smiled.

'Here together.' He pecked her on the lips. 'Shall we stop at the gelateria with the big blue cone? It's on the way to the hotel.'

Stella considered. She was already having trouble doing up the zips on some of the slightly too tight dresses Joe had bought her. But she *was* on holiday. 'Yes, that's a nice idea. We're not having dinner until half-eight.'

'I think you'll like the restaurant.'

'I'm sure I will. Shall we go to the casino afterwards? It's such a beautiful, famous building, I've always wanted to see inside.'

Joe turned to her, his brow troubled. 'I didn't know you were a gambler.'

Stella laughed. 'We don't have to have a bet – and anyway I don't think a few spins of a one-armed bandit will corrupt us.' An image of Fernanda waggling her finger entered Stella's head. In Gino's mamma's eyes the casino was akin to Sodom and Gomorrah, a sinful den of bright lights. Fernanda didn't even like to see Gino play cards with his mates like all the other kids – and men – in the village did.

'Not for me.' Joe shook his head.

Stella felt a sudden stir of something. Daring? Rebellion? That was daft, Joe would never stop her doing anything. 'Come on, just one go on the roulette. It will be fun. We might even win!'

'You don't want to set off down that rocky road.' Joe's laugh seemed a bit forced. 'I don't think it's a good idea, Stella. I don't want you to do something you'd regret.'

'I guess you're right, I'd probably just lose my money.'

She pushed aside the uneasy feeling. Joe was just being responsible. And that was a good thing. She didn't want another reckless husband like Ricky.

There'd been too many nights when Stella had woken up to find her ex-husband's side of the bed empty. She'd find him passed out on the sofa more often than not. She didn't know how she'd put up with it all: caring for Lauren; sorting out Ricky's debts; the lonely nights listening to the click, click, click of his cigarette lighter as he crumbled a lump of hash, the sweet grassy smoke wafting up the stairs.

They set off towards the gelateria, Joe holding her hand. The pedestrianised area was quiet save for a large family group jostling to take multiple photographs by the bronze statue of Mike Bongiorno, arm raised in his familiar pose.

'Who's Mike Bongiorno? They seem very excited,' Joe said.

'He organised the Sanremo festival and hosted family game

shows. When I was a kid he was one of the most recognisable people on TV. They called him The Quiz King.'

Mamma and Papà had been huge fans. The whole family had gathered around their small portable set, never missing an episode of *I Sogni nel Cassetto* – the dreams you put away in a drawer. Stella hadn't put her dreams in a drawer. She'd buried them far deeper than that.

8

Amy stepped out of the train station, struck at once by the aura of tranquillity. Alassio bore no resemblance to Rome, the only Italian city she'd previously visited, where the ghosts of ancient civilisation, the tourists of the world, the power of the Catholic church and the glamour of Italian high society clashed in an intoxicating mix. Here, fine buildings and tall palm trees created a feeling of elegance; not a scrap of litter swirled along the well-kept street. She could almost imagine Grandpa Lance, who never considered himself dressed without a shirt and tie, walking along this same pavement. She took another swig from her trusty water bottle. It was daft to feel so nervous. Her brother Jack would be in Central America by now, probably dangling from a high wire somewhere. She was only a two-hour flight from home, negotiating a wheelie case down a pedestrianised road past handbag shops, art galleries and houses of yellow and terracotta.

The concierge at Amy's small hotel was welcoming, allowing her to stow her case until she could officially check in.

She walked back into the sunshine, her red suede bag dangling from her shoulder, clutching her new fold-out city map. The hotel's location was marked by a big green arrow but she was at a loss as to where to begin. She'd been nursing some fanciful idea that once she arrived in Alassio, Grandpa Lance's spirit would somehow guide her. Had she expected him to float past on a fluffy cloud, pointing the way with his walking stick? She'd be waiting a long time for that; the sky was an unbroken blue, vivid as a kingfisher.

She unfolded the map: the famous *muretto* with its hundreds of ceramic tiles; the oratorio of Santa Caterina d'Alessandria; the sixteenth-century watchtower: where would young Lance have spent his time? She decided to start with the sea. The beach at Alassio was known to be the best in the region, more than two miles of golden sand. Grandpa must have walked there a hundred times and with the curve of the coast as her guide she couldn't get lost. She headed for the front.

The walk along the promenade didn't disappoint, the sea a vibrant turquoise, the water so clear she could see through to the rocks below. But after a while her view was blocked, obscured by the bars and changing facilities of the rival beach clubs whose hundreds of colourful umbrellas and loungers were arrayed along the shore with military precision.

She passed a set of ride-on animals: a dolphin, an orange fish, an unlikely bear. A small boy with a huge grin grasped the neck of a big blue whale. The animals looked like a long-loved fixture but they certainly weren't pre-war. She tried to imagine Grandpa as a skinny boy in knee-length shorts and a Fair Isle tank top with some 1930s toy – a spinning hoop perhaps – walking along this same seafront holding his mother's hand. If only she could feel him here, it might help her cope with her loss. But at least in Italy she wasn't surrounded by well-meaning people telling her Grandpa had had a good innings, that instead of feeling bereft she should be moving on with her life, as if grief had an in-built expiry date she'd failed to observe. Of course, nobody actually said that out loud, but the unspoken words hovered behind their nervous smiles and hasty changes of subject.

Amy kept on walking, the sun warming her bare shoulders. The beach clubs petered out as she approached the outer reaches of the town. Beyond the high wall to her left she glimpsed the top floors of elegant villas, soaring palm trees, a cascade of purple bougainvillea spilling over a wall.

The road widened; holidaying couples wobbled along the adjacent cycle path. Ahead of her stood the little seafarers' chapel her mum had recognised on the memory box postcard. The old stone structure sat on a high platform overlooking the sea covered by a shady roof positioned to take in the views from each of its open sides. Below the promontory the cliff fell away. A group of teenage boys sprawled across the rocks, their smooth torsos brown as conkers.

There weren't many steps but Amy felt each one, the back of her newly purchased leather sandals rubbing against her heels. Thumping beats from some portable sound system accompanied her as she climbed. As she took the final step, a swift flitted inches from her ear, causing her to stumble and almost face plant the floor.

Another swift flew above her head through one open side of the chapel and out the other, launching itself into the blue. Another came, then another, perhaps a dozen flitting past, screeching. Nothing like the silence she'd expected. But when she looked out over the sea to the tiny snail-shaped island of Gallinara she felt strangely calm.

The board she'd seen near the entrance told her the chapel had been there since 1929.

'Did you ever come here, Grandpa?' Amy said.

But no answer came. Just the pounding boom, boom, bass from the boys down on the rocks.

9

The day was already warm, sun glittering on the surface of the swimming pool. Stella toyed with a slice of watermelon. The morning would be perfect if only her brain didn't have the annoying habit of releasing memories she'd kept tidied away. Walking along the seafront with Joe brought back memories of lying on the sand with Gino. And passing the flower-bedecked roundabout where the fountain spurted up jets of water above the letters that spelled out SANREMO, it was impossible not to relive the thrill teenage Stella had felt when Gino rode his moped around it three times as if it would prove they were really there.

'Enough breakfast, Stella?'

'Yes... Of course.' She quickly drained her orange juice.

In the lift, Joe was silent, a strange smile on his face. Stella swiped her key card and opened the door. The place looked so tidy she thought the cleaners had already been in until she noticed the rumpled bedsheet. Her suitcase lay on top of the covers. Then she noticed Joe's own case standing on end by the wardrobe, its pull-along handle up, ready to wheel away.

'Surprise!' Joe said.

'We're leaving? But we're not due in Portofino until tomorrow.'

'That's right, but we're going somewhere else first. Go and brush your teeth then I'll tell you.' His grin was maddening.

She stepped quickly into the bathroom, wanting more than anything to be alone for a few minutes. She knew just where they were heading without him saying a word: Leto, the place where she'd spent her childhood. Of course, he'd think it a marvellous, nostalgic treat. He wasn't to know.

She cleaned her teeth half-heartedly. Her eyes looked back at her from the mirror above the basin. She hoped they wouldn't betray her. She inhaled deeply, stepped out of the bathroom, a happy smile pinned to her face.

'So, where are we going?' She held her breath, praying she'd got it wrong, that he'd chosen pretty Apricale, or Dolceacqua where they could see the bridge that Monet painted.

'Your old village. The travel agent did wonders – she's come up with a one-night stay in an apartment right on the main square. The hotel reception has arranged us a taxi at ten. I'm so excited to see where you grew up.'

'We'll be the talk of the village turning up in a taxi instead of taking the bus!' She was conscious of her false, bright voice. A taxi was the last thing people would be talking about.

* * *

The taxi negotiated another hairpin bend. Beside her, Joe took a sharp intake of breath. Stella had warned him not to look down to where the hillside fell away but the sparkling sea below was hard to resist.

Anxiety knotted her gut. *It's only twenty-four hours, Stella, you can do this.* She focused on the back of the driver's neck, the dark hairs sprouting there. She put her hand to her forehead; the strong artificial, fruity scent coming from the air freshener, shaped like a bunch of cherries hanging from the driver's mirror made her feel nauseous. A fluffy pompom, like the one that dangled from Carol's designer bag, swung back and forth, knocking against a hologram of a cathedral, Milan's, she thought.

They were passing through another village now, past a bar spilling onto the narrow pavement. The driver stopped to allow a woman with a pram to cross. Outside a general store, an elderly lady grimly clutching the arm of a young girl was examining a stand with rolls of patterned oilcloth. The windows were crammed: scales, crockery, pans and clocks, just like the shop Papà and Uncle Domenico had run. Her family's shop was probably long gone. Neither Stella's brother or sister had remained in the village and Domenico's only child, Stella's cousin Luisa, had left for the university of Pisa and better things. Mirtillo, the blue budgerigar that had chirped from the cage hanging outside the entrance, would have been entombed by the war memorial under cover of darkness where her uncle had made an unsanctioned grave for his pets.

'Is it far now?' Joe said.

'Nearly there.' She didn't need to consult the blue and white road sign ahead.

The road turned again past the bus stop where no one ever got on or off. There'd been nothing at this bend in the road for decades but an overgrown mule track leading up to the woods, a tumbled down *rustico* the only building in sight.

'That looks abandoned, poor old place, it's a shame no one lives there any more,' Joe said.

'The *rustici* weren't designed to be lived in all year round, they're far too basic and cold,' Stella said. 'Places like that were mainly used for storage of farming equipment. Originally the farmers would stay there in the summer months to save walking to and from the fields but once the roads were developed and more people had motorised transport it was easier to come back to the village at night.'

'Wouldn't it make more sense to build their farmhouses on their own land?'

'To live without close neighbours, that's not the Ligurian way,' Stella said. Foreigners sometimes moved into the old places and restored them. The idea was romantic but when the snow came they soon realised why the locals wanted to live somewhere where they could walk to the bar and the church.

'Nearly here.' Their driver spoke for the first time. Stella could see the campanile of the big church of Sant' Agata ahead. They reached the car park on the edge of the village. The driver pulled into the only free space. It was always hard to find one. That had to be a good sign, didn't it?

'Driver, we're staying on the main square,' Joe said.

'We park here.' The driver opened his door, went round to the boot.

'That's a bit off,' Joe said.

'We can't get much further. Even with the wing mirrors folded in you can't get through the *caruggi* in a great wide Mercedes. We may as well park where he can turn around easily,' Stella said. She clambered out in a rather ungainly fashion, smoothing down her rucked-up dress. Joe climbed out, paying the man from a wodge of notes and waving away the change.

Stella took the handle of her case, checking carefully for traffic before leading the way up the main road towards the square where the war memorial stood. She was going to have to make quite a detour to avoid the main part of town where she might run into someone who recognised her. She took a right turn, past the house on the corner with a view across the valley where her best friend had lived, along a winding street, through an archway cutting across the small courtyard where Signora Togliatti had run the old *alimentari*. The shop now stood deserted, the paintwork peeling. A faded sign read *Vendesi – For Sale*. Judged by its state it had been pinned to the door for quite some time. Stella should have expected things to change but somehow she'd imagined the village would be no different from the day she'd left it.

'Are you sure we're going the right way?' Joe sounded a little impatient.

'Wait a moment.' She peered through the smeared window. The old counter was still visible and the stool where Signora Togliatti sat. 'We used to shop here...'

'What! In that tiny place?'

'There was a bigger minimart on the main street down from the bar, a *fruttivendolo* and a *salumeria* too.' But this was where her mamma sent her with an old string bag to collect the chestnut flour and the creamy round cheeses from the Togliatti family's goats that the signora fetched up from the cool cantina below.

'Now we need to go through here.' She led him under a low archway into a stone passageway, a small shrine to the Madonna high up on the wall. Someone still polished the glass but the plastic flowers, once scarlet, had faded to palest pink. Below, the heavy doors of the carpentry workshop stood open, the scent of wood shavings in the air. A man in dusty blue overalls bent over what looked like an old *madia* – the traditional short-legged chest where flour was stored – she hadn't seen one of those in years. The carpenter was probably the grandson of the family who had always run the old place. She turned away before he chanced to look up.

'This is quite a walk. I'm sure we've gone around in a circle,' Joe muttered.

She ignored his grumbling. 'It's just here, down the steps.'

They descended into the main square. She was relieved to see that Da Luca, the village's one smart restaurant, was still open, the façade now a faded olive green. On the other side of the piazza, Sant' Agata's hadn't changed at all, the old carved doors and golden decoration above the round window just as she remembered them.

There were two churches in the village, three if you counted the abandoned Old Chapel up past the vineyards, but Sant' Agata's was the one where she'd come to mass and dressed as a little bride for her first communion. Every Sunday and feast day she'd see Gino there, the two of them sharing glances across Fernanda's bowed head. Church was the only place where their families came together. Stella couldn't help but feel the tension when her parents crossed paths with Fernanda, Papà giving a curt nod when Mamma reminded him with a look that they were in God's house, where judgement was the preserve of the Almighty.

'Wow, what a beautiful church!' Joe said. Stella felt a swell of pride. She quickly chided herself. This wasn't her village any more.

'There's number four, isn't that the property we're staying in?' She pointed at a yellow five-storey building, window boxes brimming over with white geraniums and pink petunias beneath each row of bottle-green shutters.

'Yes, that must be it. At last!' Joe wiped his brow.

'I can't wait to unpack, have a glass of water and freshen up.'

'Your wish is my command.' Joe grinned.

* * *

The oak wardrobe was vast but Stella only needed two hangers. There was no point unpacking her whole case for just one night's stay. Joe sat on the edge of the bed, his empty water glass already in the sink, drumming his fingers on his thigh. She couldn't expect him to understand why she wanted to linger, arranging her cosmetics and stripy washbag by the bathroom basin, putting off the moment when they left the safety of the apartment's four walls. She was tempted to lie down, feigning a headache or some minor illness. It wouldn't be a complete untruth; the tension was tightening around her skull. But she couldn't face Joe's smothering attention or worse, the thought that he might suggest that if she was too incapacitated, they should stay on for a second day.

   Outside the apartment's window a three-wheeled truck was pulling up. She hoped it was coming to clear away the pile of scaffolding at the far end of the piazza but its back was piled with wooden planks, on top of which was furled a long white banner: everything needed for a makeshift stage. A band must be playing in the village tonight. Joe couldn't have picked a worse date for their visit; the inevitable summer festivities had begun. They lasted for weeks, the village playing host to visiting musicians, dance competitions, food festivals, not to mention their own brass band. She'd played the triangle (the limit of her musical talent), her cousin Luisa the French horn. Papà and Uncle Domenico sang folk songs with the other men, dancing with their arms aloft after too many tots of *Amaro*. She'd been so embarrassed but now she'd give anything to see

Papà dance again. The memory sweet and painful all at once like sugary *canestrelli* on sensitive teeth.

She took out her phone and started to compose a message to Lauren, careful not to reveal any misgivings about Joe's change of plan.

'Stella! What are you doing?' Joe had given up drumming his leg and sighing. He stood by the door, his small nylon rucksack slung over one shoulder, gripping the door key's acorn-shaped fob.

Stella stuffed her phone into her bag.

'I'm ready,' she said. As ready as she'd ever be.

10

Amy hadn't planned to stop on her way back down the beach. It was only the leaping dolphins on the wooden sandwich board that had caught her eye. But now that she'd been ushered to one of the beach club's white tables and a basket of bread placed by her elbow she realised how hungry she was.

She helped herself to another piece of bread. The American couple on the next table hadn't touched theirs. They hadn't picked up their menus either, their eyes and hands too busy exploring each other's ears, noses, lips, the bar just another piece of shifting scenery, a backdrop for their love.

Amy turned her head towards the sun-glittered sea. She had no desire to be pawed in a public place but it might be quite nice to think that one day someone might look at her the way the two lovebirds gazed at each other. She'd had a handful of short-term relationships and her share of dates, a few of them set up by friends, but she always felt she was playing a game where she didn't know the rules, or where the rules were arbitrarily changed from day to day. And although she found things to talk about with her boyfriends, the silences in between were never the truly comfortable ones like the ones between her and Grandpa Lance working on their pots in Mum's garden shed. He had been the one who really got her, who never made her feel like she was saying or wearing or doing the wrong thing. He never nagged her to be more adventurous or to come up with some impressive plan for the rest of her life.

The waitress placed a great glass bowl of salad before her.

'That's a pretty necklace you are wearing, isn't that an old Italian coin?' she said.

'Yes, my grandpa left it to me.'

'Beautiful. But I would not wear it until you can get a new chain. That leather looks quite worn through. You do not want to lose it.'

Amy's hand went to the thin thong. She could feel the worn patch and despite the oil she'd rubbed in, the leather was terribly dry.

'Oh, it must be my fault, tying and untying it the way I have. I had better not wear it again until I can string it on something else.' She undid the necklace and slipped it into the inside pocket of her bag. The waitress was right; she couldn't risk losing the precious coin.

Amy picked up a forkful of lettuce. Rabbit food, Grandpa would have said. She wondered when she'd ever stop hearing his voice. She forced herself to sip some water, tried to compose herself. She'd never swallow her food with a lump in her throat like this. She dug into her salad. The *cuori di bue* tomatoes burst with sweetness; tangy taggiasca olives nestled amongst salty anchovies, peeled cucumber and slices of red onion. The sound of laughter made her turn her head: a group of children playing on the beach. The sand was golden, the sea sparkling like a million crystals had fallen from the cloudless sky. She shouldn't be sitting feeling sorry for herself on a perfect day like this. She ordered a coffee and unfolded her map, searching for inspiration, checking each numbered place of interest against the photos and descriptions. Her finger hovered over the Hanbury Tennis Club. Tennis was something Lance had loved. He'd taught Amy to play when she was no more than four or five, replacing the net she couldn't see over with a length of Mum's washing line. She'd run backwards and forwards, swiping her little racket through the air until she was almost dizzy whilst he stood still, rocking from foot to foot, his thin, veiny arm wielding his old-fashioned wooden racket with deadly precision. She had her destination. She threw back her espresso and called for the bill.

Amy set off back along the seafront. Instinctively her hand went to her chest. She'd only been wearing Grandpa's necklace for a couple of weeks but it already felt strange that it wasn't dangling there.

* * *

A lipstick-red George VI post box stood at the entrance to the tennis club. Amy couldn't help but smile at the ridiculously English touch. Behind the high wire fencing, two women in traditional white skirts were engaged in a spirited rally, their bright yellow ball bouncing off the clay surface. The other courts were unoccupied, most members probably having the sense to keep out of the mid-afternoon sun.

Amy crept a little closer, conscious of the private property sign she'd ignored. Surely no one would care if she stood and watched. No one except the man striding towards her with a not terribly friendly look on his face. His salt and pepper hair told her he must be at least sixty. He was probably in charge of the club, come to send her on her way. It was only as he drew nearer that she realised he wasn't frowning, just squinting into the sun.

The man said something in Italian. She responded with what she hoped was a harmless shrug and friendly smile.

'Can I help you?' He switched smoothly to English.

'I was just looking.'

'Looking? Looking to join? Looking for a person?'

'For a person... except he's... umm... not here.'

He raised his eyebrows. No wonder.

'My grandpa...'

'Ah! He used to play here?' His green eyes softened.

'I don't know if he did but he lived in Alassio when he was a child and he liked tennis.'

'And that is why you are here? To see where your nonno played? Would you like to see around? Why not? I am not so busy. We can go into the Club House. There are some interesting old photographs on display and of course a wonderful view over the courts from the veranda.'

'That's so kind! If you're sure it's no trouble.' She had to stop herself hugging him.

He led her along by the courts and into the yellow-ochre Club House. She couldn't help but smile at the sight that greeted her: cane tables and chairs, an elegant grandfather clock, vintage posters and old wooden tennis rackets mounted on the walls – the place was straight out of Agatha Christie. But she didn't get much chance to look around before the man led her onto the covered veranda.

'I come out here whenever I can. This is the most perfect place to sit, whether there is a game taking place or not,' he said.

'I can see that.' Below them, a second couple had just started warming up.

'You can imagine your nonno playing tennis on these courts?'

'Yes, and sitting up here with a gin and tonic.' But the Lance she could see was at least eighty years old, wearing a shirt and tie and a woolly waistcoat despite the heat, ice cubes clinking in his cut-glass tumbler. Maybe she lacked imagination, but it was hard to picture him aged eight or ten, slurping on a can of bitter orange *chinotto*.

She put her hand to her breastbone, her fingers seeking the lira coin nestled beneath her top before remembering it wasn't there. Italy hadn't brought her any closer to Lance. He was gone for good. Her favourite person in the world. Why had she thought coming here would make her feel any better? But she couldn't dissolve into tears in front of this stranger. She looked beyond the courts to the dark green hills.

'Thank you so much for showing me around.'

'It was nothing. Unfortunately, I cannot stay longer, I promised to meet my daughter when she finishes her work at the English Library. She's helping there this week, the usual librarian is away holidaying in Spain.' He stood up, Amy did likewise and followed him back down the stairs and out through the car park.

He paused by the red post box. 'So, where will you go next? I'm sure you have already seen our famous *muretto* – the wall covered in ceramic tiles. It is opposite the Caffè Roma, the coffee there is not to be missed.'

'I haven't gone to look at the *muretto* yet but I'll make sure I do. Thank you again.'

'My pleasure, signorina...'

'It's Amy.'

'Amy, that is a lovely name. Enjoy your stay. And if you wish to return to the club, there is no problem. Just ask for me, Signor Perillo... Gino Perillo.'

11

'I can't imagine you living here,' Joe said. 'All these dank alleyways, funny little houses and uneven paving.' He bent to rub the back of his ankle.

'I'm sorry, I should have warned you,' Stella said automatically. They were walking towards the edge of the village to admire the views across the hills.

'Will you take me to where you used to live? I'd like to see your old house.'

She was about to protest but it gave her the perfect excuse to go the long way round, bypassing the end of the main street and the general store that Uncle Domenico had run alone after Papà's death. She spoke very little as they made their way through small courtyards, and sloping streets with steps leading up to some houses and down to others, where layers of the hillside had been cut away to build the village long ago.

It didn't take long to reach Stella's family home. She wasn't sure if she was relieved or sad to find it barely altered, even down to the little scroll carved into the lintel above the door. The new occupants had changed only the colour of the paintwork and put a few terracotta pots by the front steps. The shutters on her old bedroom window she had shared with her sister, Marta, were closed. She couldn't see her parents' room from here, that was on the other side looking over the hill. She used to sneak in there sometimes when Mamma was out, peeking in the wardrobe at Papà's clothes still hanging there. Then she'd stand on tiptoes looking across the vineyards towards the place where Gino's family's *rustico* stood, wishing senselessly that the two of them had braved the cuts and scrapes from the thick brambles and the climb in the heat to go there that day. Fernanda would never have found them then. One change of plan, one rev of a red moped and everything changed. She felt a lump in her throat, Joe's arms around her.

'Stella, you're crying. I'm so sorry, I didn't realise bringing you here would upset you.'

'It's nothing, just feeling nostalgic, I suppose.'

He took her hand. 'Let's see if we can find somewhere we can have one of those nice Italian ice-creams.'

She smiled weakly. As if gelato would solve anything! But Joe was trying, bless him. She set off, trying to concentrate on the here and now. Before she knew it her feet had carried her the shortest way. They were back on the main street. Across the road stood Uncle Domenico's old shop. A silver Magimix took pride of place in the window surrounded by boxes and cartons faded by the sun. Above the doorway, painted in green capital letters, was FERRANDO, her family name. She tried to turn her gasp into a cough.

Perhaps it was just a coincidence, there weren't many different surnames in the village; most of the families had intermarried over the years. Or, she tried to tell herself, the shop had new owners who hadn't yet bothered to paint over the sign. But a blue budgerigar chirped in the cage hanging by the entrance – one of a long line of replacements for the original Mirtillo.

'What is it, Stella? You look like you've seen a ghost. Is that shop something to do with your family? That's your surname above the window.'

She hesitated. She could fob Joe off but there was already too much she hadn't told him.

'My grandparents used to run that shop, then later my great-uncle, then my papà and his younger brother Domenico took it over. It looks like Domenico is still there. He and Papà had two elder brothers but they were both killed in the war and there was a sister who moved away. Nonno didn't survive the war either. He wouldn't have been conscripted, he was too old for that and anyway he had a dodgy leg and his eyesight wasn't too good. I believe he was a civilian casualty but I don't really know what happened. When you're young you're too wrapped up in yourself to be interested in what old people did.' Stella stopped, suddenly exhausted. It was the most she'd spoken about her family in years.

'Your uncle must be ancient. Surely he can't still be working, that's ridiculous!'

'Domenico must be in his mid-to-late eighties but he probably thinks it's more ridiculous to sit around at home. Growing up, the old folk around here worked until they dropped. It looks like he still opens the place five days a week.' She gestured to the sign with clockfaces marking the opening and closing hours.

Joe peered in the window. 'I can't see anyone but it should be open. Shall we go in?'

'Oh, no, let's not bother. We don't need anything.'

'He's your uncle, Stella.' Joe sounded incredulous.

Stella searched for an excuse. But there was no time to

ponder. A woman was walking along the narrow pavement straight towards them. Although she hadn't set eyes on her for more than forty years, Stella recognised her at once.

Domenico's daughter dropped her head, rummaging in her bag. If Stella moved quickly she could get away but her legs felt weak, as though if she moved she'd collapse in a heap.

Cousin Luisa looked up. She hurried towards them.

'Oh my word, it's you, Stella!' Luisa gasped and raised her arms. For a moment Stella thought she was going to hit her but Luisa grabbed her by the shoulders, kissing her. 'How incredible to see you. Whatever are you doing here?'

'I could ask you the same, didn't you move to Genoa after university?'

'That's not an answer.'

Joe coughed softly.

'This is Joe – my fiancé.' She slipped her arm through his. 'We're just visiting for a day... and one night. We've been staying in Sanremo, we're travelling on to Portofino tomorrow.'

'Portofino, ooh, very nice. I don't know why Papà didn't tell me you'd be here.'

'He didn't know. We were just... umm... just passing.'

'He'll be so excited to see you. He's very late opening up today. I rang the shop earlier and he didn't answer but I'm sure he won't be long. No, wait a moment, Mirtillo is in his cage, Papà must be here. Maybe he just didn't hear the phone. He is a little deaf, though he'll deny it.'

She pushed open the door. A bell jangled. The shop was empty, the counter unmanned.

'There's no one here,' Joe said.

'I'll go and look downstairs in the cantina,' Luisa said. 'He must be checking on the stock.'

'Okay, sure.' Stella looked around. The place seemed larger

than she remembered. She couldn't put her finger on why until she realised it must have expanded through into the small milliner's shop next door which had stood empty since the war.

A piercing scream cut through the silence. Her cousin's voice called from the cantina below. 'Stella, Stella, please help!'

Joe hesitated. Stella brushed past him, clattering down the stairs.

Uncle Domenico lay slumped on the floor, his face grey and racked with pain, Luisa kneeling beside him.

'He must have fallen getting something from a high shelf.' Her cousin gestured at a ladder leaning up against the wall. 'Wait here with him, will you? I'll run outside and call an ambulance.'

Stella sat down on the floor beside him, hoping her presence wasn't going to make things worse. Uncle Domenico's rheumy eyes fluttered. A puzzled look crossed his face.

'It's Stella... your niece.'

'Stella? Little Stella? Is it really you? Am I dreaming? Am I dead?'

Stella couldn't help laughing. 'Yes, it's me, Uncle. And you're not dead and neither am I! We're both still here.'

'Well, help me up then. I can't lie here all day. I've got customers.'

'You're not moving. Not until the ambulance arrives. But you're going to be okay. Everything's going to be okay.'

It had to be okay. Domenico might have broken a hip or a leg but he wasn't going to die on her. Not like Papà did. For a moment she was back there: Domenico pumping frantically on Arturo's chest. The paramedics arriving too late. The look Domenico gave her when all hope was gone.

* * *

Stella handed Luisa the battered canvas holdall. She'd worked quickly to find everything her uncle might need: three pairs of socks, underpants, vests, pyjamas, the razor from the bathroom cabinet, the half-read detective novel by his bed.

'Thanks, Stella,' Luisa said. 'The ambulance should be here soon. Let's hope there's not too much traffic on the road to Sanremo.'

Stella bent down. She squeezed Domenico's dry, bony hand, glad to have this quiet moment alone with her uncle and cousin whilst Joe stood outside, waiting to point the paramedics through the shop and down the stairs.

'What happened to Arturo – your papà – it wasn't your fault,' Domenico murmured.

She shook her head angrily. She knew that wasn't true.

'I never blamed you, Stella,' Luisa added. 'We were shocked, angry, upset when Uncle Arturo died but it wasn't your fault, whatever you may think. You might as well blame Gino's mamma for finding you. You and he were teenagers, having fun like teenagers should.'

'What I never understood is why Papà hated Gino's family so much.' Stella had pondered the schism for years. But she wasn't going to find the answer to that now. A heavy tread on the floor above, voices calling out. The ambulance was here.

'I'll go with him to the hospital,' Luisa said.

'The shop... my customers...' Domenico's voice was agitated. 'What will happen to my shop? What about Mirtillo?'

Stella took a breath. She couldn't undo the past, couldn't bring Papà back but she could do something for his little brother. It was one small sacrifice she could make, one small way to try and put things right.

'I'll look after the shop for a few days, and Mirtillo, of course. Just leave me the keys,' she said.

12

Amy walked slowly along the Corso Dante Alighieri. If she stopped to study every plaque fixed to the famous *muretto* it would take her half the day. She concentrated on picking out a few, finding an autograph left by Max Bygraves, her grandma's favourite entertainer, and a simple line drawing by Jean Cocteau. Confraternities, rotary clubs and musical organisations had all left their mark since 1953 when Ernest Hemingway and the Caffè Roma's owner had snuck out after dark to fix the first decorative tile. But she was all too aware that the modern tourist attraction hadn't existed when Grandpa was a boy. The feeling she should be doing something else nagged at her.

She let out a sigh. Alassio was a charming town but she'd found nothing of Grandpa here, the only connection the seafront and tiny chapel depicted in the black and white postcard he'd left her, a reminder of the stories he planned to tell.

Her phone buzzed. She snatched it up.

'Jack? You're actually calling me! What is it?'

'That's a nice greeting.' She could hear the laugh in her brother's voice.

'It's not that! You send messages and memes but you never make an actual call.'

'I thought you'd like to hear a friendly voice.'

'Yes, I would. What are you up to?' She stopped walking, resting an elbow on the wall.

'Not a lot, drinking beer, dodging man-eating crocodiles.'

'Crocodiles?' Amy winced.

'I quite fancy a pet one,' Jack joked. She hoped. 'How's Alassio?'

'Beautiful.' She looked over at the bronze sculpture of the two lovers atop the *muretto*. 'Relaxing. Perfect.'

'And how are things really?'

'It's also… Oh, I don't know.' Amy paused.

'Sad?'

'Yeah, I can't help wondering what I'm doing here. Grandpa didn't set foot in Italy after 1938.'

'I'm not sure that's true. Maybe he was there during the war.'

'He can't have been. He was captured in Libya. You've got his old medal. I know there was some story about him escaping but he'd damaged his leg. The army would never have sent him back out to fight in the Italy campaign.'

'But what about the necklace with the Italian lira and the other postcard of the little village?'

'He could have picked them up anywhere.'

'Hang on a minute, Amy.' Jack broke off. She could hear voices and laughter in the background. 'Sorry about that! I met a bunch of guys earlier. They're all about to go off to the Irish bar.'

'You go, join them, have a good time.'

'Good to speak to you, sis.'

'You too,' Amy said. But Jack had already gone.

The rest of the day stretched ahead of her. Perhaps she'd stop at the café across the road. Gino from the tennis club had recommended it and she could see there was one spare table outside.

She crossed the road, heading for the table, but it seemed that someone else had just the same idea. She was a stride too late. A tut of exasperation escaped before she could stop herself. It turned into a gasp of surprise. The man who'd beaten her to it was Gino and it was obvious from his startled response that until that moment he hadn't noticed her.

'Oh, it's you. Amy, isn't it? Please, share my table, it is the last one.'

'Oh, no.' She stepped backwards. 'I don't want to disturb you.'

'Please.' He waved his arm towards the other seat. 'It was only talking to you yesterday that reminded me how many weeks it is since I came here. And you are a visitor. I would feel bad if I deprived you of the chance to sit in this nice spot.'

'If you're sure.'

'Of course. Coffee? I will buy you one, no arguments.'

'Thank you, there's no need.'

'No need but even so...' He twisted his head towards the waiter. The two men exchanged a few words at a speed she could not follow. 'Now tell me, what have you been doing, are you still enjoying our fine town? Have you found any more connections to your nonno?'

She rested her elbows on the table. 'No. Somehow, I just can't imagine him as a boy living here. I'm beginning to have a strange feeling that if I want to find out more about him, I need to go somewhere else. Grandpa left me a postcard of this town and I knew he grew up here but he left me a postcard of a small village as well. Of course, it could just be one he picked up anywhere, even at a flea market back in England. Something that reminded him of another place in Liguria he once knew.'

'You have it with you?'

'Yes.' She rooted in her shoulder bag.

He reached over the coffees the waiter had just set down. 'Let me take a look, would you?'

'Sorry it's so battered.' Amy made another attempt to smooth the postcard but the creases were too embedded to flatten out. She handed it to him.

He let out a strange gasp. 'But this is Leto... This is the village I grew up in! How extraordinary.'

'Really?' Amy felt a frisson of excitement. It was such an odd coincidence. Perhaps Grandpa really was guiding her after all.

'Yes, really.' Gino shook his head in wonder. 'I wonder when this was taken. It cannot be later than the 1960s; the old school building is still in the picture.'

He took a sip of his espresso and leant back, studying the picture through narrowed eyes. 'Whenever I visit, it seems nothing has changed for decades. My son Leo still lives there, in fact. He finds the countryside inspiring for his work. And he keeps an eye on my mother. Or perhaps it is his nonna who keeps an eye on him.' He gave a wry smile.

'There's a message on the back,' Amy said.

He turned the card over. '*Allora... Baci e abbracci dall'Italia* – that's our way of saying love from Italy. But there is no clue who wrote it, not even an initial, and the name of the village has been struck through, that's odd. It is strangely impersonal and yet it seems to have been folded and unfolded many times, as if your nonno had carried it around in his pocket.' He held the postcard out to her. She tucked it back into her bag.

'I'd like to visit the place. Would you know a reasonable hotel there where I could stay for a day or two?'

'Stay longer if you can. I know it seems there may be nothing to do but it's such a picture-perfect village. You can wander the old mule tracks up into the hills and just take in the views. You will not find a hotel there but my mother has a spare room she rents out from time to time to help make ends meet. It is simple, you will not have your own bathroom or anything like that but it is convenient and clean. When would you want to go? Tomorrow? I can ring her if you like.'

'That would be so kind of you. I don't need anywhere fancy,' Amy said, trying to push down the doubts. Would she have to search out her own breakfast and cram her things into a wardrobe alongside some old lady's spare clothes?

He stepped away from the table to make the call, speaking in a language that didn't sound like Italian. After what appeared to be a protracted goodbye he sat back down, tore a strip off the edge of the newspaper he was carrying and wrote down a name, address and phone number.

'You are expected tomorrow afternoon. Mamma speaks in the local dialect but her Italian and English are both excellent too. She spent hours making sure I learnt the language when I was a boy. Mamma believes that the devil makes work for idle hands.'

'Oh.' Amy took the piece of notepaper, half wishing she hadn't agreed to the odd arrangement so hastily.

'Do not worry. She may seem a little strange, stern and devout but her heart is good.' He touched his chest. 'Just do not allow her to catch you smoking, drinking excessively or taking the name of the Lord in vain.'

'I don't smoke.'

'So you have only two things to worry about.' She wasn't

sure from his tone of voice if he was joking or not and Gino did not mention his mother again, talking instead about the walks Amy might take in the surrounding countryside and recommending a pizza place he was sure she would enjoy.

'Thanks so much for arranging this for me and thank you for the coffee.' Amy made to get up.

'*Di niente.* It is nothing. Good luck with the village – and Mamma.' He picked up his newspaper.

Amy stepped back into the street. She could hardly wait until tomorrow. She was off to the village in the postcard but she'd only solved part of the puzzle. *Baci e abbracci dall'Italia.* Love from Italy. Whoever had written those words – and when – remained a mystery.

13

'You agreed to do *what*? Stella, have you gone stark, raving mad?'

Stella stopped coiling her linguine around her fork. She'd thought it best to let Joe relax with a couple of glasses of wine before broaching their change of plan but judging by the way he was raising his voice, the alcohol hadn't had the effect she'd hoped for.

'I'm only going to look after the shop for a few days until Luisa's husband can arrange to take time off to look after their grandkids. Then she can come and hold the fort.'

'Well, you'll just have to tell her you can't do it. We've got a private car taking us to Portofino tomorrow, everything's booked and paid for.'

'They're family,' Stella said.

'Not exactly close, are they? In all the months we've been together you've never mentioned them. In fact, you implied you'd no family left in the village.'

'I didn't realise Domenico was still alive.'

Joe forked up a great coil of pasta. 'I think that rather proves my point.'

Stella stared at the remnants of her *linguine ai frutti di mare*. Were they really having their first argument? She hadn't expected him to be overjoyed at the turn of events but she had expected a calm discussion, not an outright 'no'.

'You were the one who wanted to come here. You were the one who said I should pop into the shop and see him.' It was a pretty pathetic argument to make but she couldn't think what else to say.

'You haven't thought this through, have you?' Joe said patiently. 'Where would we stay? We've only got the apartment here for one night. And I'm sure your uncle wouldn't want to ruin the holiday of a lifetime.'

Stella frowned. Joe had already been abroad three times this year, he could afford to jet off whenever he felt like it.

'I know it's not what you planned but we can stay at Domenico's place. It's a funny little house but this is just a short trip, it's not like it's our honeymoon. We can go to Portofino anytime.'

'I spent hours planning a special treat for your sixtieth and that's all this is to you? Nothing important?' His voice was getting louder. The other diners at Da Luca were beginning to stare.

'Joe! You know I didn't mean it like that.'

The waitress was approaching. Stella gave her an extra-big smile, trying to make up for the tension radiating from their table. The woman cleared away the plates from their first courses. Joe poured himself another glass of *rossese*, not bothering to offer Stella any.

They sat in awkward silence until the main courses arrived. Stella had chosen fresh fish with creamed peas but her appetite had gone, her stomach as tangled up as her linguine starter. Joe shovelled his steak down, ignoring her attempts to lighten the atmosphere. He finished the last of his potatoes and drained his glass.

'We'll need to have breakfast early, Stella, our taxi comes at nine thirty. We won't be able to get into our room in Portofino until two but we'll drop our cases, take a look around and have a long lunch at this very special restaurant I've booked.' He spoke as if their earlier conversation hadn't taken place.

'I can't do that, Joe, I have to help out, even if it's just for a day or two until Luisa can arrange someone else to cover the shop. I know this is a special trip but we've got a lifetime of holidays to look forward to.'

Joe leant across the table, dropping his voice to a whisper. 'You just don't get it, do you, Stella? You and I are getting the taxi I booked. You're not going to work in that shop, not for one day, not for one hour. We're leaving in the morning and that's that. Have I made myself clear?'

Stella stared at his closed-up face, the glower that marred his good looks. She looked down at her lap and picked a piece of squid off the new dress he'd bought her.

Joe signalled to the waitress for the bill. 'I'm beat, I could do with an early night. You didn't want dessert, anyway, did you?'

14

'I'll see you in Portofino when you've come to your senses.' Joe slammed the taxi door. The Mercedes drove off.

Stella stared at the receding number plate. She couldn't believe he'd really gone. But she didn't have time to dilly dally, wondering what she could have said or done differently. She had to wheel her case over to Domenico's shop and open up. Luisa had messaged her last night and again this morning. Her uncle had been very lucky: plenty of bruising, no broken bones. But Luisa was insisting her father stayed in Genoa with her and his great-grandchildren for a few days, knowing that as soon as he returned to the village he wouldn't be able to keep away from his beloved shop.

Stella set off up the road from the car park, calling out *buongiorno* in response to a workman's greeting, but her voice wobbled. The sun was bright, the sky a cloudless blue, but it was hard to find any joy in the holiday weather. Joe had gone. She was alone again. She could already hear Carol's admonishing voice: *Falling out over some relatives you haven't seen for forty years and a tatty old shop – you must be joking! Stella, go after him!* And worse, the inevitable, *You're practically sixty, Stella, you won't find anyone else.*

She passed the war memorial. This time she took the direct route to the bar. Yesterday she'd hovered awkwardly outside whilst Joe bought the gelati, worrying she'd run into someone from the past, but now she no longer cared. She was hungry, she hadn't been able to face any breakfast, and she was desperate for a decent coffee before she started work. If people were still judging her for what she'd done so many years before, she would have to learn to cope. Somehow.

She squared her shoulders and stepped into the cool tiled interior. The bar was almost exactly as she remembered it: the long counter, the speckly grey-tiled floor, the stacks of waffle-textured cones lined up from little to large on the ledge above the enticing array of Italian ice-cream. The pairs of chairs at each small table were the same ones she'd sat on with her brother and sister on days when the sun was too hot to risk taking their rapidly melting treats outside. Now, her brother and sister had their own children and quite probably grand-children. Did they have a favourite local gelateria where their families went without fail every week? She'd probably never know.

The person behind the counter was the same one who'd served them yesterday, a trim woman in her thirties, she wouldn't have been born when Stella left. This morning she'd be treated like any other stranger passing through. Stella waited whilst the woman prepped the orders for the customers who'd arrived before her. The *cavolini* and almond meringue-filled *pinolata* they'd chosen were the same favourites the place had served for generations but the display case looked shiny and new.

The only other upgrade was a pinboard on one wall

covered in photos, many with cheerful greetings: *Ciao! Saluti! Che bella!* scrawled across them with smiley faces and rows of kisses. Old folk holding hands outside Sant' Agata, toddlers clinging delightedly to the pink and turquoise horses on the mini roundabout that was set up in summer, families with grins as wide as their pizza slices. Thanks to the spread of social media, the once unknown village was beginning to attract its share of day trippers.

Stella ordered her breakfast *al banco*; she'd save time and money standing up at the bar. She tore a piece off her sweet focaccia to dip into her cappuccino. Its surface was decorated with a pretty leaf. How many visitors had ordered the same coffee and taken a photograph of that?

She ate quickly, wiping her fingers on the flimsy paper napkin. Domenico's shop was calling. She felt in her pocket for her uncle's reassuringly heavy bunch of keys, paid quickly, and set off up the narrow pavement. She could hardly believe she was doing this without Joe by her side. She'd been so sure he was going to apologise in the morning and in turn she would have apologised herself. She'd believed he'd come to a compromise, that they'd stay in the village for just one or two days – enough time for Luisa to rope in somebody else. But he'd gone off with barely a backwards glance. The Joe she knew wouldn't do something like that. It must have been a knee-jerk reaction; he'd soon be back. She pushed away the thought that perhaps she didn't really know him at all.

The shop key turned easily in the lock. Stella laid her case on its side behind the counter; she'd take it over to Domenico's place when she closed up for lunch. She removed the old cloth draped over Mirtillo's cage; the budgie gave a small chirp. She hung the cage back outside and sent a quick message to Luisa to tell her she was opening up. A thumbs-up back and a report

that Uncle Domenico had got some sleep: those were the easy
parts.

A leatherbound book lying on the shelf beneath the
counter proved to be the order book, nearly identical to the one
the two brothers had used back in the 1980s. Not much had
changed, thank goodness. No computerised systems with
unhackable passwords to worry about, no unfamiliar software
with unfathomable glitches. The great grey metal till opened
with a satisfying ping. Stacks of euros were arranged neatly in
its five drawers. There were plenty of coins too and the till roll
was nearly full. No reason why she couldn't turn the shop sign
from Closed to Open.

Stella took a deep breath. She could do this. She walked
over to the door, flipped the sign and took up her position
behind the counter.

Her phone buzzed in her bag. Stella jumped. It had to be
Joe! He must have got part way to Portofino only to change his
mind. Everything was going to be all right.

She grabbed her phone from her bag. Her daughter on a
video call. Stella would make this brief. She didn't want to tell
Lauren about Joe's departure. Not yet.

'Mum!' Lauren's face filled the screen. Her cheeks looked a
little pink, as though she'd caught the sun.

'Hi, darling! You look well. Is the weather good?'

'Beautiful.' Lauren swung the phone in an arc. Stella caught
the tip of her daughter's chin followed by part of the garage
roof, an explosion of yellow flowers in a hanging basket, then a
close-up of tarmac and immaculately painted toenails.

'Err, lovely,' Stella said, not quite sure what she was
supposed to have gleaned from the rather dizzying tour.

'Where on earth are you?' Lauren said.

'Oh, just in a shop. In fact—' Stella laughed nonchalantly

'—it's actually the old general store your grandpa used to run with your great-uncle Domenico. Isn't that a funny coincidence!'

'What are you doing in there?'

'Just, umm, shopping. There wasn't a corkscrew in the apartment.'

Lauren's nose loomed large against the screen. 'Mum, you're behind the counter!'

'Am I?' Stella looked over her shoulder. 'Oh, so I am. Aren't I daft!'

'I know you've been missing your old job. You'll be asking to have a go on the till next!' A frown creased Lauren's forehead. 'Wait a minute. You're right next to the till and the drawer's open. I can see all the cash.'

Stella elbowed it shut. She groped for some plausible explanation.

'Mum, why are you still in Leto? Weren't you supposed to go to Portofino today?'

'I... I can't really explain right now, Lauren. I've got to go.'

'Tell me what's going on. Is Joe with you?' Lauren had switched to her doing-business voice. Stella was tempted to accidentally cut her off. But she'd only phone back.

'Joe's gone,' she said.

'Gone? What do you mean, gone?' Lauren twisted her head, her hair catching a trailing strand of ivy.

'Gone. You know – left, departed, scarpered, whatever you want to call it.'

'I know the meaning of the *word*, Mother.'

Mother. Stella was definitely in trouble now. She could feel one of Lauren's little talks coming on. They were even worse than Carol's.

Stella stumbled out an explanation as quickly as she could.

Lauren let out an exasperated huff. 'Of course Joe's going to be cross! Of course he's going to be fed up! Any normal person would have told this cousin of yours to sort out her own family dramas. I'm sure if you send her a message apologising and call a taxi firm, you can meet up with Joe. You'll sort everything out.'

'But I...'

The doorbell jangled.

'*Buongiorno!*' A man in paint-splattered overalls entered the shop. He looked like a local who'd hopefully find what he wanted without Stella's help.

Stella signalled a 'be with you in a moment'.

'You know what the problem with you is, Mum?' Lauren's head continued to spout. 'You're a soft touch. For once in your life will you stop thinking about other people and do what you want.'

It was a creed Stella had once lived by. She'd ignored everything but her own feelings the day she'd jumped on that moped with Gino and sped off to Sanremo. Doing what she wanted had caused nothing but heartache.

The customer was picking up an electric strimmer. He turned it over to read the back of the long oblong box. Stella had to finish up this call.

'I'm not running after Joe. I'm staying here, looking after the shop. This *is* what I want.'

'But you've had nothing to do with your family for decades.'

'I have to do this, Lauren. I have to do this for Uncle Domenico... to make up for the awful thing I did to his brother.'

'Whatever are you talking about, Mum? You're the kindest person. You wouldn't hurt a fly, let alone your own father.'

'That's where you're wrong.' Stella's voice shook. 'I did something terrible...'

'Oh, honestly! I expect you're worrying about some bit of nonsense everyone else probably forgot about decades ago.' Lauren tutted. 'But if you've been brooding about it all these years, you'd better tell me about it. You won't move on until you've opened up.'

'It's not that easy.' Stella gripped the counter with her free hand. She'd never move on. Never forget.

The man with the strimmer had swapped the box for another model, opening up the packaging and pulling out the operating instructions. Seemingly satisfied, he came forward and placed it on the counter.

'Wait a moment, Lauren.' Stella took the man's cash, handing over a few euros' change. He nodded, departing with a cheery *buona giornata*. She picked up the phone. Lauren was wearing her best 'I'm listening' face.

'I'm waiting, Mum. Talk to me! Get it off your chest.'

Stella sighed. After all these years, it had taken less than twenty-four hours back home to bring everything to a head.

'I killed him,' Stella said. 'I killed my darling Papà.'

15

It was dark, the shutters blocking any light. Amy had slept remarkably well in Fernanda's narrow single bed. It was only the sound of the front door clicking that had broken her dreams. The old lady must have left for church; she'd mentioned the night before that she attended morning mass every day.

Amy scrambled out of bed and fixed back the shutters. Fernanda's small house lay on the outskirts of the village. Beyond the mesh that kept the insects out, the view across the hillside took her breath away. It was so calming, Amy felt she could stay there all morning with her nose pressed up against the window, but she had a funny feeling Fernanda wouldn't approve of her wasting the day away.

There was no reason to hang around the house. Fernanda wasn't providing breakfast; Amy would have to go to the local bar for that, though she was welcome to use the kitchen to fix herself a drink. Last night she'd been shown a fiddly-looking coffee pot and a jam jar full of rather dusty-looking teabags that she decided she wouldn't bother with once she'd learnt Fernanda didn't keep any milk in the fridge.

She put down her phone on the Holy Bible Fernanda had left on the bedside table. Pulling down the edge of Jack's old T-shirt she was using as a nightdress and dragging a hand through her tangled hair, she picked up her towel and washbag and headed for the shower. It would make sense to use the shared bathroom whilst the old woman was out.

Gurgling sounds came from behind the bathroom door, the plumbing no doubt as ancient as the terracotta floor tiles and well-worn rug in the hall. Amy turned the round handle. The door flew open, sending her tripping over an uneven tile and almost pitching her straight into – what the heck! – a rather fit young man, naked from the waist up.

Amy let out a shriek. She folded her hands across her body, relieved she'd packed her brother's baggy old top to wear in bed rather than the pink T-shirt with a hem that barely reached her knickers.

'*Che diavolo!*' The young man grabbed at his towel as it threatened to fall to the floor. Amy couldn't prevent a nervous giggle escaping, her initial fear tempered by his obvious embarrassment.

The man ran one hand through his damp hair, clutching the edge of his towel with the other. She tried not to stare at his golden brown chest – whoever this was, he definitely worked out or did some sort of physical job. The rest of him wasn't bad either: medium build, medium height, strong tattoo-covered arms and a smile that lit up his golden-brown eyes.

'*Scusi*... umm...' The few words of Italian she knew weren't any use to her. 'What on earth are you doing here?' she said instead. Amy was sure Fernanda would have mentioned if she had another guest staying. In a house this size, three people would be constantly under each other's feet.

'You're English.' He frowned into the mirrored cupboard on the wall, retrieved a comb and swept it roughly through his hair; a pointless exercise as the strands that had fallen over his eyes flopped straight back down again.

'Yes, I am and *I'm* staying here. Now I've answered your question, are you going to answer mine?' She laughed nervously.

'I just came in for a shower, mine's broken, the plumber can't come until this afternoon. I knew Nonna Fernanda would be out, she goes to mass every morning, never misses a day.'

'Oh, Fernanda's your grandmother!' This must be the son of the man from the tennis club; no wonder his English was so good.

'Did you think I just walk into old ladies' houses to use the hot water?' His lips twitched with amusement. 'I'm Leo, by the way. I am sorry I startled you. Nonna rarely rents out the room nowadays. Well, I'd better let you have the bathroom, umm...'

'Amy.' She shifted awkwardly, clutching her towel.

'The shower makes a little spluttering sound before the first few drops of water come out but after that it is okay.' Leo squeezed past her into the hall.

'Sure, err, thanks.' She hung her towel on the back of the door, engaged the so-called lock – a flimsy latch held in place by a single nail – and stepped onto the plastic tray, drawing the nylon curtain. The pipes made a sound like a cough but after a couple of violent splashes, the water gushed out, just as Leo had said. Amy squirted out a large blob of shampoo, glad she'd packed her own. She closed her eyes, working up a generous lather as she inhaled the scent of lime and basil. How Leo had emerged smelling so good after using Fernanda's workaday shampoo and cracked sliver of soap was a mystery.

Amy didn't linger in the shower, mindful not to run down the old lady's hot water. Wrapping her towel around her very firmly in case Leo hadn't left, she hurried back to her room, grabbed some underwear and pulled her blue sundress over her head. She rummaged in the inside pocket of her case for her teardrop-shaped pendant. It was one of her favourites but her neck felt strangely naked without Lance's coin necklace.

'Coffee?' Leo called from the hall. 'It's okay, I have clothes on!'

'Same here.' She opened the door. Leo stood in the hall, now fully dressed. His jeans were worn at the knees, covered in what looked like white paint, his light green shirt similarly stained and frayed around the collar.

'Not my best look.' He flashed a rueful grin. 'I am going to work.'

'What as? Sorry, that sounded a bit rude.'

'It is okay. I would be surprised if you were dressed like me instead of looking so lovely.'

Amy felt herself flush. 'So, what do you do?'

'I am a *scalpellino*, a stonemason, you call it. By the end of the day my skin is full of dirt, clothes covered in dust. Sometimes I wonder, why do I have a shower in the morning? But I do not like to start the day feeling – how do you say – grubby?'

'Icky?' Amy suggested.

'That is a good word. I do not know it. You like coffee? Nonna will be okay if I wash the pot.'

'Yes, *grazie*. I haven't had breakfast.'

'You will not find much here. Nonna eats like a sparrow.'

'She told me to go to the bar.'

'Good coffee and the best *gobeletti*.' His face broke into a wide grin. 'We will go there instead so I can show you.'

She already knew where the bar was but she guessed he knew that too.

'I don't want to make you late.'

'I work for myself.' He shrugged. 'And now I am thinking of *gobeletti*. They are a small kind of tart; have you tried them yet?'

'No but they sound like good fuel for carving or whatever stonemasons do.'

He opened the door, locked it and put the key under a terracotta pot filled with geraniums. Amy followed him down the street, the sun hazy on the hills in the distance. The village was coming to life. Three old men stood talking on the corner by the turning to Sant' Agata, hands clasped behind their backs. One had a dog's lead looped over his wrist, another had his fingers threaded through the handles of a plastic bag full of groceries. A smartly dressed lady passed by using a walking stick; perhaps she had come from the same church service as Fernanda.

The bar was busy, it seemed many of the local folk were as keen on their pastries as Leo was. And their enthusiasm wasn't misplaced. The *gobeletti* were delicious: thick sweet apricot jam under a little pastry lid. Leo had an espresso, Amy a cappuccino, a leaf drawn on the surface.

'So, what sort of things does a stonemason do?' She cringed at her boring question.

He opened a sachet of sugar. 'Lettering mainly, carving names and dates on headstones and plaques, that is the day-to-day work. I like to do it, even the simple things, they are important. A name spelt wrong on somebody's grave can be devastating.'

Amy nodded, wondering how to continue the conversation,

it seemed a rather gloomy subject. She took a bite of her *gobeletto*, stalling for time.

'What I really enjoy is the chance to be creative, to add decoration,' Leo continued. 'Some people ask for scrolls, flourishes, fruit, flowers. Of course, I sketch a design for them to approve before I start carving.'

'That sounds fun. I do a bit of pottery. Well, I did when my grandpa was alive, he had a potter's wheel and a little studio in my mum's garden shed.'

'And do you not make things now?'

'It doesn't seem the same since he's gone. I can't get motivated somehow. Not just the pottery, everything seems so much harder. He only died a few weeks ago. Sorry, I don't know why I'm telling you all this.'

'Sorry? The English say this word a lot, usually when there is nothing to be sorry for. You miss your grandpa, that is natural. Maybe that is the reason you are here in Italy.'

She nodded and took a sip of her coffee.

Leo leant forward, one hand resting on his chin. 'He had a connection to this village?'

'Perhaps. He spent his childhood in Italy, at the seaside, in Alassio. The family returned to England in the late 1930s. I don't know what connection he had to this place, but there was a postcard of Leto in the memory box he left me.'

'Then it must have meant a lot to him. Did he come back to Italy after the war?'

'No, I don't think so, but he went off on all sorts of adventures; he found it hard to settle after being demobbed. He even drove tanks for the British Army in Yemen for a time. He settled down in England eventually after meeting my grandma and finally had a child when he was in his fifties.'

'That was your dad?'

'No, Grandpa was my mum's dad. My dad's parents were quiet and conventional: holidays on a canal boat, gardening, knitting, playing dominoes.'

'I never knew my other grandparents, only Nonna Fernanda. I spent hours in her little house during the summer holidays. Anyway, that is enough about me.' He popped the last piece of tart in his mouth.

Amy hastily downed the dregs of her coffee. 'I should let you get to work.'

'Yes, I must. I have a deadline for something important.'

She reached for her purse.

'No, I will go in and pay. We will call it compensation for scaring you this morning.' His eyes sparkled.

A vision of him half-naked came unbidden. Her cheeks burned. 'Thanks, that's kind of you. I think I will stay here for a few minutes more, take a look at the map your nonna gave me and make a plan for the day.'

He stood up. 'See you, Amy, *ciao!*'

She sat and watched him walk down the street, the sun brightening his mid-brown hair. Once he was out of sight she unfolded the map, tracing a route with her finger. There were plenty of streets and paths to wander down, a couple of churches to explore. But she was pretty sure there was nothing she would find in Leto that would provide a link to her grandfather's past. The small village would probably turn out to be another dead end, like Alassio. But there was something about this place. She didn't know why, but she was in no hurry to leave.

16

Stella's daughter's face filled the phone screen, her mouth now open but no words spilling out. Lauren, who'd happily give a speech to a room of five hundred advertising executives, had been shocked into silence.

'I killed him, Lauren,' Stella repeated. 'Did you hear me?'

'Yes, yes, of course I did. But I don't understand what you're saying. If you'd killed your papà, you would have been sent to prison. You wouldn't have gone swanning off to England.'

'Swanning off?' Slunk off more like, unable to live with the mother who blamed her for her husband's death, unable to comfort her grieving brother and sister, unable to face the curious stares.

'Mum...' Lauren prompted. 'You can't just drop a bombshell like this and not tell me what you're going on about.'

The shop's doorbell jangled.

'I can't talk right now,' Stella said. 'We'll speak tonight, after you've finished work, after I've tidied up here.'

'Make sure you ring me.' Lauren snapped back to her usual brusque self. 'I don't like the thought of you stuck in that village by yourself, brooding over whatever you think you did or didn't do in the past.'

'I promise I'll call you.' Stella switched her phone to silent. Even though she longed for Joe to ring and tell her he'd acted in haste and was on his way back, his call – if he made one – would have to go to voicemail. She couldn't cope with Lauren interrupting her day with more questions. Stella already had another customer to deal with.

An elderly lady was making her way towards the counter, clutching a set of boxed light bulbs in one hand, her stick in the other. Instead of the colourful smocks sported by other elderly village folk she wore a frilly collared blouse nearly tucked into a sunray pleated skirt that fell to her ankles. A gold cross dangled from a length of black beads double looped around her wrinkled neck. Despite her painfully slow gait, she held her head high, almost as though she were defying anyone who might suggest she was old and frail. The quiff of white hair above her high forehead made Stella think of a proudly hoisted flag.

'*Buongiorno!*' Stella said.

The woman responded with a nod.

It was now that Stella focused on the woman's face and the beady eyes that, despite her age, had no need of glasses. Those eyes! Stella recognised them at once: lake-water green, searching Stella's for some evil rooted deep in her soul. The eyes of Fernanda, Gino's mamma.

Fernanda placed her purchase on the counter. 'Where's Domenico?' She twisted her head as though he might have sneaked up behind her. A bone in her neck creaked. Stella winced.

'He had a fall, he's at the hospital.'

'I'm surprised I hadn't heard. But then I don't get out as

much as I used to... Wait a moment, I know you. It's Stella, isn't it?' she said sharply.

'You remember me?' Stella tried to sound casual, even though her heart was racing faster than the time Carol had dragged her along to her Wednesday night spin class. She rang up the cost of the bulbs.

Fernanda gave a brief nod. 'You remember me too, I see, though you were just a young girl when you left.'

'Of course I remember.' Stella watched the old lady's face but Fernanda didn't react, merely counted out the exact change from her plum-coloured pigskin purse, dropping the coins onto the counter with a clatter so Stella had to scoop them up.

Fernanda placed her shopping in her brown cloth bag. 'Give Domenico my best wishes.' And with that, she turned and left.

Stella clutched the edge of the countertop, her heart still thumping. When she arrived in the village, it hadn't crossed her mind that she'd see Fernanda again, imagining she'd be long in her grave. Even as a teenager, Gino's mamma had seemed ancient, her stern looks and mutterings about sin something from another era. But now here she was, large as life. The woman who'd set off the chain of events that had upended Stella's life.

17

The church bells were chiming. Half past twelve. As a teenager, Stella had been frustrated by the way the village shut down for hours in the middle of the day. Her younger brother and sister had been content to rest, do their schoolwork or play cards after lunch but Stella had railed against the enforced downtime, longing to slip out and make the long walk to the abandoned *rustico* where there were no adults and no rules, just two teenagers in love. The only comfort had been knowing Gino was similarly confined, ploughing his way through an English-language novel, a giant dictionary by his elbow. Now, totting up the morning's takings and tidying the counter, Stella could appreciate how beneficial it was to take a break and for those working amongst the olives, in the vineyards and labouring at the goat farm to escape the hottest part of the day.

Today, she didn't want to go back to Domenico's house for her siesta, knowing that even if she was resting her body, her mind would be far from calm. She'd be constantly churning over what had happened with Joe, leaping up at any notification on her phone, hoping he would get in contact.

Stella glanced up at Mirtillo's cage. The little bird seemed happy enough pecking at his seed bell under the shade of the shop awning. She locked the shop door and walked down the street, passing the drawn shutters of the other shops, towards the bar. The dread of bumping into her old neighbours had evaporated. A steady stream of the villagers had dropped past Domenico's shop that morning, some in genuine need of an obscure household item but most driven by the desire to learn the latest news about the old man's health or to catch a glimpse of Stella, news of her arrival having spread faster than a cut-price deal at the village pizzeria. To her surprise, no one had seemed hostile. Over forty years had passed, her father Arturo's death was old news. Decades of births and deaths, betrothals and betrayals had supplanted her own tragic tale. But she knew it wasn't forgotten. This was a place that held its past close, where alliances and feuds could endure for generations. Like the bitterness between her family and Gino's.

The bar was quiet, just the odd tourist passing through, eating their lunch at the outside tables. She ordered a panino filled with salami and cheese, tearing at the chewy bread with her teeth, trying not to miss the butter she would have slathered on back home.

A quick espresso to finish and she was done. She paid inside at the counter and walked slowly back to the shop. The heat of the sun was made bearable by the light breeze but it was still a lot warmer than the English summers she'd become used to and though she was glad of the relative cool of the shop, she rather wished Domenico had had the resources to install some air conditioning. She set her handbag on the counter and descended to the cooler cantina, a spiralbound notepad and pen in hand.

The basement was quiet, no hoot from a passing car, no dog

barking. There was no better time to concentrate on the job in hand. If she was going to continue to look after the shop, even for a few days, she needed to familiarise herself with her uncle's stock. She'd been too worried about him to notice much about the basement on the day of Domenico's accident but now she could focus on the extraordinarily packed space. The floor was so cluttered she was surprised he'd found room to set up his ladder. And it was a miracle he'd landed on the pile of outdoor cushions and picnic blankets that had cushioned his fall instead of on the box of sharp-edged secateurs or the crate of crockery just nearby. It might be fanciful to imagine Papà had been looking down on his younger brother but someone up there had decided it wasn't Domenico's time to go.

She started to jot down the contents of the nearest boxes, soon realising the task she'd set herself was as great as attempting an inventory of Aladdin's cave. Except here there was no tree of glittering jewels or genie's lamp but box after brown box. Some were labelled in the handwriting she recognised from Domenico's notices behind the till but most were unmarked and could hold just about anything; the task was overwhelming. She sank down onto one of the crates.

Come on, Stella, you can do this. She'd managed a whole supermarket branch in the years before Lauren was born and afterwards she'd juggled working behind the till in another branch with bringing up a lively toddler and coping with Ricky's chaos. The only way Stella had managed was to tackle one chiller cabinet, one display stand, one toy box or one pile of washing at a time.

She decided to start with the smaller area behind the pillars that marked what was once the division between her family's shop and the one next door. Although upstairs the wall between the two had been completely knocked through, down here part of the wall that had once stood between their place and the old milliner's shop remained.

Stella knew from comments her parents had made in the past that Fernanda's older sister, Violetta, had run the shop successfully until her death towards the end of the war. Who could afford to buy hats during those lean times was a mystery. The villagers had become more impoverished with every passing year. Crops were requisitioned by Mussolini's troops, rations reduced, stocks of stewed fruits, bottled tomatoes and olive oil all run down to nothing. Her parents rarely mentioned their hungry childhoods, but her mamma had told Stella about her own mother grinding acorns to make a rudimentary coffee and her childish fear – neither confirmed nor denied by her parents – that the homeless cat she'd made friends with had ended up in the stew. Those had been years of patching and repatching old clothes, of lining leaking shoes with cardboard. Who had the money for the fancy new titfers Violetta made and sold?

Stella looked around the small space. Her eye caught boxes of fairy lights, Easter decorations, artificial Christmas trees. This area was clearly used to store out-of-season goods. There was nothing here she was likely to sell in the next few days but curiosity got the better of her.

Investigating a corner cupboard half hanging from the wall, she uncovered stacks of brown boxes, their lids secured with butterscotch-coloured sticky tape, split and peeling. She ran a finger across one, tracing a line through a layer of pale grey dust, thick and soft as rabbit's fur. Knowing Domenico wouldn't mind, she ripped off the sticky tape, revealing bundles of feathers, brown and mottled, grey and white, not much use to anyone. She picked up the next box, it nearly fell apart in her hands. Inside were ribbons in every shade, neatly coiled. A scrap of yellowed paper lay amongst them: a receipt, the ink faded but still readable: an amount in Italian lire, the date 1942. This must be part of Violetta's old stock, untouched for decades. The task of sorting through it all put off year after year.

Sifting through the rainbow of ribbons brought up images of neat fitted suits, peekaboo veiling and cute cocktail hats dipped flirtatiously over one eye. Stella picked up a wooden dome, not far off the size of her own head. Had Fernanda's sister used this to mould the shape of the hats or to show them off to good effect? There were other blocks of wood in the cupboard too but whilst retrieving them, her fingers brushed against something soft, a hat fashioned from leaf-green felt, flattened almost beyond recognition. She blew on it softly, immediately regretting the puff of dust that made her sneeze. This had been a pretty thing once, decorated with a delicate spray of silk violets, the centre of each fashioned from a tiny jewel. She turned the hat over, revealing a lining of patterned silk. It didn't seem right to put such a carefully made object back to languish for goodness knows how many more years. Perhaps she could restore it and try to return it to its former glory.

A bell jangled. Stella must have forgotten to relock the door. Picking up the hat, she hurried up the stairs. A young woman – late teens, early twenties perhaps – stood just inside the door.

'*Buongiorno*,' Stella said, installing herself behind the counter and popping the hat beside the till.

'*Buongiorno*,' the girl replied. Her accent marked her out as English, as did her milky white skin and light reddish hair. 'I wasn't sure if it was okay to come in. The sign said closed but then I saw your handbag on the counter and realised the door was unlocked.'

'I am supposed to be closed but I'm happy to help you.' Stella switched to English, to the girl's obvious relief.

'Thank you.' She glanced towards the till. 'That's a cute little hat.'

Stella tweaked one of the silk flowers. 'I found it in the back of a cupboard downstairs. I was just wondering if I could salvage it somehow.'

'Do you have a kettle?'

'We might have a travel version, it depends what size you need,' Stella said, surprised her customer had changed the subject so abruptly. But that was young people these days. They never seemed to have the time to just stand and chat.

The girl smiled. 'It's not for me. You could use it on the hat. You could steam it back to shape.'

Stella pulled the felt in her hands. 'Clever you. I hadn't thought of that.'

'I went to a make-your-own-fascinator session on a friend's hen night. The milliner shared all sorts of odd hints and tips.'

Stella didn't want to think about hen nights. Carol was insisting on organising Stella's: something over the top with a theatre matinee, cocktail making and cupcakes. Her friend would have a blue fit if she knew there was a chance Stella wasn't going to walk down the aisle. *Stop it*, she told herself. Joe would come around. He'd apologise for his impetuous behaviour soon enough. He just needed a little time.

'So, you don't want to buy a kettle.' Stella gave a laugh that she knew sounded a little false.

'I was hoping you might have something for this.' The girl fished something out of her handbag and laid it on the wooden counter: an old coin strung on a length of leather.

Stella rubbed the coin between her thumb and forefinger. 'One lira, from Mussolini's time. I haven't seen one of these for years. There's something engraved on the back but it's not clear what letter it is.'

'I don't know whose initial it could be. This necklace was amongst a few bits my grandpa left me. The leather is old and cracked. I'm scared it will break and I'll lose it.'

'Was your grandpa Italian?' If so, this girl didn't take after him; she was a classic English rose.

'No, he was English but his family lived in Alassio up until the end of the thirties.'

'But this was minted in 1941.' Stella squinted.

'I don't know where he got it from, it's a bit of a mystery. As far as I know he never came back here.'

'Not as a soldier?'

'He – Grandpa Lance – fought in North Africa. I wish I'd taken the time to talk to him about it.' She chewed the edge of her thumbnail.

'Mmm... well, you don't want to lose it. I'm not sure we have a leather thong like this, though. Have you thought of a chain? I will need to have a rummage to find something that will fit, the hole drilled here isn't very big. What time does your bus leave?'

'Oh, I'm not just here for the day, I'm staying at least until after the weekend.'

'With friends? There isn't a hotel as far as I know.' Stella turned the coin again, running a finger over the eagle's spread wings.

'A man I met at the tennis club in Alassio arranged for me to lodge with his mother, Fernanda.'

Stella took a breath. 'I can't imagine Fernanda taking paying guests.'

'You know her? Oh, I suppose you know everyone when you live here.'

'I'm only passing through myself, but you're right, everyone knows everybody here.' Stella paused. She knew she shouldn't, but she couldn't help but ask. 'The man at the club, I might know him. Did you catch his name?'

'He was called Gino.'

'Gino Perillo.' It was the first time Stella had spoken his name in years.

18

Amy stepped back into the street. She hoped she'd done the right thing leaving the necklace at the shop. She wasn't like her brother Jack, who'd happily leave his passport and phone with some guy he'd met in a bar. Maybe she was too cautious, the village didn't seem like a hotbed of crime, and Stella seemed lovely. She couldn't believe they'd been chatting for the best part of half an hour.

The rest of the morning passed by in a flash and by the time she decided to search out some lunch it was a quarter to two. For such a small place it was amazing how she'd managed to walk round in circles, getting lost in the maze of streets. It was the layering of the village she couldn't quite get her head around. It seemed so odd to find front doors half-hidden beneath the steps to the neighbouring property and doorways that seemed to lead into rocky walls. Sometimes she'd see a house that looked poky and dark, only to round a corner and realise the views from its upper windows looked out upon hills. She'd stopped to admire an old lantern, a painted saint in a tiny shrine, a flight of steps with a potted plant on every tread. It was easy to see how her grandpa would have fallen in love with the place but the message on the reverse of the postcard told her there was something more.

The bar she'd gone to with Leo that morning was surprisingly quiet, it seemed the local folk had disappeared indoors. She found a spare table and picked up the menu. She wasn't too sure what was in a *torta verde* but when the waitress wandered out she ordered it anyway and asked for a glass of white wine. Drinking at lunchtime was probably on Fernanda's list of sins, but the old lady wasn't likely to spot her, she was bound to be at home snoozing in her armchair.

There only seemed to be one member of staff looking after both the bar and the gelateria counter but Amy had time to kill. She lingered over her lunch, trying and failing to identify which dark, leafy green vegetables were encased in the golden pastry and ended her meal with an espresso, toying with the cup and saucer long after she'd finished the teeny drink.

She glanced at her phone, it was now almost three. She didn't want to waste away the afternoon and she'd already made a plan. She hadn't visited the church of Sant' Agata yet. Grandpa had been a believer; if he'd come to this village he must have gone inside. Amy wasn't likely to find a connection to him in the church but it would be nice to walk in his footsteps.

She paid and left, cutting through the passageway. The main piazza stood deserted in the afternoon sun, the only signs of life a girl of about nine or ten riding her pink bicycle around and around. Perhaps she'd sneaked outside whilst the rest of her family were having their siesta. Amy approached the church. She gave the panelled wooden door a push but it remained resolutely closed. A small notice she hadn't spotted before stated the opening times: 8–12, 4.30–8. Another hour and a half to wait.

'*Salve!*'

She turned at the man's voice. He was dressed in a black cassock, a silver crucifix dangling low. A round, friendly face smiled at her from beneath a crop of short curly hair. Chubby cheeks and a small mouth gave him the look of a cherub. If it hadn't been for the lines around his eyes she might have put him at twenty-two or three, but he was probably nearer thirty. She'd always thought of priests as white haired, wise and old, not young like this one.

'Oh, umm, *salve!*'

'You wish to enter the church?'

'Yes, but it looks like I need to come back later.'

'Wait.' He put a finger to his lips. Almost on cue, the church bells began to chime. He laughed. 'Now it is three. Let us go inside.'

'But it says four thirty.' She gestured to the notice.

'The Lord is available twenty-four hours a day.' He smiled, reached into his pocket and pulled out a great key.

He unlocked the door and ushered her into the vestibule. Ahead of her lay another hefty wooden door.

'*Attenzione!*' He pointed out a small step.

The church was even bigger than it looked from the outside, the ceiling so high she couldn't imagine how anyone had managed to paint the faded frescoes.

'Welcome to our glorious church.'

'*Che bella!*' She tried out a couple of words of Italian, feeling her cheeks burn at her clumsy pronunciation.

He smiled. 'You must look around in peace but afterwards I hope that you can help me.'

'Me?'

'I have a decision to make and you will be...' He rubbed the fingers of his left hand together, searching for the word. 'Unbiased. Now, please enjoy our church, signorina...'

'Amy.'

'Father Filippo. I will leave you to contemplate. Perhaps start with this picture; it is very beautiful, I think.'

He pointed to a classic *Madonna and Child*, Mary's face pale and serene, the infant's remarkably long legs dangling below his white dress. The proportions were rather odd but Filippo was right, it was beautiful. Amy turned to say so but he had moved away, sitting head down in one of the pews, silently praying.

Amy moved around the church, conscious of the silence. In front of a painting of Sant' Agata a row of candle-shaped bulbs stood next to a metal money box. Amy dropped in a fifty-cent piece; one light flickered. She closed her eyes for a few seconds, thinking of Grandpa Lance. When she opened them the priest was standing in front of the altar, gazing at the cross with a look of wonder as though he were seeing it for the first time. She waited for him to turn around before she spoke.

'You said I might be able to help you.'

'Oh, yes. It is a small question but a rather long story... Of course, if you are in a hurry...'

'No hurry,' Amy said.

'Good. We have a ceremony in the village next week, a special service to commemorate the life of one of our young men. He fell in 1944 but it is only now that we are able to lay his body – well, his bones – to rest.'

'Where has he been?'

'Lying peacefully under the soil, a good few kilometres from here. A man from Paris purchased an abandoned *rustico*, dreaming of a retirement making wine. A wealthy man, with time for leisure, he spoke to the right people and got permission to dig out a swimming pool. It was a shock when his workmen found a skeleton, and when they saw the bullet hole in the back of the skull, the police were called. It was a crime, of course, but one from long ago. When the story spread, we knew he must have been a local man to be found in a place like that. Only someone from the village would have known the old mule path up through those woods. He must have thought he'd got away. And then...' The priest crossed himself.

'Who was he?'

'Of course, at first we did not know, but once we knew the skeleton dated to the war years, people began to come forward with their stories, hoping for answers. Old Signora Togliatti whose family owned the little *alimentari*, for example. She had a teenage brother who was sent to the Russian front, missing presumed dead. More than eighty years later she hoped that somehow it would prove to be him so that she might find some closure.'

'How sad. And this man, you now know who he was?'

'Pietro Parodi, dead at barely twenty-one. He had been one of Mussolini's soldiers. At first he was proud and happy to fight for Italy but when Mussolini was overthrown and Italy surrendered, he was one of many cheering. Perhaps it seems strange to celebrate the humiliation of the country whose uniform you wore. But ordinary people had become weary, sick of the war. Il Duce – Mussolini to you – was no longer invincible, he had showed that by his foolish adventures in Ethiopia and by dragging us into Hitler's war. Many wanted peace with the Allies whatever the price, but the Germans turned on us, installing Mussolini as a figurehead for their puppet government in the North. He insisted those fit and able present themselves to fight on for fascist Italy but thousands like Pietro refused.

'Some joined partisan bands up in the hills but others lay low in their village homes. Pietro joined the local communist party, so I am told. Loyalties were divided but in a place like this we still had to live together. The butcher had a picture of Mussolini on the wall right up until the end but who could afford to starve themselves or their families? And those here who supported the fascists did not want to betray their neighbours' sons like Pietro, whatever their politics. Then one day the Germans came.' The priest's voice tailed off. He gazed back at the altar.

'What happened?' Amy said quietly.

'They called it a *rastrellamento*, it means a sweeping up. Their soldiers stormed through the village looking for partisan fighters and deserters. Pietro's sister told me she urged her brother to flee. Her family thought he had got away; they made excuses to themselves for why they never heard from him again. But others...' The priest shook his head. 'Something terrible happened here. Something that makes men lose their faith or cling to God, our only hope amidst the horror.'

Amy waited, she couldn't imagine terrible things happening in such a peaceful pretty place.

'Have you seen our village hall?' Filippo continued. 'That was built where a row of cottages once stood, burnt to the ground, their inhabitants with them. Others were dragged from their homes and shot in the square across from this church, against the far wall. Seventeen people died that day, the youngest victim a boy of thirteen. They had information that he acted as a messenger for a partisan gang up in the hills.'

'How absolutely awful.' Amy couldn't begin to imagine it.

Filippo twisted his hands together. 'Pietro's return has brought old memories to the fore but it is not good to dwell on these bad things. We will parade his casket through the streets,

the village band will play, after the service there will be feast-
ing. In Italy all is celebrated with food, the good and the bad.'

'And you wanted my help?'

'The villagers have raised the money for a permanent
plaque in honour of those innocent victims. Unfortunately, a
lorry carrying cement reversed into the original commemorative obelisk some years back and it has taken all this time to
agree on a suitable replacement.'

Amy nodded, not sure how she could possibly fit in.

'There has been much discussion about where this tribute
should be placed, no one could agree. The mayor placed a box
on the counter of the bar for people to vote and the majority
believed Sant' Agata to be a fitting place. But where? I cannot
decide on which wall, north or south? You appeared at the
church door just as I prayed for God's guidance. What better
person to make the final decision?'

Amy put her hands to her face. 'I can't... I feel over-
whelmed.'

'Do not be, my child. I saw you light a candle. Think of that
loved one.'

'My grandpa Lance.'

'He will guide you. Is he not up in heaven?'

In Alassio she'd found it so hard to imagine a younger
version of Grandpa but now he seemed to materialise in front
of her, the parting in his hair as neat as the crisp crease down
the front of his trousers. She saw him walking down the aisle,
his wheelchair gone. He turned towards one wall and then the
other, his eyes settling on a space to one side of an oil painting
of Saint Jerome in the wilderness. She waited for the doubts to
come but she had none.

'Just there.' She pointed.

'Thank you. I think that will be perfect. I hope you will be here to witness the unveiling, Amy. I understand you are lodging with our parishioner, Fernanda.'

'I would love to come but I'm not sure how long I will be staying here.'

'Of course, I understand.'

They walked in silence down the aisle. The priest stopped to lock up the church. Amy wandered across the piazza feeling slightly dazed. The priest's surprising request had helped her as much as it had helped him. Inside Sant' Agata she had felt closer to Grandpa than ever. Even if she never discovered the connection between him and the village, her visit had been worthwhile. She'd come to the right place.

An elderly lady she'd seen that morning smiled and wished her *buonasera*. Another man nodded in recognition. Amy nodded back and smiled. It seemed that in less than twenty-four hours, she'd become part of the village.

* * *

Fernanda still hadn't changed the bulb in Amy's bedside light. She'd been sitting in the kitchen for the best part of the afternoon staring at the wall. Remembering.

It had been the weirdest day. Encountering that dreadful girl Stella Ferrando again had shifted something in Fernanda's carefully constructed world. There was an English word for how she was feeling, she tried to remember it. She took Gino's school dictionary down from its place next to the cookbooks on her high shelf and flicked through the much-handled pages. Discombobulated: that was the word. The English had good words like that, so did the Germans but she didn't remember much German any more, it had been so many years since Violetta had tried to teach her.

Fernanda was still amazed how quickly she'd recognised Gino's old love. Stella must be nearly sixty now. She looked it too, her forehead lined, her jaw a little droopy. Stella's hair was a deep brown, she must dye it, no one that age had so little grey. But despite all that she was an attractive woman, her hazel eyes had kept their flecks of colour. Stella still had that certain something that had turned Gino's head. Unforgettable, that was the word, in any language.

Fernanda put the dictionary back, she couldn't bear anything untidy or out of place. But her orderly kitchen didn't put her mind at ease. She'd spent years convincing herself she'd done the right thing but the appearance of her son's old girlfriend had flooded her mind with doubts as unstoppable as a landslip in the Alps. If only she had kept quiet that day, contented herself with punishing Gino for taking the moped without permission. Instead, she'd incurred Arturo's wrath, wreaking havoc on his family and hers.

She'd tried to tell herself it was only natural that Gino would leave the village, move to a bigger place, find his own way. Wasn't it a mother's job to protect her young but also help them fly the nest? But Gino hadn't flown, he'd hobbled away like a bird with a broken wing. If she'd sat back and let Stella and Gino's relationship fizzle out of its own accord, the wretched girl would have become a fuzzy memory instead of a first love put on a pedestal, the one that got away. If Fernanda hadn't destroyed their love affair, Gino might have stayed in the village and been close to his mother in her old age. He and his wife Gaia might have taken over his grandparents' land when the farmer renting it came to the end of his lease. Her country-side-loving son could have grown his own olives, maybe even restored the old family *rustico*. Instead, her precious boy was an infrequent visitor, a disembodied voice at the end of a phoneline.

Sometimes she allowed herself to believe she'd saved Gino from an inevitable heartbreak. Arturo would never have allowed Stella to marry him. Decades might have passed but the wound Fernanda's family had inflicted on Domenico and Arturo had cut too deep. But heartbreak was part of life. Gino would have survived. She should have let things run according to God's will. Instead, she'd driven away her only child.

19

The girl on the pink bicycle shot past, disappearing behind Sant' Agata's only to emerge again. Round and round she went, over the cobbles, disappearing and reappearing. A family clutching cones of gelati wandered by, the dad gripping the shoulder of one small child. The mother moved in a strange crablike fashion, trying to walk whilst simultaneously swiping a wet wipe across vanilla-tipped noses and chocolate moustaches.

It was Amy's second morning in the village. She'd gone to the bar and eaten the delicious jam-filled *gobeletti* for breakfast again, kidding herself she wasn't hoping that Leo would choose to do the same. But there was no sign of him and she had no plans other than wandering around hoping that some connection with her grandfather would mysteriously materialise.

She left the church behind and set off down the main street, past a pizzeria where the windows were shuttered and the chairs piled up under the outside awning. From there she took a winding street down into the shadier part of town, crossing through dim passages, up and down twisty lanes where even in her trainers she had to watch her footing.

Amidst the small houses an enterprising artist had set up a gallery. Amy browsed for a while amongst the bright brush-strokes and abstract art. A yearning to sit in Grandpa's shed and do something creative seared through her. The yellows, greens and terracotta colours of the village houses and the vibrant pinks and reds of the cascading flowers had her longing to create some new designs for the pots she'd been planning to make. But Grandpa wouldn't be there whilst she worked. When would the spikes of grief stop coming out of the blue like this? She'd thought she was okay.

Excusing herself from the gallery assistant's concerned gaze she carried on walking, passing under a small lantern she assumed was lit up at dusk. There were a couple of bigger workshops ahead. What strength and sweat must have been used to carve them out of the rock with just mules to carry the building materials, the stones and the earth away.

Music drifted towards her. Oasis playing 'Wonderwall'. A male voice sang along. *How I feel about you now-ow!* He dragged out the last word. The next verse started up, the voice contin-ued, singing fractionally behind the lead vocal. She imagined whoever it was strumming an air guitar, swaggering like one of the Gallagher brothers. Biting her lip to stop herself from laughing aloud, she glanced through the workshop's open door.

Through a haze of dust, a familiar figure bent over a stone plaque shaped like an arched window. She tried to shrink away, not wanting to be caught looking in, but it was too late.

'Amy?' Leo lowered his safety goggles.

'Err, hi!'

He reached behind him to where a paint-splattered CD player sat on the floor-to-ceiling shelves and turned it off.

'I haven't seen one of those for years,' Amy said. 'Sorry, I didn't mean to be rude, it's just everyone seems to stream their music these days.'

'Good luck getting a signal through these rock walls! And anyway the fine stone dust causes havoc if it gets in your phone. It's bad enough when it gets in your hair!' He ran a hand through his, only succeeding in messing it up even more.

'I didn't mean to spy on you. I was just wandering around the village...'

'Did you hear my singing and think, wow, who's that?' His lips twitched.

'I'd stick to the day job,' she quipped.

'You haven't seen my work yet. That might be equally talentless.' He set down his chisel.

'Fishing for compliments?'

'No one apart from Father Filippo has seen this project yet. I am starting to convince myself it's not good enough.'

She stepped nearer. 'I can take a look but only if you're sure.'

'You will be honest? You were honest about my terrible singing. But I am nervous, this is an important commission.'

'The commemorative plaque for the church?'

'Yes, for the wartime massacre. You heard about that?'

Amy nodded. 'I met Father Filippo when I looked round Sant' Agata yesterday.'

'Come round this side of the bench, otherwise you'll be looking at it upside down.'

'Sure.' She squeezed past a headstone etched with a cross and a simple script.

There wasn't much space between the workbench and the

wall. Leo was so near their hips were almost touching. Her breath caught. She forced herself to concentrate hard on the plaque. She'd expected to find lettering, perhaps a list of names enlivened by a cursive script, not these plants, flowers and trees. Two doves perched on top, olive branches in their beaks; three-dimensional butterflies fluttered around the sides. At the base, crinkle-edged poppies seemed to burst from the solid stone. The detail took her breath away. A date was inscribed below the doves; at the bottom there were two lines in Italian.

'What does it say?'

'*In memory of our seventeen innocent citizens. Cruelly struck down, they live forever in our hearts.* The doves are a bit of a cliché but Father Filippo and the others on the committee wanted an easily recognisable symbol of peace. We need to remember who died at the hands of the Germans and their collaborators but we must come together as a village so that their souls rest untroubled.'

'I think it's utterly beautiful. I saw a butterfly just like that one earlier today, a yellow one.'

He swept his hand across his work. 'All the plants and creatures I chose are native to this area. It is a reminder that the beauty of the place lives on, that Mother Nature provides, whatever terrible things humans do. That peace will always win. Of course, not everyone appreciates the sentiment.' He rubbed his hand across his jaw.

'Whyever not?' She studied the carving of the doves, trying to distract herself from the enticing scent of his woody cologne which mingled with the scent of the damp and the stone dust.

'Some people believe that something full of life and beauty is an inappropriate way to commemorate a massacre.'

She felt a surge of indignation on his behalf. 'What do they want depicted? Blood and gore?'

'The alternative design had a pair of doves at the committee's request. But they were perched on a fascist helmet and swastika broken in two.' He made a face.

'I can't imagine it was a difficult choice,' she joked.

'Closer than you think. The other proposal was submitted by the mayor's nephew. He lives in Florence, he has rarely visited the village.'

'People must be glad that someone local got the job. It seems only right that they chose you.'

'That is not what everyone thinks.' An odd cloud passed across his face.

'Why not?'

He did not answer, just picked up his chisel. Had she overstepped some invisible line?

'Well, thanks for showing me the plaque. I'd best get going, you'll want to get on.'

'Sorry,' he said, forcing a smile. 'It is a complicated question to answer. Let us just say that people here have long memories.'

Amy nodded. 'Well, I'll see you then.'

'Amy?' He stopped her as she reached the door. 'I was planning to walk up to the Old Chapel tomorrow morning. Have you been there? Only, I was wondering...'

She smiled; he looked so awkward, fiddling with the handle of his chisel. 'I haven't been there, but I'd love to.'

'Shall I see you at Nonna Fernanda's around nine o'clock?'

'Will you be wearing more than a towel this time?'

He laughed. 'Maybe...'

'See you tomorrow.' Amy made a quick exit. What had possessed her to make a quip like that? It would make it even harder to get that image of him half-naked out of her head. She carried on her walk, smiling to herself.

20

Stella ground rock salt and garlic to a smooth paste; Domenico's small kitchen filled with its tantalising scent. The bunch of basil she'd picked up on the walk home lay waiting on the old wooden chopping board, she'd found a hunk of parmesan in the larder and supplemented this with a triangle of pecorino. She concentrated on the rhythm of pestle against mortar, humming the tune of an old Ligurian folk song as she worked. She could almost be back in her mother's kitchen at a time when struggles with mathematics and teenage spots were her only cares. Mamma always gave her the job of preparing the cheese ready for the pesto, a task Stella rarely accomplished without scraping her knuckles on the grater. How she wished she'd known to cherish those days instead of rushing through her chores, longing to escape, jump on her bike and cycle up the mule path to meet Gino at their secret hideaway.

She began picking off the basil leaves, tearing them roughly, inhaling the scent of home. Her phone lay just in reach. She couldn't quite believe Joe wouldn't follow up his earlier message with another. He'd sent a photograph from the hotel in Portofino: a bare-chested selfie, a lurid coloured cock-tail in his hand. A James Patterson novel rested on his pink swimming trunks. An attractive blonde woman, face half-hidden behind oversized sunglasses, occupied the adjacent lounger by the turquoise pool; she appeared to be in the process of rubbing suncream into her caramel-coloured thighs. Stella felt a frisson of irritation. Had Joe deliberately angled the camera to capture his shapely neighbour? Was he trying to make her jealous? Stella didn't play games; she'd had enough of that with Ricky.

She couldn't resist picking up her phone again, even though it meant she'd have to re-wash her hands to finish preparing the basil. She read Joe's message once more in the vain hope she'd somehow got the wrong end of the stick but his words were plain as the nose on his now slightly sunburnt face.

JOE

Waiting for you to join me x.

No *missing you,* no *how are you?* No hint of apology for leaving in a strop, no enquiry after Domenico's wellbeing. Just an assumption she'd hotfoot it to Portofino, strip off down to her swimwear and grab an Aperol Spritz, leaving her papà's beloved younger brother in the lurch. She knew her insistence on staying in the village was frustrating for Joe, but her gut told her she had to stay, whatever Joe, Lauren and Carol – if she ever found out – might think.

Stella filled Domenico's great pan with water and chucked in some salt but she wouldn't start to boil the water yet. If Lauren called halfway through the cooking, her dinner would turn into a soggy mess. And there was no way Stella would get away with not answering the phone. Instead, she laid the table using a placemat and a battered coaster for her glass of wine, even though the kitchen table was decorated with the round rings from a hundred previous mugs and glasses.

She found a bottle of kitchen cleaner under the sink and sprayed some on the tiles, killing time until she received Lauren's call. Communication had been so much less fraught when Stella could tuck the landline phone under one ear and potter around tidying whilst she talked. Now, Lauren's fondness for FaceTime meant Stella couldn't shy away from her daughter's scrutiny. She'd have to watch her eyes widen in horror when she heard how Stella had been responsible for dear Papà's death.

The theme tune from *Succession* rang out. Stella tucked her hair behind her ears, drank a big slug of wine and picked up her phone. Lauren's face swam into focus. She looked tired, washed out in her black work jacket and pale blouse. Her daughter's fancy stainless-steel cooker was just in shot, she must be in the kitchen, probably perched on one of her leather-topped barstools.

'Lauren, hello, love. How was your day? How did your presentation go? I don't know how you do it, standing up in front of a roomful of people.' Stella was aware she was babbling.

The vertical frown lines between Lauren's eyes deepened. 'It was fine. I'm pretty confident our pitch swung the deal.'

'Sounds like you'll be getting another promotion soon. Now, have you got everything ready for your trip to the States?'

'I haven't called to talk about me,' Lauren said briskly. 'I want to know what's going on with you. What's happening with Joe?'

'Joe?' Stella was all psyched up to tell Lauren about the

worst day of her life – and her daughter wanted to hear about a lovers' tiff!

'Yes, the man you're walking down the aisle with in less than eight weeks.'

'Joe will come round, he'll be fine.'

'He'd better be. I've bagged an appointment on Saturday with the personal shopper at Selfridges to pick out my outfit. They're like gold dust.'

'Oh, well, I'll have to get married then,' Stella quipped.

Lauren glowered. 'I don't understand you these days, Mum. Is it something to do with the change? Maybe your hormones are making you do strange things.'

Stella stayed silent. She didn't have the headspace to cope with a row.

'Sorry,' Lauren said. 'I shouldn't have said that.'

'Maybe it's coming back here, stirring up old memories.'

Lauren tapped a pen on her granite worktop as if encouraging a junior colleague to sit up and pay attention.

'Okay, Mum, you may as well tell me: what *is* all this nonsense about killing your papà?'

21

1981

Stella looked up, the mother of the woman who ran the *salumeria* was resting her skinny arms on the balcony. Stella called out, '*Buongiorno.*' The old lady gave a toothy cackle; she made it her business to know exactly what everyone was up to and where they were going but Stella knew she wouldn't give her away.

Stella walked on to the top of the street, the ancient stone archway at its end acting like a picture frame for the view across the terracotta rooftiles to the hills beyond. She checked her watch and hurried along the road until she reached the shallow steps climbing up through the countryside. The ground was uneven, weeds growing between the mismatch of stones that made up the path. A lizard scurried into a gap in the rough stone wall. Vivid red poppies bobbed their heads in the slight morning breeze. She felt as free as the yellow butterfly that fluttered past.

Now she'd got this far, she wasn't likely to be seen by anyone except for old Francesco tending his vineyard. His plot was so small most people wouldn't bother with it; rumour had it he consumed the whole harvest. This morning the old man wasn't in sight but his scruffy crossbred dog stood at the perimeter barking and barking as she passed.

The steps became steeper the nearer she got to the Old Chapel. As usual there was no one around. The one-room building had long ceased to be a place of worship. Only Fernanda came here on a regular basis to clean the windows and sweep the step. Today, Stella and Gino were safe. Both their mothers were on church cleaning duties at Sant' Agata and Papà and Uncle Domenico would be occupied at the shop. Stella could safely climb the mule track to where Gino would be waiting at his grandparents' abandoned *rustico*. Their special place.

'Stella!' Gino's voice came from out of the blue. He stepped out from behind the chapel, a small rucksack slung over one shoulder. Her heart leapt. She loved him so much and he was hers. How could she be so lucky?

'What are you doing here? I thought you were going to meet me at our place.'

'I have a surprise for you.' His eyes were shining. 'We'll need to meet at the car park in half an hour.'

'The other side of the village.' Stella gave a great huff of irritation.

'I wish I could have saved us both the walk but I couldn't exactly phone you at home.'

'I know, I don't really mind. But why the car park?'

'It's a secret. You'll see.' He gave her a maddening grin. 'We'd better go separately. You go first and wait for me, go the long way round.'

'Okay.' She bounded down the steps two at a time, sending Francesco's dog into a fresh frenzy of barking.

She passed under the archway, making a detour through

small piazzas where steep flowerpot-lined stairs led to unpainted front doors, down gloomy stone passageways under unlit lanterns, past tiny shrines set into walls, past the carpenter's workshop where clouds of dust hung in the air. Eventually, she arrived at the war memorial by the winding road that led to their meeting place. Hugging the kerb, she walked downwards until she came to the car park.

She leant nonchalantly against a post; a three-wheeled truck rattled past. A few minutes later, Gino appeared, sweeping his hair back from his nut-brown forehead, a huge grin on his face.

'What are we doing?' She bounced from foot to foot.

'Your carriage awaits, my lady.' He gestured to a red moped between two parked cars.

Stella gasped. 'Where did you get that from?'

'Mamma's cousin has come for the weekend. He knows Mamma doesn't approve of his flashy transport so he's parked it here for the day.'

'And he's letting you borrow it?'

Gino kicked a stone towards the fence. 'Not exactly, but the keys were on the side in the kitchen and as long as we bring it back in one piece...'

'Oh.' Stella knew she should refuse. Papà and Gino's mamma, Fernanda, would go spare if they found out.

He swung one leg over the seat. 'Are you coming or what?'

'Where are we going?' She hoped he didn't hear the wobble in her voice. What if they crashed? They didn't even have helmets.

'Sanremo.'

The beach, the palm trees, the glamorous casino. Paradise.

Glad she was wearing jeans, she climbed on behind,

needing no prompting to wrap her arms around him, burying her face in the back of his shirt.

'Hold on tight.' He glanced over his shoulder and they were off. Down the winding road, leaning into the bends. Now she knew what freedom felt like! Her and Gino together, and not another soul knowing where they were going. Pressed up against his back, she couldn't see the traffic on the other side of the road until it was upon them; cars and trucks flashed past in a blur. Adrenaline coursed through her. And suddenly she was laughing and laughing with the sheer joy of it.

They parked near the seafront. She climbed off the moped. Her legs felt weird and wobbly, her heart still racing from the exhilarating downhill ride. She ran her hand through her hair. Her styling mousse had set solid in the sun.

'Let me.' He smoothed a rogue strand away from her face and kissed her. Right there where anyone passing by could see. But it didn't matter. They were in Sanremo now. Far away from Fernanda's talk of shame and sin. Far away from her parents' warnings to keep away from the boy she loved. Blinded by some old feud with Gino's family, they couldn't see how kind and funny and clever and generous he was. She couldn't understand why Papà wouldn't give him a chance.

He took her hand, their fingers entwining. 'Where shall we go?'

'Anywhere.'

'Gelato?' His eyes sparkled.

She was about to point out that it was only nine thirty but there were no rules now. No Mamma poking Stella in the ribs, tutting at a non-existent roll of flab, no Fernanda rationing sweet things and treats as if God himself must approve before she dished them out.

They found a gelateria almost immediately. Gino ordered:

three flavours each and a wafer poking out. Blobs of purple *frutti di bosco* fell on Stella's trainers. She couldn't eat it fast enough. Gino licked the drips off her fingers, laughing.

There were so many things they could see in Sanremo: the cathedral, the Russian church, Alfred Nobel's villa, the famous casino. But they couldn't be bothered. They just lay on the sand, him and her entwined in each other's arms. They left the beach only to queue up with the tourists for slices of pizza, which she ate so fast her stomach hurt.

'I want to stay here forever,' Stella said.

'Maybe we'll live here together someday.' Gino tilted her chin and kissed her. He tasted of pizza and the sea, his mouth warm as the sun.

'I love you,' Stella said before she could stop herself.

'I love you too,' Gino replied.

It was the best day of her life.

* * *

Stella didn't tell Lauren all of it. She didn't want to let her daughter's comments spoil the magic of that memory. It was still the best day of her life. Until it turned into the worst.

'So, you went for a joyride to Sanremo and sat on the beach,' Lauren said, picking up on the little she'd gleaned. 'I expect you were in trouble when you got back. Did your parents ground you?'

'No,' Stella said. Sometimes she wished there had been a punishment, but no punishment could fit her crime.

22

1981

They pulled up in the village car park. It was all as they'd left it: Uncle Domenico's Fiat Panda with the bent door panel in the far corner, the rusty Ape truck Signora Togliatti's husband drove to and from the goat farm still in its usual place.

'We did it!' Gino said.

Stella nodded, biting her lip, still half shy, half excited after their exchange of 'I love yous'. She was scared of looking at him, seeing wariness in his eyes but when she did they were full of love. This time they didn't go their separate ways at the top of the road but recklessly walked through the village together, high on happiness, not wanting to hide away any longer, careless of the consequences. They reached the passageway beside Sant' Agata's. Instead of a quick goodbye, Gino pulled her to him, kissing her deeply. He pressed her up against the wall, uneven stone scraping against her sun-sensitive shoulders.

'*Ti amo, ti amo,*' he gasped out. She could feel he wanted more.

'*Ti amo.*' She sounded like a sexy temptress, nearly grown

up, nothing like the virginal schoolgirl who'd sneaked out of the house that morning. She slid a hand beneath his shirt. Would she dare do something more?

'Not here, we can't.' He seemed to come to his senses, backing away from her.

'Where shall we go?'

Gino didn't answer. A strange expression crossed his face.

Stella swung around. Fernanda stood at the entrance to the passageway, lips pursed, a tin of polish in one hand, an old rag in the other. All three of them stood frozen like actors in a strange, silent tableau, waiting for the curtain to fall.

Fernanda stuffed the polish into the pocket of her apron. The rag fluttered away; she didn't seem to notice it.

'Mamma...' Gino began.

'Don't you "mamma" me.' Fernanda's voice was measured, cold. She grabbed her son by the arm, pulling him away so roughly that he stumbled on the cobbles. The key for the moped clattered on the ground. Puzzlement then understanding crossed his mamma's face.

'You disgusting, shameless girl, where have you been? Where did you take my son?'

'Me? He was driving.' Stella instinctively defended herself, immediately regretting getting Gino into more trouble.

'Don't blame him, you little tart.'

'Don't call Stella that.' Gino's eyes flashed.

'I told you not to see her, I told you not to get mixed up with her.'

Gino opened his mouth but the look on Fernanda's face would have silenced a mafia boss.

'Go home!' Fernanda said. 'Now!' She gave him a small shove.

Gino looked at Stella helplessly. She gave him a tiny nod.

Fernanda waited until Gino had reached the end of the passageway. Stella knew how much it had cost him not to turn around.

'Say what you want to me, I don't care.' Stella raised her chin.

'You'll care by the time I've finished with you, young lady. We're going to see your papà.'

Stella's stomach lurched. She'd be grounded for a month; she wouldn't be able to see Gino. She had to stop Fernanda.

'No, no, you can't!'

'Oh, I can.' Fernanda smiled.

Stella flicked her hair, trying to look nonchalant. 'There's no point speaking to Papà. He won't take any notice of what you say. He hates you and your family.'

Fernanda winced. For a beautiful moment Stella thought she'd won, that she could turn around and go home and hope her parents never found out. Gino would have to face whatever punishment his mother served up but Stella knew Fernanda was too scared of losing her only child's love to be angry with him for long. Instead, she'd blame Stella for the whole escapade.

Fernanda laughed, a cruel mocking sound. 'Good. I am glad. If Arturo hates us, he'll make sure you stay away from my precious boy.'

Stella had played her cards all wrong. She groped for words, desperately searching for a way out. Fernanda's bony fingers gripped Stella's lower arm as she steered her towards home. It was pointless trying to shake her off. Stella had nowhere to run.

Mamma opened the front door. Her hand flew to her face.

'Go!' Mamma hissed. 'Please, Fernanda, go before Arturo sees you.'

It was too late. Papà lumbered into the hall, yawning as though he'd just woken up from a doze. His trousers were held up by braces and his sleeveless white vest was splattered with spaghetti sauce. Stella couldn't help wishing he looked more dignified.

Fernanda launched into a tirade. Papà frowned, trying to grasp everything she was trying to say. Stella couldn't follow it all either but she couldn't mistake the list of crimes: joyriding, theft, fornication, corrupting an innocent boy.

'I didn't...' Stella began.

'I told you not to see that boy,' Papà said quietly. 'As for you, Fernanda, I've heard enough, you can go.' He ushered her out into the street.

Papà waited until the door was firmly shut. Then he began to yell. Never had Stella seen her father like this, waving his arms, shouting, eyes bulging. She could hardly make sense of what he was saying. Her younger brother and sister, who had been loitering wide-eyed and silent at the top of the stairs, had the sense to make themselves scarce.

'You defied me! What do you have to say for yourself?' he raged.

'I love him!' Stella wept.

'Love him? You don't know the meaning of the word, you silly girl.'

'Yes, I do.'

'Don't answer me back.' Papà raised his hand. Stella reeled back, whacking her hip on the edge of the hall table.

'Arturo!' Mamma's voice was shocked.

'I wasn't going to hit her.' Papà stood looking at his palm as if not sure what he'd been planning to do with it. Seizing her opportunity, Stella ran up the stairs two at a time.

'I haven't finished with you yet!' Papà yelled.

Stella burst into the bedroom she and Marta shared. Marta fell backwards against the wardrobe, she'd obviously been listening at the door. Stella grabbed one end of the blanket box but it was too late to barricade themselves in. Papà burst into the room.

'Stella!' Papà panted, his face red.

'Get away from me!' Stella screamed.

'I told you...' Papà stopped abruptly. His face contorted. He slapped one hand to his chest, grabbing at the bed's headboard with the other, doubled up in pain.

'Papà?' Stella said.

Papà gave a strange groan. His body seemed to crumple. Marta screamed. The bed broke his fall.

Stella stumbled onto the landing. 'Mamma, come quickly.'

'Stella, call an ambulance!' Marta yelled.

Mamma burst out of the kitchen screeching: 'I'm coming!'

'I'll get Uncle Domenico.' Her brother Giovanni brushed past Mamma on the stairs. The front door slammed shut behind him.

Stella ran to the hall. She grabbed the phone from its cradle, dialled 112, her fingers fumbling out the number. Upstairs Mamma screamed, 'Arturo, Arturo,' over and over again.

Her sister walked quietly downstairs, hand gripping the banister.

'Oh, Stella,' Marta said. 'What have you done?'

* * *

For once in her life, Lauren was silent. Apparently, none of her management training had prepared her for this. No pithy soundbite culled from a PowerPoint presentation could save the day. Stella almost felt sorry for Lauren. She'd never seen her daughter flounder for words like this.

'It wasn't really your fault, Mum,' Lauren said at last. 'You were just a foolish teenager; you didn't mean any harm.'

'Sometimes it doesn't matter what our intentions are, the results are just the same. It didn't matter to your Uncle Domenico whether I meant to kill his brother or not. I'll never forget his face that day.' And she'd never forget the terrible groans Domenico made, thumping up and down on his brother's chest. They might have saved Papà if it happened now, Stella thought. Earlier that day she'd noticed a glass box holding a defibrillator, screwed to the wall of the bar.

'Domenico was probably just in shock. What about your mamma and your brother and sister?'

'Mamma couldn't look at me. At the funeral I put my hand on her arm and she shook me away. I know Marta and Giovanni blamed me too. Of course, they said they didn't but I knew.'

'Is that why I never met them? Why we never went out to Italy to see your family?'

'My sister did invite your dad and me to her wedding years later but I didn't even tell Ricky about the invitation. I knew she didn't really want us there. I never heard from Marta or Giovanni after that.'

'And Gino? What happened to you and him?'

Stella swallowed. It was still so painful to go there. 'Gino wanted us to keep seeing each other but after we met up once or twice, I knew it had to end. When I closed my eyes to kiss him all I could see was Papà collapsing, clutching his chest. As soon as I could, I left the village for England to stay with an old friend of the family. She got me enrolled into a school for my A levels and looked after me. I thought at first I might go back to

Italy after that but I could tell when Mamma answered the phone that I would never feel truly welcome there. I never blamed her. Papà was the love of her life, as important as Gino was to me.'

Lauren's face clouded. 'Is that why you married Dad? For security, to create a new family because you couldn't go home?'

'I never thought of it like that. I fell for your dad because he seemed so like Gino, wild and full of life, fun and exciting. Not the best qualities for a marriage, I suppose.'

Ricky had the same sparkling green eyes as Gino, the same untamed hair. He would have jumped on that red moped just the same. With Ricky she could dream those same crazy dreams. But her ex-husband had turned out to be nothing like her first love. Gino was a charmer, spontaneous, occasionally reckless too but underneath he had a serious side. His anchors were family – no matter how much he railed against Fernanda's rules, he loved his strict mamma – and community. If there was a stage to be built for the village festa he'd be helping the men to secure the scaffolding, if there was an appeal for funds for Sant' Agata's he'd go through his old books and toys finding something he could donate or sell.

Ricky had been all surface charm, no substance. When she'd looked for something more, her husband had made her believe that she was at fault for being boring. In Ricky's words she was 'no fun any more'. It wasn't until she sat alone for hours with baby Lauren that she finally saw him for what he was but she had stuck it out until Lauren went off to college, determined to give her daughter a stable home.

'Dad was always fun though,' Lauren said.

'He never picked you up from school.'

'Somehow that never seemed to matter. But that's because I had you.'

'And I had you, so everything worked out for the best.'

'I thought you were rushing into this marriage but I can see why you want to be with Joe. He's so different from Dad... I saw Dad in town the other day, did I tell you?'

Stella plucked a leaf from the basil plant, holding it under her nose and breathing in its comforting scent. 'No, you didn't. He didn't ask you for money again, did he?'

Lauren laughed. 'Dad gave up asking me the day I offered him a loan and presented him with a list of repayment conditions. He seemed shocked that I equated the concept of lending money with getting my cash back.'

'I'm so sorry.'

'It's not your fault, Mum. Anyhow it doesn't really bother me. Dad's a loveable rogue. He'll never change. He was with another new girlfriend, Maya she's called. Apparently, she plays the tambourine in his new band. I'm not sure how old she is but I'd say she's younger than me.'

'Oh dear.' Stella cringed.

'It's not a good look. You're so much better off with Joe.'

'But Joe's not here.'

'He will be, Mum. He'll come back.'

'Of course he will,' Stella said briskly. 'Now, tell me about this personal shopper business. I'm sure she can help you find a nice outfit but I do hope you're not going to spend too much money.'

23

A key turned in the lock.

'I'm back!' Amy called, entering the kitchen. She'd caught the sun; she looked happier, healthier, Fernanda thought.

'*Buonasera*,' Fernanda said. 'Will you join me for a coffee?' She'd filled the Bialetti hours ago but hadn't lit the stove.

'Yes, that would be nice.'

Fernanda rose from her chair and put on the pot.

'Tell me about your day. Did you do anything nice?'

'I just strolled around, went into the little gallery, ate gelato.'

'Gelato – delicious!' Fernanda couldn't think of the last time she'd indulged. She took two mismatched cups down from the cupboard. Sometimes she toyed with the idea of purchasing a new smart, unstained set from Domenico's shop before checking herself. These were good enough for her; a sinner didn't deserve anything more.

Amy's eyes strayed to the fridge.

'Did you want milk? We haven't any, I never thought.'

'Don't worry, I'm getting used to espresso now.'

'So, you like Leto?' It was important Amy did, though why that should be, Fernanda wasn't sure.

'Yes, very much.' Amy paused, licked her bottom lip. 'Did you manage to fix the lamp in my room? It's not a big deal but it is nice to read in bed.'

'It only needed a new bulb, I bought some today. I meant to replace it earlier. I'll do it now.' She made to get up.

'Let's have our coffee first. Shall I pour?'

'Thank you.' Fernanda accepted the cup, bringing it near to her nose to inhale the rich aroma. 'If everyone was like you, I'd have paying guests more often.'

'Oh, it's nothing.' The girl blushed, actually blushed at Fernanda's compliment.

They drank their coffee together, her young guest's chatter a welcome replacement for the intrusive thoughts that had earlier filled Fernanda's head. She could have sat there for longer but she wanted to sort out the lamp whilst it was still light and before she forgot again.

'We'll change that bulb now. Where did I put the box? I should have left it on the table. I must have put it away some-where.' Fernanda tutted. 'I am getting absent-minded.'

Amy took both cups over to the sink. 'You sit down. I'll look. Where do you think it might be?'

'There's a big wooden cupboard in the other room,' Fernanda said, before she had time to think. She wanted to cry out, 'No! Stop!' but Amy was already at the kitchen door. Fernanda sent up a silent prayer that Amy would somehow find the light bulbs, and nothing more. But as the minutes ticked by, she knew her young guest must have found the pictures. The ones that reminded Fernanda of the sin she must absolve.

Slowly, creakily she rose from her kitchen chair and walked

down the hall, her house shoes silent on the tiled floor. Amy was standing stock still, staring at a black and white photograph: a young, soft-focus Fernanda, one hand proudly raised in a straight-armed salute.

'Amy?'

The girl twitched. She swung around.

'I see you have found my photos.'

Amy bit her lip. 'Is that you?'

It was too late to lie, and besides, lying was a sin.

'Oh, yes, that was me. I was a good little fascist.'

Amy gawped.

'I've shocked you,' Fernanda said.

Amy shifted awkwardly, not sure where to look. 'No... well, yes, actually, a little bit.' She *was* shocked but now her conversation with Leo was beginning to make more sense. His grandma was a fascist. No wonder he'd been wary of talking about the war.

'That is the uniform of the *figlie della lupa*, the fascist organisation for the youngest children. Children of decent folk, friends and neighbours. But the way people talk nowadays, you would think all Mussolini's followers had a forked tongue and a tail like the devil himself.'

Amy peered more closely. 'How old were you when this was taken?'

'Just turned six, proud as punch. "Believe! Obey! Fight!" – that is what we used to chant. I am not proud of it now, of course... such terrible things... but I was so young, how could I have known?'

'You kept the picture.' And put it in a frame, Amy could have added.

'It is important not to forget what happened back then. To

admit my small part in it all.' Fernanda took the photograph from her and stashed it back in the cupboard.

'You were just a little girl.'

'I was seven years old when the German soldiers came to this village. I had no more understanding of politics than a goat in the field. But my sister, Violetta, was thirteen years older than me and she supported Mussolini until the very end.'

'Is this her?' Amy pointed to the beautiful young woman in the framed painting on the wall.

Fernanda nodded.

Amy gazed at the painting, drinking in all the details. Violetta wore a fitted dress with a pointed collar and a row of covered buttons. Big eyes looked up from beneath a cute felt hat, decorated with feathers and flowers, artfully tilted to one side.

'She was very pretty,' Amy said.

'Yes, a real beauty. Violetta was so much older than me, she was almost like the mother she had to be. I was a late baby, a surprise, I expect. Papà was killed at the beginning of the war and our beautiful mamma died of cancer not long after that. Violetta worked so hard as a milliner to provide for both of us.'

'I'm sorry,' Amy murmured.

'Violetta taught me so much. How to cook simple things. Yes, even at five years old I was shaping my own pasta. She gave me a love of languages, music and even mathematics too. But most of all she loved me. She never let me know how hard it was for her. You might not believe me but I never heard her speak ill of anyone. She supported Mussolini as a patriot, from a place of love, not hatred. She was beautiful inside and out. Oh, yes, I can see by the look on your face that you do not think this is possible.'

Amy felt herself flush. 'People are complicated.'

'You, my dear, are very diplomatic. I hope what you have discovered has not made you think ill of me. I hope that you will not want to leave.'

Amy paused. Fernanda's revelations had made her feel rather uncomfortable but she couldn't dismiss the image of Leo's face that flitted unbidden into her head.

'Of course I don't want to leave. But now I need to freshen up. I thought I'd go out to the pizzeria.'

'I made some fresh pasta earlier. I had thought to suggest we might eat together. But now...' The old lady looked away.

'Do you have a bottle of wine?' Amy said.

'Of course. Just local wine from a vineyard nearby.'

'That sounds perfect. Shall we have a glass? I'd love you to cook for me.'

She followed Fernanda into the kitchen. The old lady opened a low cupboard, pulled out a bottle of red with a brown paper label. 'Thank you for staying, Amy, for not judging me too harshly.'

'Why would I judge you for what your sister did? That wouldn't make any sense to me.'

'Others do. Would you mind opening the wine, I haven't much strength in my wrist.' Fernanda handed her a wooden-handled corkscrew.

Amy ripped off the metal foil and eased out the cork. She poured them both a glass, glad of the feeling of warmth and wellbeing that followed the first few sips. She wouldn't bother Fernanda with more questions this evening, but Amy had a strong suspicion there was a lot more to Violetta's story that had been left unsaid.

Domenico's shop stocked endless versions of stovetop coffee
pots but so far Stella had only spotted one kettle. It was a ludicrously expensive, garishly patterned Dolce and Gabbana
designer item that some sales rep must have talked Domenico
into ordering in a moment of madness. Stella wasn't going to
splash that sort of money around. Maybe there was something
in the basement, perhaps in the overflow area below the old
milliner's shop. There wasn't much call for kettles in this part of
the world. Any villager who wanted to boil up some water
would probably use a small saucepan. And there certainly
wouldn't be many customers looking to steam an old cocktail
hat back to its former glory.

24

Domenico's shop stocked endless versions of stovetop coffee
pots but so far Stella had only spotted one kettle. It was a ludicrously expensive, garishly patterned Dolce and Gabbana
designer item that some sales rep must have talked Domenico
into ordering in a moment of madness. Stella wasn't going to
splash that sort of money around. Maybe there was something
in the basement, perhaps in the overflow area below the old
milliner's shop. There wasn't much call for kettles in this part of
the world. Any villager who wanted to boil up some water
would probably use a small saucepan. And there certainly
wouldn't be many customers looking to steam an old cocktail
hat back to its former glory.

Stella didn't have time to go downstairs right now to take a
look, she was about to open up and her phone was vibrating on
the counter. Joe! She snatched it up. Why had she worried? Of
course he wouldn't sulk for long. Of course he would be
missing her. She hadn't missed him all that much but that was
because she was so busy with the shop. He, on the other hand,
had nothing to do but lie by their Portofino pool, thinking of

what they might do together. But it was hard to feel sorry for him when she looked at the photos he'd sent her: dining in the hotel's fancy restaurants, enjoying its luxurious spa, lounging by the pool.

'Hi, Joe! How happy I am to hear your voice!'

'So, you've come to your senses. Which train are you catching?'

'You know I can't leave today.' Stella kept her voice steady despite irritation bubbling up like an overfilled milk pan. 'Domenico is making great progress but Luisa wants him to stay with her for a few more days. If he comes back here too soon, he'll only run before he can walk.'

'He can't walk? Is he in a wheelchair? Stella, this could take weeks!'

'I didn't mean it literally. It was just a turn of phrase.'

'Oh.' Joe didn't sound any happier.

'So, what have you done today?' Her voice sounded too bright, just like when she'd quizzed a teenage Lauren after a day at school.

'We went on a boat trip to the Cinque Terre. It was marvellous.'

'We?' Stella turned a page over in the ledger where Domenico jotted down the day's sales.

'Rachel.' Or at least that's what she thought he'd said. The line wasn't terribly good.

'Rachel? Who's Rachel?'

'*Raquel* is staying at the hotel. We've palled up together for some outings, seeing as we're both on our own.'

Was she the blonde at the pool? Stella didn't like to ask.

'I hope you're leaving something for us to do when I get there.' She tried to sound breezy.

'Well, you'd better hurry up. I'm getting impatient, Stella. I won't put up with any of this when we're married, you flitting off on a whim. I need a woman who wants to be with me and to do what I want to do, 24/7.'

'Like Raquel?'

'Raquel's cultured and charming and she plays golf too. Look, Stella, I can't stop and talk all day. Raquel and I are playing tennis. She booked the court as soon as I mentioned I used to play. Raquel wants to make me happy, to do what I want to do. Actually, perhaps there's no point you coming here after all.' And with that he rang off.

Stella stared at the handset. Had she really just been dumped over the phone? She could already hear Carol's voice scolding her: *Us women have to compromise, Stella. If you want to hang onto a man like that, you have to do what he wants to do. This could be your last chance of happiness.*

About to turn sixty and alone again: she should be feeling devastated but instead she felt strangely calm. She switched her phone to silent and stuffed it right into the bottom of her bag. For too long she'd been ignoring the warning voice in her head. Joe had never tried to boss her around before, never been so uncompromising but maybe he hadn't needed to assert himself. After all, she'd gone along with everything he wanted: the elaborate tasting menus, the dull dinner parties with his friends, Sunday lunch at the golf club where the portions were far too big, the concerts and bands that were his taste, not hers. She'd even let him buy her those slightly too short, slightly too tight dresses. She had bent to his will. Why had it taken her so long to realise?

The truth was, she'd fallen for Joe because he seemed so different from Ricky. But underneath the smooth exterior, the solicitous compliments, the expensive gifts and faultless manners lay the same selfishness. And she'd picked Ricky because his devil-may-care cheekiness reminded her of Gino. Both times she'd failed to look any further, like an optimistic second-hand-car buyer taken in by a new paintjob. It had been different with Gino. Beneath the surface was a solid foundation: kindness, family values and an honest heart.

She caught a blur of colour in the corner of her eye, a woman in red peering in the window. Stella glanced at her watch; she hurried to open the door.

The woman had specks of dried paint in her hair as though she'd been decorating. '*Buongiorno*! I don't suppose you speak English by any chance?'

'Yes, I lived there for many years... I still live there. I'm just taking care of this shop whilst my uncle recuperates from a fall.'

'How kind of you, and lucky for me. I've just bought a holiday home a few streets away. It came with a few sticks of furniture but now I need everything else.'

'You've come to the right place.' Stella tucked her hair behind her ears; somehow it made her feel more businesslike.

The woman produced a sheet of lined paper, a list of items written on both sides. Stella was glad to immerse herself in the task, knowing it was going to be quite a challenge to unearth some of the more esoteric items.

Two hours later, she helped the woman and her bulging bags out of the shop, the Dolce and Gabbana kettle sitting proudly on top. Stella sank down onto the stool behind the counter and began carefully transcribing each item into Domenico's book with a sense of pride she hadn't felt since winning Area Manager of the Year in her twenties. This morning, she'd sold almost four hundred euros' worth of stock. She reached for her phone to share her morning with Joe. And then she remembered. He'd be playing tennis with the glamorous

Raquel, followed by what? Cocktails by the pool? Sunset drinks overlooking the harbour? Joe had met Stella only weeks after he'd split up with his ex. Maybe that was how he'd always operated, clutching onto the next woman who came along.

Stella was done with men; every one she'd picked was a dud. Except for Gino. A physical pain shot through her at the thought of her first love. Despite the bad blood between their families, loving him had been so simple. No guessing games, no keeping of scores. She should have reached out to him once the wound of Papà's death was less raw but the months ticked past until she'd convinced herself he wouldn't love her any more.

Now Joe was gone, she could admit to herself that one of the reasons she'd been scared to come to the village was fearing that her relationship with him would flounder if she chanced upon her old love.

For the first time in years, she let herself imagine what Gino would look like now, his dark hair turning to grey, his green eyes framed by folds and lines. His jeans would no longer fall off his slim hips, they'd be belted into the groove beneath a well-fed Italian papà's tum. She pictured him in an orange shirt, a colour he loved to wear, tackling his favourite *quattro stagioni* pizza surrounded by a big, loving family – a beautiful wife and grownup children drinking wine, laughing and joking.

The bell tinkled; Stella snapped out of her reverie. A man of around her age, carrying a reusable carrier bag, had entered the shop. He looked so much like the Gino of her imaginings she had to stifle a laugh.

'*Buongiorno,*' she greeted him, pushing aside Domenico's accounts book.

The man did not respond in the expected fashion, just

stood and stared. Something in Stella's world shifted. She gripped the countertop. Was she hallucinating or was it really her old love standing there?

'Stella,' Gino said. 'Stella, I can't believe it! What are you doing here?'

25

Amy held her short-sleeved yellow blouse to her nose; miraculously, the mothball smell of Fernanda's wardrobe hadn't transferred to her top. It was a little try-hard for a walk in the hills but she'd dress it down with denim cutoffs and trainers and tie back her hair.

It was still early. Fernanda had woken her up clattering around, clearing up last night's meal before heading off to her daily mass. Amy had offered to help after supper but the old lady had insisted she do it all herself before promptly falling asleep in her chair. Amy had rinsed off the plates and put the pans to soak in the sink but she strongly suspected that she'd face Fernanda's wrath if she did any more chores before bed.

She drank a glass of water and headed for the bar, not fancying a walk up to the Old Chapel on an empty stomach. As she approached the scattering of outside chairs, Leo raised his hand. She took in his half-drunk espresso, the golden pastry crumbs scattered across his plate.

'Great minds think alike,' she said.

'Want to join me?' He shifted a discarded menu and sugar bowl out of the way. 'Oh, watch out for the bucket!'

'Thanks, I would have fallen over that.' She used her foot to nudge a pail full of bleach, polish and cloths out of the way. 'Do you think the cleaner meant to leave this here?'

'He did.' Leo grinned.

'They're yours?'

'Now you've spoilt the surprise!' he joked, smiling at the waitress and ordering himself another *gobeletto*. Amy quickly chipped in to ask for a caffè latte and the same.

'I thought we were going for a walk to the Old Chapel this morning. Are we stopping off on the way?'

'I've got a few jobs to do when we get there. Do not worry, I will not ask you to scrub the floor! You can sit and admire the views before we walk back.'

'I don't mind helping.' It wasn't what she'd imagined they'd be doing but she didn't have anything else planned.

'I hoped you might say that.' He plucked a pair of discoloured rubber gloves from the bucket and waggled the empty fingers. 'I think these would suit you.'

'Cheeky! At least I'll work off some of these calories.' She bit into the delicious little tart that had just appeared.

'You will use up all those calories walking there.'

'Sounds like a challenge.' She took a sip of her coffee, closing her eyes for a second. Sunshine, warmth, just milky enough coffee, a jam-filled pastry: a perfect start to the day. She opened them again to find him smiling at her. Her face heated. There was something about him. She didn't know what it was but it made even a morning scrubbing an old church sound appealing.

'Shall we go? Or do you need to go back to Nonna's first?' he asked.

'No. I'm all set. Looks like you've got everything I'll need.' She looked meaningfully at the bucket.

They left some cash under the saucer and headed off. She walked by his side, the bucket swinging between them. The church bells were ringing. Nine o'clock: Fernanda would be emerging from Sant' Agata. The three men she'd spotted yesterday morning were standing by the old water trough on the other side of the street, talking with their hands as much as their voices as she and Leo walked past.

'We need to head to the end of the village, through the big stone arch, up some steps, past a couple of old vineyards...' he said.

'Then up more steps?'

'You've got it!'

They carried on walking. Outside the *fruttivendolo* the owner looked over her wooden crates of apricots and cherries. Her twenty-something daughter was arranging some peaches in a velvety pyramid. This will be the same again tomorrow, and the day after, Amy thought. A daily ritual – except for Sundays and holidays – perhaps unchanged for years. But everyone she passed seemed quite content.

They stopped for a moment under the stone archway, the lower part of the village falling away, a mishmash of terracotta roofs beneath them, dark green hills stippled in the sunshine like an oil painting.

'Is that it?' Amy pointed to a pale building on the horizon.

'No, we don't have to walk that far but we can go there on another day. That's the way to my great-grandparents' old *rustico*.'

'A sort of farmhouse?'

'Yes, a rough sort of dwelling mainly used for storage but

the farmers would sleep there in summer to make use of the long days.'

'I'd like to see it another time. Shall I carry the bucket for a bit?'

He switched hands. 'No, it's nothing, you concentrate on the views, I've walked up to the chapel a hundred times.'

Amy strode on in the fresh air, breathing in the scent of thyme, marvelling at the delicate two-tone purple petals of the wild sweet peas. Past the vineyards, the steps became steeper. Red valerian sprouted from the gaps in the stone walls, its stems curving outwards towards the sun. Across a scrubby patch of ground dotted with clumps of light blue harebells bleached pale by the bright light was a single-storey white building with a simple wooden cross over the entrance. A small stone fountain stood nearby.

Leo reached above the lintel, retrieving a key on a piece of string. He turned it in the lock and pushed open the plain wooden door. Amy followed him in.

The chapel felt even smaller than it looked from outside. Whatever seating there once was had been removed, leaving just an empty space. Three of the walls were painted a soft white but one still bore the patchy remnants of its original fresco. It was sad there were no longer any worshippers to appreciate the carefully executed drapery in the faded portraits of the saints.

Leo emptied his bucket and went back outside, leaving her gazing at the wall. She heard the sound of running water; he returned with a pailful.

'It would be an easier job if we could heat this water up but there's no electricity here and I can't risk lighting a fire, it's so dry this time of year.'

'So, why is this your job?'

'Nonna Fernanda has looked after the place for years. She came every week to clean and dust, to check the windows for cracks and the corners of the floor for mouse droppings. But now, finally she admits she cannot easily walk up here, though she's still incredible for eighty-seven.'

'You've taken over then, that's good of you.'

He shrugged. 'It isn't much to do but I can only get here once a month.'

He rolled up his sleeves, exposing the tattoos on his biceps. She tried not to let his well-honed golden arms distract her from the task in hand.

'Come on then,' Amy said. 'Chuck us those rubber gloves.'

They scrubbed and mopped and brushed every corner. It was cool inside the Old Chapel but the work was making her hot. It was certainly nothing to do with Leo's close proximity.

Finally, they finished cleaning every nook and cranny. There was no longer anywhere she could write her name in the dust. And definitely not a mouse dropping in sight.

'Fernanda will be pleased with you,' Amy said.

'I am glad to do it. She has always been good to me. I know grandparents aren't supposed to have favourites, but I knew I was hers. When I was a child she used to call me her little man around the house. I think she missed my grandpa a lot. Of course, I still had to behave myself. I could not swear or make a mess but she baked all my favourite treats, all the things she would not allow Papà to have when he was a boy.'

'She will be so proud when she sees your plaque being unveiled.'

'She will be there for the first part of the church service but she will not stay for the unveiling. She will come and see it the next day.'

'She must get tired at her age.' Though it had not stopped

Fernanda staying up until past eleven the night before, drinking wine and chatting to Amy.

'Some people would think it wrong for her to be there.' He crouched down, wiping some non-existent dirt off a flagstone.

'Because her sister was a Nazi sympathiser?'

Leo's head jerked up. 'Who told you this? You have only just arrived and already you hear these rumours? Honestly, this place...'

Amy sat down, cross-legged on the stone floor beside him.

'Fernanda told me herself, last night over our meal. She told me how charismatic and vivacious her sister was, how she dated a German officer. How she sold her cocktail hats to the fascist leaders' wives and went to parties with them.'

'Wow! I am surprised she told you. Nonna does not usually open up like that.'

'I think she wanted to tell her tale to someone from outside the village. It was strange to listen to her. She obviously struggles to deal with the past, she feels such guilt.'

'It is a burden she carries but when the Germans came here she was just seven years old. How could Nonna be guilty of anything? Some folk in the village still judge her because she will not condemn her sister. Violetta was like a mother to her. It was the two of them, their parents dead, no other brothers or sisters.'

'I could tell how much Fernanda loved her. But what happened to Violetta in the end? I heard they did terrible things to women who consorted with the Germans.'

'Violetta did not live to see the end of the war. The very day of the *rastrellamento*, she was visiting a pregnant friend in hospital. A stray Allied bomb fell on the building, killing many people. Violetta was one of them. A kind neighbour in the village took Fernanda in that night and looked after her until she was older. Some people did not approve, but that lady would not condemn a little child for what her sister had done.'

'Such a sad life.'

'It is lucky she has her faith, and her voluntary work means so much to her.' He got to his feet. 'We have done all we can here, shall we walk back?'

She clambered to her feet, glad to free her now numb bottom from the cold floor. She began gathering up the cleaning products whilst he went and tipped the dirty water away.

Back outside, the heat hit her like it had done when she first stepped off the plane. After the dim interior, the sun was almost blinding. For a moment she struggled to make out the small fountain and the bushes and trees. She fumbled in her pocket for her sunglasses.

Leo stepped into the shadow cast by her feet. His hand brushed her forehead. She felt her face burn, her heart beat a little faster.

'There, that is better.' He held up a straggle of grey cobweb. 'But perhaps I should have kept it in your hair for Fernanda to see. If she knows how hard you were working, she might bake you her *canestrelli*.'

'I don't know what they are but they sound pretty good.'

'They're biscuits made with vanilla and lemon zest, shaped like a flower. Nonna's are the best. I have tried to make them myself but they don't turn out nearly as good. Pity my poor papà, he is eating my cooking for the next few days.'

'He's visiting? With that and finishing the plaque, you'll be busy.'

'Yes, he is arriving today. I would love to show you more of the countryside but I had better get back.' He set off down the path. She kept pace with him, trying to think of something to say that wouldn't let her disappointment show.

The descent was far quicker than their climb up the steps. Before she knew it, they were walking back under the stone archway. In a minute or two they would pass the turning that led to his workshop.

'Well, thanks for the walk. It was fun, even though you had me working my socks off.'

'Socks off? I like this phrase.' He paused. 'I was wondering… Would you like to come to dinner with Papà and me tonight?'

'Oh, no, you must want to catch up.'

'He's going to be staying with me right up until Pietro's burial and the unveiling; we will have plenty of time to talk. Besides, Papà can be quite intense. And if you come to dinner, you will distract him from the burnt bits.'

She laughed. 'Well, in that case, how can I refuse?'

'Eight o'clock?'

'I will see you tonight, then.' She walked off quickly before he could catch a glimpse of the great big grin on her face.

26

'I'm looking after the shop. My Uncle Domenico fell off a ladder down in the cantina, he's recuperating at home with Luisa,' Stella said, amazed that she could form coherent sentences with Gino standing in front of her.

'So I heard,' Gino said. 'But what are you doing here? Here in the village?'

Stella eased herself onto the stool behind the counter, needing something solid beneath her. 'I was just, umm, passing through.'

'Passing through from England?' His expression was incredulous.

'We... I made a detour here for a night. I'm on holiday. I was supposed to be getting the train from Sanremo to Portofino.'

'You were staying in Sanremo?' The place they'd gone that day. Was he remembering the joy they'd felt before it all went wrong?

'I almost went to the casino,' she added.

'Despite my mamma's dire warnings?' He raised his eyebrows.

'I might have risked it.' Stella laughed. Was she flirting? In Gino's presence it seemed to come naturally, despite her heart-in-her-mouth nerves. 'But what are you doing here? I thought you lived in Alassio now.'

'It didn't take you long to find out who's doing what around here.'

'I saw Amy, the girl who is staying with your mamma. And I saw Fernanda too, she came in buying light bulbs. Do you come back often and stay with her?'

A frown creased his brow. 'I will visit her, of course, but I stay with my son, Leo, when I come here. He is a stonemason, creating the memorial plaque which will be unveiled after the return of poor Pietro Parodi's bones. I assume you know about that.'

'Yes. You must be proud. And the rest of your family?' She held her breath. This was when she would hear about his wife. His contented life without a Stella-shaped hole in it. And that was a good thing. It would stop this crazy urge to vault over Domenico's counter and throw her arms around him.

'My daughter is between jobs, staying with my ex-wife. She's been helping out at the English Library.'

'We went there once on a school trip when it was in the old building. Do you remember?' Stella said, trying not to show how the words ex-wife made her heart leap. *Calm down, you fool!* Just because he had an ex-wife didn't mean he was single. And she'd just sworn off men, hadn't she?

Those green eyes met hers. 'I remember everything.'

Her breath caught in her chest. She tucked her hair behind her ears, trying to get a grip.

A strange look passed over his face.

'Well, it was nice to bump into you again. I expect I'll see you around, it's a small place.'

With that, he turned and walked towards the door. He hadn't even bought whatever he'd come in to get. The bell tinkled, incongruously cheerful, as he left.

Stella stood open-mouthed. What had she done to prompt his sudden departure? Was there something hideous about her he'd only just noticed? She reached for her handbag to retrieve her powder compact with its dinky mirror. As she undid the clasp, she realised at once what had caused him to scarper. As she'd fiddled with her hair, she'd brought something to his attention: Joe's great big sparkling you're-mine-forever diamond ring.

27

Amy hovered outside Leo's house, clutching her bottle of wine. She'd left Fernanda's early, knowing one false turn in the maze of streets would leave her puffing up and down steps, getting in even more of a fluster than she already was. As it happened, she found her way as though she'd walked it a hundred times before and it was only bumping into Stella that had threatened to make her late.

Amy had been about to take the opportunity to ask Stella whether she'd found a chain for her necklace yet but Stella had seemed in a bit of a daze. And to Amy's shock she'd blurted out that her fiancé, Joe, had ended their relationship out of the blue. Amy had been ready to offer a listening ear, praying it wouldn't make her late. But after repeating her news, as if she could hardly make sense of it still, Stella had shocked Amy again by saying she'd probably had a lucky escape. And then the woman had practically skipped off up the road! It was all rather strange.

Leo's door opened.

'Amy! I saw you through the window. I did not hear you knock.'

'Oh, I hadn't knocked. I thought I might still be a bit early.' She felt her cheeks heat. How could any man be that attractive whilst sporting a long chef's apron splattered with sauce?

'I hope you weren't just going to stand there? Come on in.' He ushered her into the kitchen. His father, Gino, was leaning against the counter.

'This is Amy, she is staying with Nonna.'

Gino's eyebrows quirked; he put down his newspaper.

'Amy. Of course. We met in Alassio. How could I forget? You have brought wine? May I open it?'

'Of course. It's lovely to see you again.' She handed over the bottle.

Leo took some wine glasses from the cupboard.

Gino wrestled with the bottle, removing the cork. He ran his hand through his damp hair. 'Let us go into the living room. You must excuse my appearance; I have had to take a second shower today. The dust in my son's workshop gets everywhere.'

'Have you been to see the plaque?' Amy asked, taking a glass of the ruby-red wine from Leo and sitting down on a somewhat battered couch. Gino took the chair opposite, leaving Leo to sit next to her. Their knees were almost touching. She took a big gulp of wine.

'Yes, at last my son allows me to take a look! It is extraordinary. I am looking forward to seeing the unveiling and partying in the piazza.'

'Papà will be dancing.' Leo smiled.

Gino gestured with his hands. 'I will enjoy myself. Why not? I will dance and eat and drink – not too much but I will still wake up the next morning with a sore head. One finds it harder to recover these days. It is the curse of age.'

'You're only sixty, Papà!'

Gino leant back in his chair and took a great swig of wine.

'I appear ancient to you two, I am sure. So, Amy, have you found out anything more about your nonno? Since I met you, I have been thinking. Perhaps he found himself back in Liguria during the war? There were places in the woods up in the hills where they say escaped Allied prisoners of war hid out in makeshift shelters and outbuildings.'

'Mum did say something to me once about Grandpa escaping from a prisoner-of-war camp, but he fought in North Africa. He was captured in Libya.'

Gino leant forward in his chair. 'Then he could have been here!'

'How? Did he swim?' Leo joked.

Gino tutted. 'Did you pay any attention at school? Many Allied prisoners taken captive in North Africa were shipped to Italy, some to Sicily then on to the mainland, to Naples and on to other camps. Plenty ended up in Liguria. In the chaos after the 1943 armistice, English POWs broke out of the camps and fled to the countryside. Now, Amy, let me take another look at that postcard of yours.'

She took it from the bag she'd set down on the floor. He examined it carefully.

'The placename is crossed through. That makes sense if your nonno was in hiding. A person from this region might recognise this picture but if your nonno was stopped some-where en route home, a German soldier would not have a clue where he had come from.'

'I suppose it makes sense. I always wondered about how Grandpa could have made it all the way back to England from Libya. It was one of the stories he was finally going to tell me. I was going to write them all down and type them up for him. We might have put them into a book or something. But now...' She bit her lip.

'I'm so sorry, Amy.' Leo squeezed her hand.

'I don't believe there were any English POWs hiding in this village but he may have passed through,' Gino continued. 'Certainly, in the countryside around here there were those who risked prison and even death to aid them. Some helped because they despised the fascists, some because they hoped someone might be doing the same for their own sons somewhere, others just because they had good hearts. Yet there were other Italians who called them traitors.'

'Those who supported the fascists like Great-Aunt Violetta,' Leo said.

Gino looked at him sharply.

'It's okay,' Leo continued. 'Nonna has been telling Amy her old stories.'

'Really?' Gino glowered into his wine. Amy fiddled with her glass.

'I will go and check on the food.' Leo left the room, leaving her and Gino sitting there.

'It is easy to condemn women like Violetta,' Gino said carefully. 'But our country was divided: bombs falling, food shortages. It was a terrible time. Violetta was a young woman trying to survive. Her parents were both dead, she had her young sister to take care of. Violetta sold her hats to those in power, she dated German soldiers who might protect her and Fernanda – these things might have seemed logical choices. She should have done things differently, I do not doubt that, but none of us know what we might do if we were in her position.'

She should still have known right from wrong, Amy thought. But Gino had a point. Amy liked to think she would behave honourably but she had never lived through a war. She had never been tested.

'I am glad I have never had to make those sorts of choices,' she said. 'I guess I will never know if Grandpa was given food or a place to stay by people here in Liguria, but it is nice to know there were those who would have been willing to help.'

'You have no other clues? Only this postcard?'

'I have a necklace; a love token, I suppose.'

'You have it here? It cannot be the one you are wearing, that looks very modern.'

She touched the silver raindrop dangling around her neck. 'No, this is just something I was given last Christmas. The one Grandpa gave me needs a new chain. I left it with Stella – the woman in the general store – she's going to find one for me. Maybe you know her; she said she grew up around here.'

Gino's eye twitched. He laced his fingers together. 'Yes, I did know Stella but it was a long time ago. She left here when she was a teenager. It is a little strange to find her back in the village with her fiancé.'

'A fiancé? Not any more. I ran into Stella on the way here and she told me her fiancé had gone off with another woman.'

'She must be devastated.'

'To be honest, she seemed more relieved than upset.'

Leo's voice called from the kitchen: 'Papà, Amy! The food is ready!'

Amy stood up. Gino hesitated. He picked up a paperweight from the coffee table, inspected it and put it down again.

'Did Stella say anything else?'

'Err... Not really.'

'I see. It does not matter anyway. Let us go and eat.'

Amy followed him into the kitchen. Their conversation about Stella was over but she strongly suspected Gino was still thinking about her.

28

Stella flicked the shop sign round. After just a few days she was getting used to being her own boss but she wouldn't be calling the shots for long. Domenico would be back next week and no matter what his doctor and daughter advised, nothing would keep him from his beloved shop.

There's no use worrying about that now, she told herself sternly. She unlocked the door; three customers surged in. Luckily for her they seemed intimately acquainted with the stock and soon enough she was ringing up purchases of storage jars and floral coasters for one woman whilst a mother and her young son argued over a new lunchbox. After a bout of wailing, the child got his way, grinning delightedly as he plonked his frog-patterned selection on the counter.

'Twice the price of the plain one,' the mother muttered, emptying out a purse full of small coins with unnecessary force. A fifty-cent piece shot off the counter, bouncing off Stella's foot.

'Don't worry, that will count towards it, I'll get it later,' Stella said. She bent down to retrieve it, stretching as far as she could, noting the ring of the bell over the door as yet another customer entered. She was glad to be busy. The busier she was, the less time she'd spend thinking of Gino.

'Got it,' she said aloud. She straightened up, holding the coin aloft.

Gino was standing by a pyramid of boxed crockery sets. 'I was wondering where you had disappeared to.'

'I could say the same about you,' Stella snapped before she could stop herself.

'You mean yesterday? I am sorry. I will be honest: it was such a shock to see you and then to know you were with somebody else. Of course, why would a woman like you not be engaged to be married?' He paused.

'I'm not...' she began. Joe's ring had gone, a faint pale mark the only sign she had ever worn it. She'd stashed it away safely at the back of the shelf where she'd found Violetta's squashed hat. No burglar was likely to go rummaging through faded silk flowers and reams of cotton thread.

'So I hear. I now learn you are here alone,' he said.

'I suppose your mother's houseguest told you that.'

'Amy? Yes, she did. I hope you will not be cross with her.'

'Of course not.'

He nodded. 'Yesterday was a shock. To see you again and then to see you were with a man who can buy a huge diamond like that. And you said you were planning to go to Portofino. Was he not taking you to some fancy hotel for your sixtieth birthday?'

'How do you know it was for my birthday? I hadn't told Amy that.'

'You think I would forget the date? It has been many years, but I can still add them up.'

'You forgot what you came in for yesterday.' Stella smiled.

'I could pretend it was simple forgetfulness but you know that is not the reason.'

His eyes were so searching she had to look away.

A beat of silence.

'So, do you still need what you originally came in for?'

'Unfortunately, yes. The fellow who fixed my son's shower did a lousy job.'

'Plumbing supplies?' She was going to have a job finding the right things.

'They are with the electrical stuff. It will be easiest if I come down to the cantina with you. I will be able to find what I need much better myself than trying to explain it to you.'

'I had better shut the door for a few minutes.'

Gino turned over the shop sign and locked the door. The two of them were alone. She felt a frisson of excitement... expectation. How ridiculous! They were only going to search for flush valves or rubber seals.

He followed her down the stairs, his body just inches away from hers, his scent of amber and leather a sophisticated upgrade to the body wash of his teenage years.

She stopped in the gap between Domenico's crates and boxes, ridiculously conscious of the enticingly soft heap of outdoor cushions. He turned and looked at her, a spark of some long-lost passion in his green eyes. Her throat was dry. Surely he wasn't going to suggest what she felt he might. They had barely exchanged a few sentences but she was certain he was thinking of that unfinished business in the passageway beside Sant' Agata, the day they'd been so stupidly reckless. Before...

'That's where Domenico landed when he fell,' she said quickly. 'If he had been just a little further over...' She gestured to the box of sharp-edged garden equipment.

Gino put his arms around her, pulling her close. 'Don't think about that. It must have been horrible. I can feel you trembling.'

She was trembling, but not from that memory. Her heart was thudding, her body heating where it was pressed against his.

He loosened his arms. 'Now, plumbing supplies! Up there on that high shelf, see the box next to the extension cables. I will need you to hold the ladder.'

'You can't climb up! You're the customer.'

'Stella, you are not climbing any ladders. You're wearing heels and a skirt! I've only just found you. I don't intend to lose you so soon.'

She didn't need much persuasion to let him get the box down; she was far too lightheaded to climb up anything. She didn't know if anything would or could happen between her and Gino after all this time. But whatever they'd had, there was still something there.

29

Amy was back at the bar again. She hadn't arranged to meet Leo for breakfast but she'd gone there to see if she could accidentally-on-purpose bump into him and it seemed he'd had the same idea.

'Thanks so much for last night,' she said. 'It was such a good evening.'

'It was great you could come. It was good to see you and Papà get on, but I thought I wouldn't get a word in edgeways at one point!' He laughed.

'Sorry.'

'No need to be. I'm glad you cheered him up. He was moping around yesterday. I'm sure it was something to do with that woman, Stella, from the shop. He looked very shifty when you mentioned her. I've got the feeling there's some history between them.'

'He definitely brightened up when I said her fiancé had left her in the lurch.'

Leo took a sip of his coffee. 'Sounds like she's on the rebound. I don't want Papà getting hurt.'

'Do you think he's going to get involved with her?'

'He was muttering something about taking her out to the pizzeria and I got the distinct impression I'm not invited.'

'So, you're free tonight?' The words were out before she had the chance to think about playing it cool.

'Are you asking me out?' The smile on his face told her he already knew the answer.

'Maybe...' She studied the dish of sugar sachets.

'I'd love to see you tonight, but I can't make it. I have to go and help a friend and he's relying on me. I wish I was not busy all day. I would love to repeat our walk up to the Old Chapel, without the cleaning this time, but I cannot. The plaque is nearly finished but it is a lot of work. Once I get absorbed in the carving, it is like I cannot stop.'

'When you get in the flow? That's how it used to be with me and Grandpa. He'd be fiddling with his woodwork, I'd be making my pots. As soon as I got on that wheel it was like I was in another world. I would only look up when Mum brought us a pot of tea. I miss that... and him, of course.'

'I wish I had a potter's wheel in the workshop you could use.'

'Oh, I'll find something to do, don't worry about me.'

'Thanks for being so understanding.' He stood up.

She picked up her bag. 'I might take a long walk in the hills, there's only so many times I can potter around the backstreets before someone reports me to the police for suspicious activity!'

'Come with me. I can point out the start of a good path. It is a roundabout way into the countryside but a beautiful one.'

Amy had been meaning to pass by Stella's shop to ask after her necklace, but she wasn't going to turn down the opportunity to spend a few more minutes with him.

'Thanks, Leo, I'd like that. If you're sure it's no bother.'

She followed him through the winding streets until they were nearly at the entrance to his workshop. He pointed through an alleyway.

'If you cut down between those two houses, you will find a road at the bottom of the steps. It curves to the right and winds down to the stream. You cross over the little donkey-backed bridge by the old mill house and take the sloping path from there that takes you up into the hills. You cannot miss it.'

Amy nodded, hoping he was right.

'Honestly, you cannot go wrong. You will see the bridge as you descend. Once you are over it, you follow the path. It slopes upwards again until you reach a crossroads, you can see the Old Chapel from there. Don't take that path, follow the other path and keep going. After three or four kilometres you will come to an old *rustico* set amongst olive trees, my great-grand-parents' old place. It should be a nice day but if the rain comes and you want to shelter, there is a key under the urn by the front door.'

'That's very trusting of you.'

'There's not much there but old farm equipment and furniture Nonna could not bear to get rid of. Most of it is too heavy to lift. You would need a van and a forklift truck to empty the place.' He laughed. 'And anyway, why wouldn't I trust you?'

'You hardly know me.'

'I know enough. Have a good walk.'

'*Ciao*, Leo.'

'Wait a moment.' He pecked her on the cheek, just as she turned her head. His lips just brushed the edge of hers, sending a shiver of pleasure through her. 'Would you fancy coming over to the workshop tomorrow morning? I've got something you might be interested in.'

'Yes, sure. If I don't turn up, you'll know where to send the search party!'

After she'd walked a few yards, she glanced back over her shoulder. He was still standing by the entrance to the workshop, watching her.

* * *

The first part of Amy's walk had been easy enough but she could see that the next part of the path spiralled its way upwards. There would be some steep stretches before she reached the crossroads that led to the Old Chapel. She leant over the humpbacked bridge, glad to stop for a while. There was no one in sight, the gurgling stream the only sound. The stream was wider than the trickle she'd expected. It must have been the main source of water for the village, once upon a time. But now the mill it had once powered stood abandoned, its huge spoked wheel nothing more than a decorative feature for a passerby like her to admire.

After a few minutes she walked on, glad to have something more concrete to do than ambling around the village. She didn't hold out much hope she'd find further clues to the time Grandpa might have spent in Liguria. But she wasn't yet willing to leave. She'd already decided to stay for the service to commemorate the return of Pietro Parodi's bones. She was determined to be in the congregation when Leo's plaque was unveiled.

She didn't want to think about what would happen after the celebrations. She and Leo were only friends but she knew she was falling for him. And that quick brush of his lips, which she wasn't sure was entirely accidental, had her believing he was starting to feel the same way. But staying in the village and pursuing a relationship with him was just a fantasy, a wonderful way of putting off the inevitable decision of what to do with the rest of her life now that the person who'd meant the most to her had gone.

30

'One pizza *napoletana*, one *quattro stagioni* and a bottle of *rossese di Dolceacqua*. Very good.'

Gino handed the waiter their two plastic-coated menus. 'I always wanted to bring you here,' he said.

Stella laughed. The pizzeria had barely changed in the time she'd been away. A set of framed posters looked new, but the walls were still the same shade of yellowy-orange and the sepia photograph of the Bruzzone family taken some time in the 1920s still hung behind the till. She could swear the menu was identical to the one she'd salivated over as a teenager. Only the prices had changed.

'I'm glad you've brought me here at last,' she said. After more than forty years they were spending the evening together, out in the open, no longer hiding away. It was strange to think how young they'd been back then but in so many ways Gino hadn't changed at all. His eyes still lit up at the thought of a four seasons pizza; he still only had to smile at her to send miniature rockets zinging around her insides.

The waiter returned with their bottle of red, uncorked it and poured out two glasses.

'*Salute!*' Gino kept his eyes on hers as he took the first sip.

'Tell me about your family.' She had to find out how things stood with the ex-wife he'd mentioned so briefly. That might help bring her back down to earth.

'You heard I married Gaia.' The classmate who'd played the tuba in the village band. They'd married less than two years after Stella had gone.

'Yes, I heard. You were so young, still a teenager.'

'Yes. Gaia was – is – a lovely woman and a wonderful mother but it was never going to last. I cannot deny there were good times: family holidays where we mountain biked and swam. She was sporty, do you remember? One year we even skied. The kids were naturals; I certainly wasn't. I must have spent half the week falling on my bum.' He laughed.

'I could say it was a shock when she finally left me but I would be kidding myself. We'd argued a lot on and off. She always said she couldn't get through to me, that there was a barrier between us she couldn't break. And she was right, there was. The truth was, I married the wrong woman. We would probably have split up years earlier once our daughter, Isabella, was out of her teens, but when we were going through a good patch, Leo came along.'

She drank some more wine, not knowing what to say. Had he married in haste because of her? That was something she dare not ask.

A different waiter was approaching their table, a great wheel of pizza in each hand. He set down their plates. The scent of melted mozzarella and oregano made her realise she'd barely eaten all day.

'*Ciao*, Gino! Your son, he is not here today? You bring this lovely lady instead.' He chuckled. Then stopped. The grin on his already smiling face grew wider. 'No, no! It cannot be... Stella! After all this time!'

'*Ciao*, Mario,' Stella said. 'I see your family still owns this place.'

'Ah, yes, but poor Nonno died.' He jerked his head towards a portrait on the wall. 'Papà is *il capo* now. I try to get him to change the colour of the walls and he does not listen. For me, red is better. But enough of that. Stella, I cannot believe you are here! It must be thirty years since you came here with your brother and sister.'

'More like over forty, though now it seems like yesterday.'

'Over forty. That means we must both be nearly sixty and that, I refuse to believe.' Mario chortled again. 'And now Gino brings you to our pizzeria, this is marvellous! Gino, why have you not told me you and Stella are together again?'

'Again?' Stella said.

Mario spread his hands. 'We all knew, of course we did. You were teenagers in love. Do not deny it! You tried to hide it because his mamma, Fernanda, would not approve. A strict mamma like mine! But no matter, you are together again, in this romantic setting.' His fingers brushed the top of the small flower vase by the chilli oil. A red petal floated onto the tablecloth.

'We couldn't think of a more romantic place,' Gino said, straight-faced.

'Enjoy your meal. I leave you in peace.' He sauntered off, singing softly '*Senza una donna*'.

Stella spluttered out a laugh. 'Honestly! Now he's going to tell the whole village the young lovers are reunited.'

Gino cut into his pizza but his eyes stayed on hers. 'Would that be so bad?'

'I suppose not.' Stella smiled.

'Don't wait to start. This is too good to go cold.'

'I was just savouring the romantic atmosphere,' Stella quipped.

'Anywhere is romantic with the right person.' Gino's words were as cheesy as the topping on his *quattro staggioni*. But he was right. She wouldn't swap the paper placemats and wipe-clean tablecloths for all the signature cocktails and sea-view terraces in Portofino.

* * *

They strolled back through the village, Gino holding her hand. He took the long way around Sant' Agata, avoiding the passageway. Stella was glad. The memory of that dreadful moment when Fernanda found them canoodling, and all that followed, was still too raw. What would Papà think if he were looking down on the two of them? Part of her felt that she was still betraying him, even now.

Soon they reached Uncle Domenico's house. They stopped at the top of the dark flight of stairs that led down to his front door.

'Goodnight, Stella.'

'Goodnight and thank you for the pizza.'

'My pleasure.' He moved a little closer, his eyes glowing in the light of the lantern from the house above. She met his gaze, tilting her head towards his. He brought his lips down to hers, brushing them gently, sending shivers of anticipation through her. She kissed him back, all those old feelings washing over her. She could unlock the door, lead Gino up the rickety stairs to the small dark bedroom where she'd taken residence. There was no Fernanda to stop them now.

But yet... She couldn't. It didn't seem right to bring her old love into her uncle's home. Even though Domenico had assured her he didn't lay the responsibility of his brother's death at her door, he might not have forgiven Gino and Fernanda for the part they'd unwittingly played.

'I wish I could invite you in but...'

'I understand. I would not want to spend the night here behind Domenico's back.' He bit his lip. 'Or am I jumping the gun? You may have been thinking only of opening one of your uncle's digestifs.'

'I was only thinking of coffee,' Stella said in her sternest voice.

'Is that so?' He smiled. 'That would be nice but unfortunately I cannot take you back to my son's house either. I do not know what I can do except kiss you again.'

'That works.' She wrapped her arms around him, melting into him. The surge of longing felt so sweet.

Eventually he broke away. 'So, have you plans for tomorrow? I could be finding something to do around Leo's house, he'll be at his workshop all day. But for me, it does not feel right to work on a Sunday. If I do anything more than a bit of washing up, I see Mamma's face glowering at me, pursing her lips, clutching a rosary.'

'She does have a point; it's nice to have a day that's different. I'm glad Domenico keeps the traditional hours.'

'So, you are free? Will you come for a long walk with me? I wanted to go up to my grandparents' old *rustico*, to see if the place is still standing and to check on the olive trees now the tenant has left.'

'Our hideaway.'

'How could I forget? So, you'll come with me?'

'There's nowhere I'd rather go.'

'Not even back to that very romantic pizza restaurant?'

She laughed. 'See you tomorrow, Gino.'

'Shall we grab breakfast at the bar first, say eight o'clock? I'll meet you there. Or is that too early?'

'Not at all.' No time would be too early; she'd be too excited to sleep a wink.

31

Stella opened the kitchen window, blinking as bright sunlight flooded the small kitchen. She set a saucepan of water on to boil. She still hadn't got round to searching the rest of Domenico's stock for a kettle. The squashed cocktail hat sat mournfully on top of her uncle's battered copy of *In Cucina*. Steaming that was another job she needed to do, along with searching for some sort of chain for Amy's necklace before the girl returned to the shop. She'd been planning to catch up today during Sunday closing but she wasn't going to miss the chance to spend the day with Gino.

She poured water onto a camomile teabag; she was jittery enough without a shot of caffeine. In less than an hour she'd be seeing him. How easy it had been, how natural and right it felt to be back in his arms. How they might mesh his life in Liguria and hers back home was a question she wouldn't worry about now. They were back together and that was all that mattered.

She took her phone off the charger, not surprised to see a message from Lauren there. Stella had been on such a high after her evening at the pizzeria she'd thrown caution to the wind and sent her daughter a rambling email telling how she'd reconnected with her old love. Bracing herself for Lauren's brusque assessment of how foolish her mother was being, she was stunned to see words of encouragement and the comment 'he sounds hot!' Goodness! What on earth had she written in that email last night? The knock on the door came fifteen minutes before she planned to leave. She flew through the kitchen, almost tripping in her haste to answer it. Gino stood on the doorstep. The sleeves on his orange shirt were rolled up, showing arms more muscular than the boyish body she remembered.

'*Ciao*, Stella.' He kissed her lightly on the lips. 'I know we said we would meet at the bar but I could not wait to see you.'

'Lucky I'm ready, isn't it?'

He grinned, clocking the trainers already on her feet, the keys in her hand.

They were too keen to get going to linger long in the bar over breakfast. Soon they were passing under the old stone arch, pausing only for a few seconds to take in the view of the hills. Gino squeezed her hand. Was he thinking, like her, how wonderful it was to walk through the village together, nodding and smiling and exchanging greetings as they went? Some people did a doubletake when they saw them – she recognised a few of her parents' friends and a couple of old classmates – but no one was hostile or disapproving. There were no angry villagers storming out of their houses to accuse her of causing her papà's death. No one shaking their fists or raining curses upon her head. People wouldn't have forgotten but time had moved on. It seemed she'd been forgiven.

She set off along the path by the vineyard, half-expecting old Francesco's dog to run up to the fence, loudly announcing to the world that they were there. There was no dog now, just a wire mesh chicken run. A tortoiseshell cat, head low, bottom in the air was eyeing up its feathery residents.

The steps leading further up were even crumblier than she remembered, weeds sprouting between the cracks. Wiry mountain thyme grew on the scraggy hillside, the beloved snapdragons of her childhood still bloomed. The sky was blue enough to make a whole fleet of sailors' trousers; the sun warmed her right through to her bones, Gino was by her side. She hadn't felt so happy in years.

Ahead of them was the Old Chapel, smaller than she recalled but her heart leapt at the sight of it.

'Oh, look! I'm so pleased to see it's still there!'

'What did you expect? A pile of rubble?'

'I don't know. Everything's changed so much around where I live in England but almost everything here is just the same, as if I've never been away. Does Fernanda still look after this place?'

'She did until recently. It's too far for her to walk these days. But she's so stubborn I wouldn't put it past her to try and get here if Leo hadn't taken over.'

'Your son? That's good of him.'

'He's fond of my mother. He doesn't want her fretting over this place, worrying about vandals or vermin. He doesn't get out here as much as she did, of course, but he did come here the other day. He brought that girl, Amy, to help.'

'Even the windows are sparkling.' Stella stood on tiptoes to peer in. 'They gave the place a good onceover by the look of it but that's not my idea of a date.'

'The pizzeria would have been more romantic.' Gino grinned.

Stella gave him a dig in the ribs. 'Very funny. Shall we go on?'

'I hope the path isn't too overgrown. We could have taken my car the long way round but it felt right to walk.'

'I'm glad. It's a nice day. I always used to manage all right, though I was a bit fitter back then.'

'I'll have to help you along.' He took her hand. 'Come on, up the last few steps. It will flatten out soon.'

'I remember. I'd always start running as soon as I got to that bit.'

'Ah, that's why you always arrived looking so flustered. Do you remember how I used to wait for you there?'

'I used to panic if Mamma kept me back to do some chores, knowing I'd be horribly late.'

'No mobile phones back then. I'd just have to wait and hope.'

She took the last few steps and paused to catch her breath before saying: 'Some things have changed for the better. I'd be lost without my phone.'

'I'm glad we didn't have them back then; Mamma would have fitted mine with some sort of tracker app.'

'I wish we'd had something to track where Fernanda was and then...' She looked across the hills. If Fernanda hadn't found them, Papà wouldn't have worked himself up into a rage. He wouldn't have died. Stella wouldn't have caused Mamma such pain, lost touch with her brother and sister. Their reckless kiss in the alley had cost her everything. She searched for a change of subject. 'When did you last come this way?'

'Not since the spring. Week after week I've been meaning to but you know how it is, life gets in the way. My daughter, Isabella, has been back in Alassio and every time I've come here to visit Mamma and Leo, I seem to get caught up in odd jobs at one of their houses, but it's really time I checked on the trees. They didn't get harvested last year, the family who rented the place these last thirty years had all sorts of personal issues so they gave notice and left. I should have taken time out and organised collecting the olives and a slot at the *frantoio* but I didn't get around to it. A terrible waste.' He tutted and shook his head.

'These things happen. So, have you found someone else who wants to take over?'

'No.'

She expected him to say more but he strode on, a serious look on his face. For the next half hour they walked side by side along the rough stony path, speaking very little, content just to be in each other's company.

The *rustico* came into view. A couple of windows were boarded up but the sloping roof and old stone walls were just as she remembered. Gino took a key from under a chipped urn. He unlocked the door. It opened with a creak; she stepped inside.

He glanced around. 'Good, it seems just as I left it.'

'I don't suppose many people come this way. We haven't passed anyone today.'

'There would be no reason unless you were here to work on the trees. That's what made it such a good hideaway for us.'

She rubbed her hand down one of the old wooden pillars.

'Looking for where we carved our initials? I think it was lower.' He crouched down. 'Look, there!'

She joined him, tracing her finger over the marks he'd hacked with a penknife: *G + S sempre* in a heart-shaped surround. 'You and me always. Oh, yes. I remember when you did that.'

'After we first kissed. And now here we are again.'

'We haven't been the only ones. I don't remember the other carvings.'

'There were a few initials and hearts when we used to come here but not as many as this. Maybe it was the kids of the family who rented from us.'

Stella stood up, she was getting cramp in her legs. 'There's a lot more stuff in here too.'

'People accumulate things over the years: wheelbarrows, ladders, baskets...' He stretched a piece of olive netting between two hands. 'Looks decent quality, hopefully it isn't too torn.'

She walked over to a short-legged wooden chest. 'A *madia*. My grandma kept her flour in one and she'd roll out the pasta on top. Hers was in the kitchen; it's strange to see one out here.'

'It's the victim of one of Mamma's tidying sessions. She keeps her flour in cannisters in the cupboard like most people these days. But Violetta would have used this during the war. Mamma won't get rid of anything that belonged to her sister but when there was no more room in the house, she used to bring things out here. Like this.' He patted the edge of an old iron bedstead, its striped mattress saggy and worn.

'That explains how these got here.' Stella stooped to examine a pair of vases sitting on a wooden ledge. She reached inside one and plucked out a pack of playing cards, the edges splayed and curled. She blew off a coating of dust. 'Now, these I do recognise. We played for hours.'

'It took my mind off what I really wanted to do with you.' He smiled.

She stepped towards him. 'I was scared back then but now there's nothing stopping us.'

His eyes strayed to the dilapidated bedstead. 'Do you think there's a chance that old thing will hold up?'

'I guess there's only one way to find out.'

'I'm game if you are.' He slipped his arms around her.

* * *

Stella's head rested against the crook of Gino's neck, his arm lay across her shoulders. How wonderful it was to lie here luxuriating in the feeling of being held by her first true love. The bedhead had rocked alarmingly, the dust had made them sneeze and the mattress's springs had creaked in protest but none of that mattered. And judging by the look in Gino's eyes, the pitting of her thighs and the stomach that remained stubbornly round since Lauren's birth hadn't bothered him a bit.

'I dreamt of this,' he said, snuggling against her.

'Same here. I could stay here all day but I suppose we need to get up and go and check on the olive trees.'

'Yes. I believe that is what I came here to do before you distracted me.' He laughed.

'Cheeky!'

'Come on, then, we'd best get up.' He dropped a kiss on her bare shoulder.

Reluctantly, she sat up, running her hand through her mussed-up hair. He stretched his arms over his head and gave a deep sigh. Stella swung a leg out of the bed; a minute later she was lacing up her trainers as Gino fastened the last button on his shirt.

He let her step out the door first and locked it behind them. She followed him down the short path past the water butt. The olive grove was beautiful, full of carefully spaced-out trees, their silvery trunks twisted this way and that. She'd never bothered to look at the trees properly before, never noticed the wild lilies growing around their trunks under the shade of their leafy branches. Her teenage head had been filled with nothing but Gino.

'The trees have been well looked after for decades,' Gino

said. 'They didn't deserve to be neglected this last year, though it doesn't seem to have harmed them.'

She squeezed a dark bud between her forefinger and thumb. 'They seem to be growing okay.'

'We should have a decent harvest this year, even with a rookie like me overseeing it.'

'You're doing it yourself? I thought you'd be looking to rent the place out again.'

'It is a trial run to see if I have what it takes. Do you remember when we talked about going to Sanremo when school was finished, living by the sea?'

Stella laughed. 'I had visions of days on the beach, nights spent playing blackjack at the casino. It sounded so exciting. How we were going to make a living never crossed my mind.'

'I was as clueless as you, but back then Sanremo spelt freedom, the opposite of home. The people who lived there didn't care whose saint's day it was, let alone who dated who. But whenever we sneaked away here I couldn't help thinking what it would be like to work the land, for you and me to have a little house in the village, tend the olives, maybe keep a few goats.'

'You never said.'

'I thought you'd think me dull or that I'd never break free of my mamma's influence if we didn't go away.'

'But you moved to Alassio.'

'Yes and even when I began a relationship with Gaia I didn't want to move back to Leto; the village had too many memories. But working for a boss, even one as reasonable as mine, isn't how I wanted to live my life. Ever since Mamma said the old tenants were moving on, I've been toying with taking over this place myself. It was what I wanted deep down all along.'

'I wish my papà had known that. He viewed you as some

wild tearaway who'd take me away to some corrupt urban existence. Maybe he would have welcomed you if he knew.'

'It's a nice thought but your papà's distress was never about my prospects or where we might live. I was Fernanda's son, that's why he would never accept me.'

'I never understood why it riled him so much. I know Fernanda and her sister were fascists, but Fernanda was a young child. Of course, her sister didn't have that excuse but she wasn't the only one around here to keep the faith with Il Duce. They say the butcher had Mussolini's portrait on the wall until the bitter end. Why should Papà single out your family and still harbour such resentment for something that happened decades ago?'

'Oh, Stella,' Gino said. 'Do you really not know?'

* * *

Stella stretched out her legs, glad of the shade cast by the old olive tree.

'Of course, I'd heard the rumour that Violetta dated a German officer,' she said. 'It must have caused a lot of resentment, her swanning around the village in her fancy little hats and silk stockings when others were stitching old rags together to clothe their kids.'

Gino leant back against the gnarled old trunk. He plucked a blade of grass and rubbed it between his fingers.

'I have tried to understand my aunt. Maybe she thought she was protecting her little sister's future by throwing her lot in with a man she believed was on the winning side. Or perhaps he was just handsome and charming and swept her off her feet into a misguided love affair. Sometimes people hide the truth from themselves, see only what they want to see. Of course, she was wrong but I tried not to judge someone who died a long time ago, who cannot tell her side of the story.'

Stella stayed silent, knowing from his screwed-up forehead and the way he wrapped his arms around his knees how difficult he was finding this.

Gino sighed. 'It took me years to face the truth. Violetta wasn't some innocent village girl. There wasn't just one German soldier. She went to parties in Sanremo where the Gestapo had their headquarters in the Villa Åberg. She was friends with these people. Laughing, drinking, dancing. I look at those photographs Fernanda keeps; although they're black and white you can see Violetta's healthy glow, her rosy cheeks. She was having fun whilst families like yours couldn't heat their homes or find enough to eat. But she went further than that. She wasn't just a Nazi sympathiser.'

'What do you mean?' Stella edged nearer, so their thighs rested against each other's. He wiped his palm on his jeans before he laid his hand over hers.

His other hand clenched. 'I was told Violetta was responsible for the German soldiers coming to this village.'

Stella gasped. 'The *rastrellamento*?'

He stared into the distance. A butterfly landed on an orange lily, so near she could have reached out and cupped it in her hand.

'I pressed Mamma to tell me the truth about the rumours. At first she would not say anything but eventually, she admitted it was no accident the Germans came. The first house they searched belonged to the couple who owned the salumeria; they were sheltering a little Jewish boy, pretending he was their own. The soldiers burned that house down. Someone had given them a list of names; they knew who they were looking for. They shot two elderly men who'd lived together for years as more than friends, doing no one any harm. Mamma was too distraught to tell me about the other victims. And like a coward I never asked her again, I didn't want to hear.

'Mamma feels she has to atone for what Violetta did; that is what makes her so devout. And that is why she was always so strict with me. She says we are a family of sinners who cannot afford to stray from the path of righteousness. Some part of me feels she is right, that we do not deserve to be happy. It makes me sick to think that my own blood relative was responsible for that terrible day. But Fernanda still loves Violetta; she lights a candle on the day of her birthday and the anniversary of her death. No wonder people like your papà and uncle despise us.'

'No, Gino.' Stella didn't say any more. She wished she could take away his pain but there was nothing she could say that didn't sound like a cliché.

He took his sunglasses from his pocket. 'Let's go back.'

She clambered to her feet. They walked in silence back the way they'd come.

He wiped a hand across his forehead. 'How hot it is! Maybe my son is not so stupid, spending the day in his workshop out of the sun.'

'Did you go and see how he is getting along?'

'Yes. The plaque he is creating is quite extraordinary, but now you understand why not everyone is happy that a great-nephew of Violetta has been given this commission. Father Filippo spoke up on Leo's behalf, saying the victims deserved the very best memorial and it was hard to disagree. No one else who tendered for the work was anywhere in my son's league. The day before the committee met to decide, Filippo delivered a sermon about the need for forgiveness. There were still some dissenting voices but the majority took the hint. Nearly eighty years have passed. Pietro's remains are being laid to rest. It is time for the village to heal.'

'Leo must be proud he is playing a part in that.'

'He says he does not think of these things. He doesn't listen to criticism, he gets his head down and works. He gets so absorbed he cannot think of anything else.'

'I'm so looking forward to seeing it.'

He took her hand, swinging it as they walked.

'I could take you to see Leo's workshop.'

'I don't want to disturb him. I'll wait for the unveiling, it will be a nice surprise.'

'You will be there, won't you?'

'I wouldn't miss it for the world.'

She didn't want to think any further ahead. What would happen once Domenico came home? She'd have to move out and rent somewhere but her redundancy money wouldn't last forever. She didn't want to leave Gino or the village. She had to find a way to stay.

32

Stella dithered by the boxes of vegetables. Gino had invited her to have dinner with Leo and him the following evening but she'd be on her own tonight. It would give her the perfect opportunity to potter around in the kitchen cooking one of the old Ligurian recipes her mother had taught her. She wanted to try out some dishes she could cook for Gino and his son when she returned the favour. But she would phone her cousin's house first, to check that Domenico had no objection to her inviting the two men into his home. No matter how shocking Violetta's crimes, surely her practical, good-natured uncle wouldn't hold a grudge this long.

She added a bag of chard and a great bunch of spinach to her shopping basket and took them to the counter.

'*Buonasera*, Addolorata.'

'*Ciao*, Stella.' The woman scanned the barcode on a tub of ricotta. 'Cooking for a few people tonight?'

'No, just me, experimenting a little.'

'I thought you were staying at your uncle's house.'

'I am but Domenico is still with Luisa's family in Genoa.'

Addolorata frowned. 'How strange. I thought Domenico was back. I swear I saw him tucking into a great slice of *pinolata* outside the bar earlier.'

'That can't be right.' Stella took her phone from her bag, realising she'd switched it to silent on their way to the *rustico*, not wanting any messages or calls to interrupt her time with Gino. The screen was jammed with notifications. Three missed calls from Luisa. She made a face.

'Everything okay?' Addolorata put Stella's onions in a brown paper bag. 'That will be twelve euros, thirty cents.'

'Yes, umm... fine. Thank you.' She paid and hurried from the shop, dismissing her plan to pick up some wine en route. It would be better to call her cousin on Domenico's landline to see what was going on than to rely on the patchy signal out in the street.

She rested her shopping bag between her feet and put her key in the lock but it wouldn't turn. That wasn't right, she knew she'd locked up before she and Gino set off. She pushed the door; it swung open. The scent of tobacco and pungent aftershave told her Domenico was indeed back, even before she'd sidestepped the holdall in the hall.

'Anyone home?' Stella called.

Luisa appeared, looking flustered. 'I tried to call...'

'Sorry, I've been out and about all day, I've barely looked at my phone. What's happened?'

'There's, umm, been a slight change of plan.'

'Cooee, Stella, in here!' Domenico called from the kitchen.

Stella lowered her voice. 'I thought he was staying with you until after the weekend.'

Her cousin gave her a what-can-you-do shrug. 'I had to drive him back here when I found out he'd booked himself a taxi to the bus garage. He was planning to travel back here by himself, silly old fool.'

Stella laughed. She pushed open the kitchen door. 'Domenico, you're back!' She bent to kiss him. Her uncle's papery cheeks were hollowed, his complexion still pale. 'Are you sure you're well enough to be here?'

'He's not right yet,' Luisa said quietly.

'Nothing wrong with me, no need to fuss,' Domenico tutted.

Luisa jumped. 'Must have his hearing aid turned up to max,' she whispered.

'I heard that too. Come on, Luisa, make our Stella a coffee. Looks like you have been shopping, Stella, love. What are you going to cook? Luisa, you will stay for a meal before you rush off, won't you?'

'Of course you must. I'm making *pansoti con salsa di noci*,' Stella said. She had more than enough vegetables to stuff pasta parcels for three. She unloaded the shopping onto the work surface and took a bag of walnuts from the cupboard for the nut sauce.

Luisa put the Bialetti on the hob. 'Are you okay to stay here for a few more days, Stella?'

'She wants you to keep an eye on me and make sure I don't try and go back to the shop.' Domenico gave a wheezy chuckle.

Luisa raised her eyebrows. 'Papà's not ready to go back until next week at the earliest but I don't want to impose on you.'

'You mustn't stay in babysitting me if you've got other plans, Stella,' Domenico said.

She tried not to think of tomorrow's evening with Gino and Leo. 'Plans? Me?' Stella patted her uncle's hand. 'I've no plans at all.'

33

The doorbell jangled. Gino walked into the shop. Stella's heart leapt. Would she ever get over the thrill of seeing him again?

'*Buongiorno*! May I help you, *signore*?'

'Very professional. I like it.' He leant across the counter and pressed his lips on hers. She closed her eyes, hoping that no one else would come through the door.

'Mmm... How I'd like to carry you down the steps and ravish you in the basement.'

'Stop it!' She laughed. 'What are you here for? More plumbing parts? Don't tell me Leo's shower still isn't working?'

'Why, do I smell?' He frowned.

She inhaled deeply. 'Only of shampoo and good things but maybe you washed in the sink.' Her face flushed at the thought of him stripped to the waist, covered in a soapy lather. *Honestly, Stella, you're sixty in a few days. Pull yourself together!*

'Hmm. I'm pleased to say the plumbing's all fine, as is the lighting, the cooker and everything else. It's all ready for the feast I'm preparing for our very special visitor this evening.'

'Aagh!' She cringed. 'I meant to call you about tonight but I've been so caught up chatting to Domenico.'

'He must be a lot better then? That's marvellous news. You never know, when someone has a fall at that age.'

'He's back home,' Stella said.

'Oh! Do you need somewhere to stay? Please don't tell me you're leaving.'

'I'm not going anywhere for now. Luisa has asked me to keep an eye on him. She wants me to make sure he doesn't try to get back behind the counter until he's good and ready.'

'So, he's barred from his own shop. That's a bit harsh.'

Stella shrugged. 'I feel bad but it won't be for long. But Gino, tonight's going to be a problem. Domenico needs me in the shop during the day but in the evening I don't want to leave him sitting alone at home.'

'Then bring him along. Cooking for four instead of three won't make a difference.'

'Do you think he'll come?'

'I honestly don't know,' Gino said. 'I'm sure we're not his favourite people but he wasn't one of the folk who objected when Leo got his commission for the memorial.'

'I'll ask him.' Stella gave Gino a nod and turned to serve a woman who'd plonked a colander and kitchen timer shaped like a tomato onto the counter.

Gino waited until the customer was back out on the street. 'I can't wait to see you tonight, even though I'll have to share you.'

'What are you cooking?'

He smacked his hand against his forehead. 'Honestly, I would have forgotten what I came in for if you hadn't asked that. I'm not telling you, it's a surprise.'

'You mean you haven't decided.'

He put on a mock hurt expression. 'How can you say that? I've been up all night planning! But I'm not going to do a good job if I don't have a grater – one of those metal planes that you use on a block of parmigiano. My son's brilliant with his hands but that doesn't extend to his cooking skills, judging by the state of his kitchen. There's a serious lack of decent utensils.'

'Third aisle, second shelf.' She knew where just about everything was now. Except for that elusive kettle.

He laid the grater on the counter; she ran the purchase through the till, adding the item to her uncle's ledger.

'Maybe Domenico and I should bring one of those olive-wood chopping boards with us tonight instead of a bottle of wine.'

'That's a great idea. My son's wine rack is a lot better stocked than the rest of his kitchen.' Gino laughed. 'Look, why don't you come over to mine for a bit once you've had lunch with Domenico and let me know what he says about tonight.'

She crossed her fingers under the counter. Their families' feud had gone on far too long.

* * *

Stella put a lid on the pan. She left the rabbit bubbling gently. They wouldn't be eating it tonight if Domenico could be persuaded to have dinner with Gino and Leo, but it would be twice as delicious if she cooked it now and heated it up another day.

'Sit down, Stella, have the rest of your lunch,' Domenico said, patting a chairback. 'You're making me dizzy. You're up and down like a jack-in-a-box.'

Her uncle was right, she was a bundle of nerves. If he didn't agree to come to Leo's house it would make pursuing her relationship with Gino so much more difficult. She didn't want there to be a bone of contention between herself and the old man. She was fond of her uncle; she didn't want to grow to resent him.

She sat down and began cutting up a peach. Despite her anxiety, she was hungry. The scent of wild thyme and garlic rising from the stove was sharpening her appetite.

Domenico patted Stella's arm.

'I don't know what you're worrying about but I expect there's no need.'

'It's Gino.'

Domenico sucked in a breath. 'I don't suppose I need to ask if you mean Gino Perillo.'

'I ran into him. He came into the shop.'

'And you have been up to his old *rustico* together.'

'How did you know that?'

'Old Goffredo dropped in for a coffee whilst you were out. He heard it from his wife.'

Stella made a face. 'That figures.'

Domenico reached out and pinched a piece of peach from her plate. 'So, you see I already know. And I am not angry.'

'But you're not pleased.'

Domenico shrugged. 'Don't worry yourself about me.'

'But I have to. Gino... well, he and Leo have invited us both to Leo's house for dinner tonight.'

'Oh.'

Stella waited for something more but her uncle merely helped himself to a bunch of cherries, sucking each one noisily and spitting out the stones.

Stella squirmed in her seat. She couldn't see how she'd get Domenico to agree to their dinner date but he hadn't actually said the word 'no' yet.

'It would mean a lot to me if you came.'

Domenico sighed. 'Is it that important to you?'

'Of course it is. You're family.' Stella stood up and started to clear the plates away. 'You don't even have to like him all that much. I just want you to rub along.'

'I suppose I'll have to accept this invitation then. And don't worry, I will behave as I would when visiting anybody else. Leo is doing a fine job on the memorial plaque, so I'm told, and I honestly don't hold Gino or your joyride to Sanremo responsible for Arturo's death any more. Now, is that enough to stop you buzzing around like a mosquito and get you to relax?'

'But how do you feel about Gino's family? About Fernanda?'

Domenico pressed his lips together. 'That's another matter.'

'What happened here was a terrible tragedy but it was so long ago.'

'Time doesn't always heal.' His face closed up.

'But...'

Domenico raised a finger, silencing her.

The look in his eye told Stella there was no point saying anything else. She finished tidying up, kissed her uncle goodbye, reminding him to switch off the gas when the rabbit was done, and half-walked, half-jogged to Leo's house. She didn't want to waste a minute of the time she could share with Gino.

* * *

Stella jolted upright. She yanked the sheet up to her chin. 'What was that bang?'

Gino laughed. 'It's only the hot water, a pipe heating up. I thought you might want a shower before you went back to the shop.'

Stella exhaled. 'Thank goodness. I thought it might be Leo at the door.'

'I told you he'll be at his workshop all day; he won't come back for lunch. But I am a bit jumpy myself. At my age it should be my son sneaking girls back to *my* house when I'm out, not the other way around!'

'Girls?' Stella teased.

'You and only you.' He put his arm around her shoulders, pulling her closer. 'Mmm, you smell so good. I could stay here all afternoon but I suppose we had better get dressed.'

'Some of us have to go to work.' Stella padded across the room, surprised at how unselfconscious she felt. She'd always wrapped her dressing gown firmly around her when she'd been with Joe. She took a quick shower, careful not to wet her hair, and scrambled into her clothes. She glanced in the mirror, her eyes were bright, her skin pink from the shower – or perhaps flushed from her lunchtime frolicking – but she'd done up all her buttons neatly. With a slick of lipstick she'd look respectable enough to stand behind the shop counter.

'I wish you didn't have to go.'

'Me too.' It was wonderful to lie in Gino's arms but her hasty departure from Domenico's house nagged at her conscience. She should have spent the whole of the lunchbreak with him instead of rushing away to see her lover. Her uncle spent enough hours alone whilst she was running the shop.

She pecked Gino on the lips. 'I'll see you tonight, with Domenico.'

'I'm so glad he's agreed to come here. I hope he'll like what I'm cooking.'

'He assures me he eats anything.' Whether her uncle liked the food was the least of her concerns. All she wanted was for him and Gino to get along.

34

Stella replaced the budgie's water bottle. She switched the shop sign to Open, humming to herself. Her uncle hadn't embraced her relationship with Gino like she'd hoped he would but the dinner at Leo's house had passed without incident. Domenico had eaten everything that had been put on his plate and declared it all to be *molto buono!* It was a start, a slow thawing, and for now that would have to be enough. After all, Stella hadn't fallen over herself to build a relationship with Fernanda; they'd done no more than exchange the odd *buongiorno* and *buonasera* in the street.

Today was going to be a good day. She hadn't yet served her first customer but it had already been a most productive morning. After a little head scratching, Domenico had explained where she might find a kettle amidst the stacks of boxes in the basement. The green, jug-style one patterned with orange flowers and sporting a brown plastic lid looked like it had sat amongst the stock since the 1970s but it would add a positively modern note when Stella set it alongside her uncle's ancient kitchen appliances.

Domenico had also remembered the whereabouts of a box of costume jewellery bought during an ill-fated attempt to diversify into fashion accessories. But amongst the unlikely collection – a dollar sign studded with rhinestones had been ordered in triplicate – were some simple gold-plated chains, some of them surprisingly delicate. They weren't particularly pretty and the clasps were awfully fiddly but one of them would do for Amy's coin necklace until the girl was able to find a more permanent solution.

All in all, things were looking up and the day would only get better. Gino had promised to pop by. Both of them were desperate to see more of each other but her old love understood that Stella was tied up with looking after the shop. And she had no plans to repeat their cheeky afternoon siesta; she felt too guilty to leave Domenico alone during the extended lunchbreak. But they were seeing each other again tonight and this time the stakes were higher. Gino was coming to Domenico's home. Now, what should she make for dessert?

Stella drifted off into a world of *pan di Spagna* and baked peaches stuffed with amaretti and dried apricot. The jangle of the shop bell made her jump.

'Hi!' Amy said. She looked remarkably well. Village life was suiting her. Even with the pale skin of a redhead she'd developed a hint of a tan and her air of being slightly lost had vanished.

'Hi,' Stella said. 'Nice to see you.'

'I was wondering...'

'Your necklace?' Stella interrupted.

Amy's face lit up. 'You found something?'

'Perhaps one of these.' Stella pushed two thin chains across the counter. 'I've tried threading both of them through the coin.

Either works so you've just got to choose which length. Oh, and they're only five euros.'

'Really? They must be more than that.'

'To be honest, I'm probably ripping you off! These have been in the stock so long the prices were originally in lire.'

'If you're sure. That's a bargain.' Amy picked one up, winding it around her fingers. Stella retrieved the old coin from its hidey hole beneath the counter. She turned it over and traced her forefinger along the flourish carved on the reverse.

'I don't suppose you've got any nearer to finding out if this symbol means anything?'

'No, I've found nothing.' Amy took the longer of the two chains, screwed up one eye and threaded it through the coin.

'Do you want me to help do it up?'

'Thanks, yes.' Amy unwound a fringed cotton scarf from around her neck. She tentatively pressed a finger against the pink flaky patch on her shoulder.

'That looks painful.'

'I stupidly didn't realise quite how hot it was. Fernanda's insisted on lending me this scarf.'

'That's kind.'

'I know some think she's a bit odd but she's been nice to me and I like hearing her old stories. She's cooking for me tonight, just the two of us. Leo's out with a friend.'

'I'm sure she'll make something good. Now, turn around, let's fasten this then you can check you definitely want the longer length.' Stella came out from behind the counter. 'There you go, all done.'

'Thanks.' Amy slipped the coin under her shirt. Near her heart, Stella thought.

'Is that all?'

'Almost. I'm looking for an apron or an overall.'

'Fourth aisle, bottom shelf.'

Amy rooted in a box, retrieving a navy apron big enough to swamp someone twice her size.

Stella suppressed a smile. 'Has Gino got you helping with the DIY at Leo's house? I know he's managed to fix the shower but he said he's got quite a list of jobs.'

'Nothing like that; I'd be hopeless. I'm making ceramic tiles, decorating them before they're fired.'

'That's a bit random.'

'Leo's had the tiles knocking around for ages. When he was starting out he didn't know how his stone masonry business was going to go. He thought he might have to have a sideline making decorative panels to go above a basin or a cooker, that sort of thing. But orders took off and now this memorial plaque may lead to other commissions, so he doesn't think he'll ever use them. I've been making pots for years, in my grandpa's shed. I miss doing something creative, so Leo suggested I have a go at this.'

'Decorative tiles, mmm.' Stella's brain began to whirl. 'And you make pots. Small ones or big ones like great urns?'

'Little things. Decorative objects, the sort you might put on the mantelpiece.'

'Interesting. Well...' Stella stopped herself saying any more. She was already racing three steps ahead. Amy might not want to stay in the village much longer. But Stella couldn't help noticing how the girl's face lit up when she spoke about Leo.

35

Stella reached into her bag for the shop key. A ringtone burst from her phone. She snatched it up. Carol. She couldn't put off talking to her friend forever. She pressed the green symbol.

'Hi, Stella, it's me!'

'Carol! I'm glad you've rung, I've been meaning to catch you...'

'The heck you have! You've been avoiding me, Stella Ferrando. And now I know why.'

'Oh.' Stella tucked the phone under her chin and unlocked the shop door.

'I bumped into your Lauren at the shopping centre. Says you're holding the fort at your uncle's shop and that Joe's gone for good. And there's me with my new outfit hanging in the wardrobe. I've even got a hat, one with a big brim, fuchsia and black it is, cost an arm and a leg. I did worry about black being unlucky but it's only a bow and a trim. I guess it doesn't matter now...' Her voice trailed off.

'Oh,' Stella said again, placing her bag on the counter. She'd expected a rollicking the moment she'd seen who the caller was but the feeling she'd let her friend down was so much worse.

'Gone off with some rich blonde, so she said. I hope you're going to keep that stonking great ring.'

'No, that wouldn't be right.'

'Compensation, that's what I call it. In the olden days they say you could sue for breach of promise. Though that wouldn't make up for being left on the shelf.'

Stella had a sudden vision of her and Carol perched in the window of Domenico's shop, her friend in fuchsia from head to toe, a 'one not-so-careful owner' sign around her neck.

'Don't cry.' Carol's voice softened. 'I'm sorry I brought it up.'

'I wasn't sobbing, I was laughing.'

'Well, full marks to you for putting on a brave face. But I'm worried about you, Stella. If I could get the time off, I'd fly out.'

Infuriating, forthright and bossy, but Carol always had her back. Should Stella dare mention Gino? It would cheer her friend up.

'The thing is, Carol, you don't have to worry. I'm seeing someone else.'

'Already! Stella, I'm impressed! A handsome Italian?'

'You could say so.'

'Tell me more!'

'He had dinner with me and my uncle last night. But look, I can't really talk now. I'm at the shop, I've got to sort out the till and open up.'

'I'm certainly not going to hold you up. But just one thing. Do you think there's any chance I might need that hat? I've only got until the end of the week to take it back.'

Stella knew Carol was only joking but she couldn't resist saying: 'You might wear it sooner rather than later!'

She held the phone away from her ear. Carol's excited shriek was loud enough to be heard at the old *rustico*.

'Bye, Carol.' Stella rang off before her friend could say any more. She turned over the Open sign and began tidying around the counter, glad there was no one waiting outside. Carol's comments had set her off daydreaming. Maybe after all this time, her girlhood dreams could come true. Domenico certainly suspected a formal relationship was on the cards. He'd quizzed Gino about his plans last night and Gino had talked about his dreams of moving back to the village and reviving his grandparents' old olive grove. And all the time he was talking he'd looked across at Stella as if seeking her approval. She was as sure as anything that they had a future together.

They hadn't yet discussed it but Stella had no intention of living off the little Gino would make from the farm. She had to pay her own way. It seemed obvious that Domenico couldn't carry on running the shop by himself but there would need to be changes if she were to join him. They would need to diversify, not into cheap jewellery but into products that enhanced their current offering. She'd want to keep most of the shop as it was. The sale of saltcellars, gardening gloves and measuring jugs was their bread and butter, not to mention a valuable service to the residents. But Amy's talk of pots and decorative ceramics had sent her imagination soaring.

Stella would make a start today, measuring all the shelf space upstairs and down. She'd need to get all her ducks in a row to get Domenico on board. She'd arrange to give Joe his ring back and get Lauren on board with her plans. And then she'd be free to pick up the pieces of the life she'd left behind the day she fled to England.

'*Buongiorno*, Stella.' Signora Togliatti let the door close behind her.

'*Buongiorno*, Signora.' Stella put down the pen she'd just picked up. 'What can I help you with today?'

'An iron, I think.'

Stella came out from behind the counter and set up the mini steps, knowing she'd be getting down every box for the elderly lady's inspection. And knowing also that the signora would leave without opening her purse. For the first few days, Stella had been puzzled as to why nothing ever seemed suitable for such a regular customer. But she soon cottoned on that the dear old soul was merely coming in for a chat and that the careful examination of options and price tags was a way of preserving the signora's pride whilst she assuaged her loneliness.

'This is our top-of-the-range option.' Stella opened up a cardboard box, removing a steam iron fashioned from garish lime-green plastic.

'We didn't have steam in the old days, just an iron with a hotplate.'

'I expect you heated it on the stove instead of plugging it in,' Stella said.

'That's right, dear. Got ever so hot, used to burn my Aldo's shirts.' The old woman chuckled. 'Never grumbled though, like some men, bless his soul.'

'It's all different these days,' Stella said, reboxing the iron.

'Oh, you're too young to talk like that. It doesn't seem like yesterday since I saw you skipping off to school. Time flies and we're all getting older but my Giacomo will help Domenico keep up to date.'

Stella paused, one foot on the steps. 'Sorry? I don't quite understand.'

'My grandson, Giacomo. He's away at the moment, gadding about like young people do but he'll be starting here in September. Domenico's promised him part time at first but after that fall of his, perhaps he will want to give him more hours. There could be a full-time job for the boy in the end and with Domenico as his boss, he'll have no better man to learn from.'

The steps seemed to sway. Stella gripped the edge of the shelf. 'Domenico's not said anything to me.'

'He probably doesn't want to admit to you that he's beginning to slow down. Now, my Aldo, he was in denial like that...'

Stella nodded and smiled politely, forcing herself to make appropriate comments as Signora Togliatti chitchatted away about the old days. At last, the old woman departed. Stella closed her eyes for a few seconds, grounding herself. She put away her notebook and the measuring tape. The general store would never turn over enough to keep three of them. She wasn't going to build a business; she was just playing shops. There was no future for her here.

* * *

Stella locked up and pulled down the shop shutters. Signora Togliatti hadn't gone far. She was standing on the other side of the road in a patch of shade, leaning on her stick, her free hand gesturing as she spoke. A young woman stood nodding along, her little boy grizzling and pulling at her skirt. Judging by the woman's body language, he wasn't the only one desperate to get away. Signora Togliatti made one last gesture, turned and trudged off towards home. She probably wouldn't speak to another soul all day. Stella snapped out of her self-pity. Domenico was looking forward to seeing her and tonight she would be in Gino's arms. She was lucky. Whatever the future held.

Stella strolled back to her uncle's house and opened the front door. The scent of garlic frying wafted from the kitchen. Domenico was leaning over the stove.

'What are you doing?' She'd been all prepared to serve up a lunch of cheese and cold meats.

'Just making some tomato sauce. And don't fuss, I'm quite capable. You need a proper meal if you're working all day and no offence, Stella, but these picnics we've been having...' He waved a hand towards the fridge.

'I'm not complaining.' After the signora's bombshell, comfort food was just what she needed.

'I'll throw in the pasta now you're back.' He tipped the end of a packet of spaghetti into a huge pot. A froth of bubbles rose and subsided.

'Are you sure you should...?'

Domenico silenced her with a look. 'I'll be back in my shop in a few days.'

'I hear you're getting some help soon.' She kept her voice light.

Domenico grunted. 'Signora Togliatti been talking to you? Her grandson's a good lad. He's not the brightest but he'll work hard and he's tall too. Giacomo can reach those high shelves, all right. Save me going up any ladders.' He chortled.

'I'll get the bowls out and set the table,' Stella said. She opened the cutlery drawer, retrieving forks and a couple of knives in case they finished with fruit.

Domenico drained the pasta pot, a great cloud of steam obliterating his features. 'What's bothering you? Something to do with Gino, your *fidanzato*?' It was the first time he'd used the word for a serious boyfriend or fiancé.

'He's not...' Stella began. Despite her conversation with Carol, she wasn't going to tempt fate.

'Ah, that he is. For better or worse.' Domenico tossed the pasta in the sauce, his face turned to the wall. Painstakingly he divided the mixture into the two bowls and set them on the table.

Stella wound a tangle of spaghetti strands around her fork. 'Mmm... this smells good. But what did you mean by "for better or worse"? I thought you'd decided you liked Gino. You seemed to get on so well when he came over for dinner last night.'

'Eat. We can talk afterwards.'

Reluctantly she obeyed. Every mouthful was as delicious as the first but her stomach churned as though she were back sitting outside the headmaster's study, not knowing what was to come but knowing it wouldn't be good.

She laid down her fork. Domenico carried the plates to the sink, waving away her offer to help. He unscrewed the top of his ancient Bialetti, scooped some coffee grounds from a red tin into the metal basket and tapped them down. He set the pot on the hob. Still with his back to her, he said: 'Your papà didn't want you dating Fernanda's son.'

'Because of something that happened before I was born?' She couldn't keep the frustration from her voice. 'I'm not trying to belittle the horror of it, honestly, I'm not. It was a dreadful, inexcusable atrocity and if Fernanda's sister was somehow responsible, that's shocking. But you and Papà and Fernanda were all children. For you it should be history, but Papà made it so personal.'

Domenico thumped the coffee pot down on the table. The unused knives jumped. Her gentle uncle's eyes blazed.

'It was personal!'

'What do you mean?' Her voice faltered.

Silently he poured the coffee into his tiny maroon and white cups, the liquid sloshing into the saucers. He handed her one; the cup sat in a brown puddle.

'Stella, there's something your mamma and papà never told you. Something you should know.'

36

Amy added a last dab of green paint. She still wasn't completely happy with the floral design she'd created but that didn't matter too much when she had a teetering pile of unglazed wall tiles at her disposal. Being given free rein to mess around with the tiles Leo had no use for, she could afford to make mistakes. And she knew from her pot-making escapades with Grandpa that flaws, botched experiments and frustration were an inevitable part of the creative process.

Leo, on the other hand, was working on the final, crucial details of the memorial plaque. He'd even stopped playing the radio these last couple of days, fearful that a catchy tune might break his focus. At first, she'd been reluctant to join him in his workshop for fear of distracting him but he'd assured her that if she worked in silence, the way she'd done back home, he would be able to lose himself in his work.

She paused for a moment and sat watching him put down his chisel, step back and survey his morning's work. Even from her far corner of the workshop she could sense he was satisfied. A smile spread across his face, the same smile that used to cross her grandpa's face when he'd successfully nailed a roof to a birdbox or helped her form the lip of a tricky jug to get it just so. It wasn't the only similarity between the pair of them. Leo, like Lance, understood why she wanted to tie a navy apron over her sundress even though the day was beautiful, the countryside enticing and the beach at Sanremo just a bus ride away.

Despite the dust from Leo's work, which forced her to wear a mask over her face, there was nowhere she'd rather be. With him she'd found the contentment and feeling of belonging she'd only found in Grandpa's shed. Thinking of him, her hand strayed to the place where the coin necklace had nestled under her shirt yesterday, a momentary wave of panic hitting her before remembering she'd decided it was too precious to risk wearing every day.

But though Leo and her grandpa had some traits in common, being with Leo was something quite different. When she'd worked side by side with Grandpa, she'd feel her heartbeat slow down and the tensions of the week melt away. Being close to Leo had quite the opposite effect. Her heart raced, her nerves jangled and sometimes she realised she was holding her breath. If he hadn't offered her a pitch in the furthest corner of his premises, she wouldn't have a hope of creating the delicate patterns she was trying to execute. And now she realised it was time to take a break outside before she acted on the desire bubbling inside her to pull off his dust mask and goggles, flip the chisel from his hand and press her mouth against his. The almost peck on the lips he'd given her just days ago had promised so much more, hadn't it?

She laid down her brush, untied her apron and made to slip out quietly.

'Amy?'

She stopped halfway to the workshop's open door.

'Are you taking a walk? Will you wait for me?' He took off his safety goggles, giving them a quick wipe with a rag.

'I thought you didn't have time.'

'I don't. It's so important to get this memorial finished but there's something on my mind and if I don't do it soon, I'll regret it.'

She waited for him to expand further but even as they started to walk along he didn't offer any explanation and the sunglasses he'd put on made it hard to read his expression. He hadn't even said where they were going but she recognised it as the route that led to the edge of the village and the crumbling steps that had taken them up to the Old Chapel. Ahead of them stood the stone archway and he stopped when they got there, looking out over the countryside.

'This is my favourite of all the views here,' he said. 'Like a painting but one that's subtly different every day.'

'It's perfect.'

'I'm glad you think so. I wanted to bring you somewhere memorable.' He pushed his sunglasses up into his hair.

'For what?' Amy said, but looking into his eyes she already knew. And he'd already moved a little closer. She breathed in his scent of woody cologne and stone dust.

'For this.' He touched her bottom lip with one work-roughened finger. Warmth flooded though her. He wrapped his arms around her, his bare arms touching hers where the sleeves of his overall were rolled up above the elbows. She closed her eyes. His mouth sought hers. The ground seemed to shift as though the stone archway itself might crumble.

They kissed for a long time. Eventually he broke away. She

opened her eyes. Through the archway the sun bleached the red rooftops, the sky above the dark green hills a pure bright blue. But even if they'd been standing in the bin-lined alleyway behind the pizzeria, the view would have been equally memorable. This was a moment she would never forget.

37

Domenico rested his elbows on the table; he threaded his fingers together. 'Your nonno was killed in the war like your mamma and papà told you. But he wasn't a civilian casualty. The last time Arturo and I saw him alive was the day the Germans came.'

'But why didn't Papà tell me...' Stella began.

Domenico exhaled: a long, sad sigh. 'Sometimes something happens to a man that alters him so fundamentally, he fears that speaking about it will bring the whole edifice of his life crumbling down. And that is how it was with my brother.

'Arturo was just eight years old on the day of the massacre. I was six, we two were the youngest of five children. Our two brothers were much older, away fighting, our only sister was nursing at a hospital in Trieste. Only Arturo and I were still at home. I hero-worshipped your papà. He was everything a big brother should be.'

Domenico closed his eyes for a second before he continued: 'On the day of the massacre, the war in Italy was far from over. The fascist government in the North and their German masters were desperate and angry. Despite their denials, they must have known their once-inevitable victory over the Allies was now slipping away. Even at home, the partisan fighters were inflicting embarrassing losses. The Germans sent soldiers into villages thought to be hiding Allied prisoners of war or supporting the rebels. Revenge wasn't an eye for an eye, the authorities announced they would kill ten Italians for every German killed by the partisans. Danger was never far away. But nothing of that sort went on here, there were just a few local lads hiding away, ignoring the orders to go and fight. We never expected the *rastrellamento* – the sweeping up of their enemies – to happen here.

'There was no warning, no inkling of trouble until a young man bicycled into the village, sounding the alarm that the Germans were coming. Papà was calm, intent on reassuring Mamma but he told us boys to run and hide, he wanted us out of the way. Arturo and I ran past Sant' Agata's. Fernanda was playing in the piazza. I grabbed her hand and took her with us.'

Fernanda? Stella bit her tongue, not wanting to interrupt Domenico's tale.

'There was an old barn on the edge of the village, a broken-down carriage abandoned there. Arturo and I had discovered it some months before whilst playing hide and seek. We'd hollowed out a space beneath the seat; it would just about hide two. I don't know how we thought all three of us would fit in there. But when we passed under the old stone arch, Arturo broke away from us. He said it was better if we split up, that he had another hiding place. I was used to doing what my big brother told me and we had no time to argue. The roar of their engines, the shouting and the sounds of people running told us the soldiers were already here. I pulled Fernanda into our hiding place.

'We didn't know what was going on but even in there we could hear gunfire, people's screams. I've never kept so quiet and still in all my life. I held my finger to Fernanda's lips to stop her whimpering. I was shaking, scared. I admit I wet myself.

'It was several hours before we dared creep out. It was eerie, the streets quiet and still. The smell of burning hung in the air. Fernanda and I parted without a word. I ran home. Mamma clutched me to her, weeping. I asked for Papà. She broke down again.'

Domenico reached into his trouser pocket, brought out a huge spotted handkerchief and blew his nose. Stella realised she was chewing on her nails.

'A neighbour was sitting in the corner of our living room, a nice lady, I don't remember her name. She told me Papà was in heaven and I must be quiet and good and brave like Arturo and not bother Mamma with any questions. It was only then that I noticed my brother curled up in the corner. I asked him what time he'd got home and where he'd been. He didn't answer. Just stared as though he didn't know who I was. All evening, he didn't say a word.

'The next day, he was just the same, he didn't utter a sound, just lay on our bed. Mamma wandered the house in a daze. It frightened me. I wanted to cheer her up and in my childish way I thought it would please her if I tidied the bedroom Arturo and I shared. And that's when I knew Arturo had hidden away close enough to see. To be a witness. His *zoccoli* were by the bed. You know what those are, don't you, Stella? A leather strap nailed to a block of wood. All of us village kids wore them; no family here could afford proper shoes, not for feet that outgrew them in no time. At first, I didn't realise what I was looking at. Then I held them up to the light and saw they were covered in blood. I threw them to the floor and ran out into the street. When I returned that night, they were gone.'

Stella gasped. 'Did he tell you he saw it all?'

'He didn't speak, Stella. He was traumatised, struck mute. It was seven, eight months before he spoke one word. From then on, it was as if I were the elder. I took on the mantle of looking out for Arturo the way he'd looked out for me. It was another twenty years before he told me he saw our papà shot in the back of the head. When the soldiers drove away, he crept from his hiding place. He stood in the pool of blood seeping across the piazza, until that shocked neighbour scooped him up and brought him home.'

Stella clamped her hand to her mouth. For a moment she thought she was going to be sick.

'He should have told us. We would have tried to understand.'

'He just couldn't talk about it. He spoke to me that one time only and never again. It was when I made the mistake of mentioning Fernanda's name.'

'But when you were children, you were all friends?'

'Yes, we were, until that day. Of course, Papà hadn't been happy about it. He didn't like us associating with the little sister of a woman who consorted with the Germans but Mamma used to calm him down, saying we were just children playing. But from that day I hated Fernanda and her family. Even at six years old I understood the gossip I heard linking Violetta to what happened.

'I gathered together the remnants of a bottle of machine oil, an old rag, a box of matches. I was a tiny soldier preparing for my war. I planned to soak the rag, light it and put it through Violetta's door. I didn't care if Fernanda was there or not. My old friend was dead to me. But then I heard Violetta had not come home. She'd perished in the bombing at the hospital where she'd been visiting a friend. Fernanda had been taken in by a lady in the village. That woman was my teacher, a kind person who was ever patient with me. I hated Fernanda but I couldn't have burnt that dear lady's little house down, even if she had Hitler himself sheltering there.

'Over the years, I began to realise it was warped of me to blame a seven-year-old child for the actions of her much older sister. But your papà's trauma was too deep for rational thought. It was only after his death that Fernanda and I started to exchange the odd word if we met. Even so, we are far from being friends. And now you see, Stella, why Arturo tried to keep you away from Gino. The thought of you marrying into that family – it was too much for him to bear. He couldn't stand the thought of Fernanda being your mother-in-law, a woman who won't disown her sister, who even displays a painting of that fascist upon her wall.'

Stella put her head in her hands. 'I'm so sorry. No wonder Papà was so angry with me the day he died. If only I'd understood.'

'You weren't to know,' Uncle Domenico said softly. 'You're not to blame.'

38

'Gino's here,' Domenico said. He retreated into the kitchen.

Stella opened the door. Gino held out a bunch of lilies. Her heart lifted.

'Thank you, they're beautiful. I'll put them in a vase. You'd better come in for a minute.'

'No need. I'll wait.'

She scurried into the kitchen, shoved the stalks into the sink and hurried out before her uncle could say anything.

The moment the front door closed, Gino pulled her into his arms. She held him tight, inhaling the warm scent of his cologne-spritzed skin. His lips moved over hers, sending her nerve endings tingling. Any other day, she would have been in seventh heaven, but the story Domenico had told her played on a loop in her head.

She stepped away. 'We'd better set straight off. We don't want them giving away our table.'

Gino smiled. 'We're not going back to the pizzeria.'

'Oh, why not?'

'Leo's gone out with Amy tonight. You know what that

means? We've got his house to ourselves all evening. I've been cooking for us. But we don't need to stay in the kitchen.' His eyes sparkled.

'Let's go, then,' Stella said.

He held her hand as they walked along. He opened Leo's front door. They stopped in the hallway.

'Oh, Stella.' His kiss on her neck sent a shiver through her. He put his hands around her waist. Her body was melting but her mind wouldn't follow. She dropped her hands to her sides.

'Stella?'

'Would you mind if we waited until later?'

'Of course, whatever you like. You could sit in the kitchen whilst I cook. Or perhaps there is a good film on TV. I'll pour you a drink. Once I have finished preparing the *pansoti* I will join you. We can sit side by side and watch television like an old married couple.' He laughed.

'You had me at drink,' Stella said.

'A Campari and soda?'

'Yes, perfect.' Anything would do.

'You go through, make yourself comfortable.'

She did as he said, picked up the remote and surfed through the channels. There was nothing she wanted to see but she put on a re-run of a comedy series from the 1990s. It wasn't long before Gino squeezed up next to her. Soon, they were laughing along. It was good to have something to distract him from asking about her day. The news that Domenico was employing an assistant and the revelations about her papà's childhood trauma weren't things she could cope with sharing right now. Gino slipped back into the kitchen to put the pasta in the pot, re-entering a few minutes later as the credits rolled.

'Perfect timing,' he said. 'Come and eat.'

She sat in the kitchen. Gino swapped her Campari for a

glass of wine. She couldn't help smiling when she saw he'd created the exact first course she'd been practising: *pansoti con salsa di noci*, the little pasta pillows piled in a pale, creamy sauce, topped with a shower of hazelnut crumbs. She took a bite, savouring the contrast of the rich sauce with the healthy chard filling. But it was hard to enjoy her food knowing she'd left Domenico eating alone. Was he brooding on the past whilst she and Gino flirted over the kitchen table? She swallowed some more wine.

Gino attended to the next course of *verdure ripiene*, peppers and zucchini stuffed with the zucchini pulp, ricotta, mortadella and marjoram. It didn't take them long to clear their plates.

He stood up. 'If this was my place, I'd leave all this washing up until tomorrow and carry you upstairs. But I'd better clear up.'

'I'll wash if you dry,' Stella said, pushing up the sleeves of her pink linen blouse.

They worked in an easy rhythm, making short work of the task.

Gino glanced at his watch. 'Leo won't be back for at least another hour. He said he and Amy were going to go and see that rock band in the piazza. Rather them than me, but their earache is our opportunity.'

He took hold of one of her hands. Gently, he eased off her rubber gloves, a cheeky smile on his face as though he were peeling off a pair of stockings. He leant back against the kitchen sink. He pulled her close.

'My beautiful Stella.' He ran a finger across her lips. His mouth brushed hers, light and teasing. He undid her top button, dropping a kiss on her collarbone. She felt as stiff and unyielding as one of his son's memorials.

'What is it?'

'Nothing.'

'Is it him – Joe? It was stupid of me to think you'd be over him so quickly.'

'It's not. Honestly. I don't know how I ever imagined myself with someone like him.'

'Then what? Is it me, something I've said or done?' His brow was creased in bewilderment.

'No. Really, it's nothing.'

It was obvious she was lying. His face clouded. But how could she tell him that when she looked into his eyes, all she could see was the face of an innocent little boy, standing in a pool of blood?

39

The church bells of Sant' Agata chimed eight o'clock. Leo was now ten minutes late, which wouldn't have been so bad if Amy hadn't been ten minutes early.

People were streaming into the piazza from all directions, eager to attend the evening's entertainment. Three young women passed by, a gaggle of long legs and laughter. An elderly man in a pressed shirt, hands clasped behind his back, moved slowly in the direction of the stage. He looked an unlikely fan of the heavy rock mixed with a dose of seventies punk they were promised. But judging by some of the elegant outfits being worn by the women of the village, this was an evening for seeing and being seen as much as for listening to the music.

The girl on the pink bicycle was circling the church again despite the crowds. A man snatched a toddler out of her way and popped him on his shoulders. Amy recognised him as Mario from the pizzeria, here with his grandchild, and gave him an awkward smile. Did it look as though she'd been stood up, hovering here?

'Amy!' The sound of Leo's voice made her jump. He'd changed out of his overalls into a light blue shirt, the sleeves rolled up, revealing those muscular arms again. His hair was half mussed up, his breath coming fast, as though he'd been running.

'Leo!' Relief surged through her. She melted into his hug, inhaling his fresh-from-the-shower scent.

'So sorry I'm late. I went to meet you and got caught up with Nonna.'

'I thought we said to meet here.'

'I was early so I thought I would catch you before you left the house.'

'I was early too.' They stood smiling at each other.

'You look great, by the way, I love that top,' he added.

'Thanks. Was Fernanda okay when you left? You look a bit flustered.'

'She is now. She was in a bit of a state when I arrived. She'd mislaid some trinket of her sister's.'

'I'm always mislaying things.' Amy laughed.

'Nonna never normally loses anything, she's so tidy and careful.' Leo frowned. Someone patted him on the shoulder and his smile returned. '*Ciao!*'

'*Ciao*, Leo.' A boy with a leather jacket over his arm, despite the warm evening, gave him a half salute and looked Amy up and down. He said something in Italian with a cheeky grin and wandered off; she didn't like to ask what it was. Leo made a disapproving noise.

'Sorry about that guy. He used to date my sister, they got together one school holiday. I haven't seen him for an age.'

'I can't believe it's so busy here. I hadn't realised this band was so popular.' The crowd around the stage was now at least ten people deep and it was impossible to see what snacks the formidable army of local ladies were serving up, there were so many people thronging around the trestle tables.

'It doesn't matter much who the band are. People here just like a night out, whether it's rock, some guy in a wig singing ballads or our local brass band.' Leo smiled. 'It looks like the whole village is here.'

'Except for Stella and your dad.'

'Stella is a nice lady but I'd rather not think about those two being alone together in my house whilst I'm out.' He pulled a face.

Amy laughed. 'Do you think we'll be able to get a beer?'

'It might be easier now than later.' He took her hand; they walked towards the temporary bar erected in the far corner. Their progress was slow, Leo stopping every few paces to chat to friends and neighbours. But she didn't mind when she clocked the pride on his face as he introduced her.

'How do you know so many people? Didn't you go to school in Alassio?'

'I spent a lot of time at Nonna's in the holidays. Kids here tend to play outside so it's easier to get to know each other.'

'I thought Fernanda kept you stuck inside chained to your schoolbooks,' she teased.

'I'm glad she did, all those hours studying English vocabulary are coming in very useful.'

'I should thank her. Maybe I should start learning Italian.'

'Why is that?' He gave her that look again, the one that turned the edges of her world all fuzzy.

'Maybe I'll come back.' She felt herself blush.

He bit his lip, looking as if he was going to say something, but a guy with a nose ring and arms tattooed with italic script said something that made him swing around.

'This is Amy,' Leo said. 'Amy, this is Ettore, Black Rat's bass guitarist. That means he stands at the back and looks moody.'

Ettore frowned, obviously not quite understanding what Leo was saying. 'Like some *cuculli*? I have plenty.' He handed Leo a paper cone of fried snacks. Amy could smell sage and rosemary.

'They're like chickpea fritters,' Leo said to her, popping one in his mouth.

'Sure, great, I'd love some,' Amy said.

Ettore gave her another cone, high-fived Leo and slapped him on the shoulder. '*Ciao ragazzi!*'

Ettore didn't take long to weave his way through the crowd. He was up on the stage two minutes later, a black and white electric guitar slung round his neck. A big man with a black T-shirt shouted *uno, due, tre,* into a microphone. Another man leapt onto the stage, his hair slicked back, a white shirt open to the navel. He fired out a string of rapid Italian. The audience responded with clapping and a few cheers. The drummer dropped his head, the singer grabbed the mic with both hands, twisting his body as he launched straight into a cover version of 'I Fought the Law'. The lead guitarist whirled his arm in a circle, strutting across the stage like he was playing at Wembley. Amy finished the last of her *cuculli*, her fingers greasy with oil and salt. She found a tissue and gave them an inadequate wipe.

The band played one rocking track after another. Even the songs they had written themselves got the villagers dancing. Teenagers leapt around, some playing air guitar, young mums swayed behind their pushchairs, couples bopped.

The lead singer said something Amy couldn't catch. A murmur of appreciation rose from the crowd.

'They're going to play some old rock and roll,' Leo said.

Amy recognised the first bars of 'Jailhouse Rock' straight away. Next to her, an elderly lady in a crocheted cardigan took dainty steps in her high-heeled shoes, singing along in a surprisingly gusty voice. The band switched to a Chubby Checker number. Mario from the pizzeria started doing the twist, holding hands with someone who looked like his father. The older chap got right down to the floor, needing his son to yank him back up again. Leo swung Amy around until she was quite dizzy.

The MC jumped back on stage. It seemed it was time for a break. The band laid down their instruments. The ladies behind the trestle tables braced themselves for a surge of hungry dancers.

'Another beer?' Leo said. They joined the throng around the makeshift bar. It must have been at least twenty minutes before they were served. Finally, they extricated themselves from the mass of bodies clutching much-needed bottles of Peroni, just in time for the second half. The lead guitarist was already back on the stage.

Amy chugged back some beer and fanned herself with her other hand.

'Got a bit warm?' Leo said.

'Yes.' She undid a couple of buttons on her short-sleeved blouse, hoping she wouldn't leave a greasy mark. Her fingers made contact with her precious coin. It had felt right to wear it on such a special evening. On stage, the drummer sat down and picked up his sticks. Somebody whooped.

'What is that?' Leo's voice sounded odd, as though someone was squeezing his throat. He was staring at her necklace.

'It's an old one-lira coin. Grandpa left it to me.' She put her hand to her chest, feeling strangely vulnerable under his searching gaze.

'Your grandpa's necklace, is that so?' He raised his eyebrows.

'Why are you looking at me like that?'

Leo didn't reply. Someone knocked into Amy's back, sending her flying into him. He didn't look amused.

'*Scusi!*' a teenage girl laughed, whirling away again.

'We're leaving,' Leo said.

'Let's not go just yet.' Amy's feet itched to dance. She grabbed Leo's hands to swing him around but he wouldn't budge. Why was he being so boring all of a sudden?

'Amy, we're leaving. We're going to see Nonna.'

'Oh, okay, if you want.'

He led her through the crowd and down the street. She had to half jog to keep up with him.

'What's the rush? Why are you in such a hurry to see Fernanda?'

He made a kind of snort. 'I thought you might have something you want to say to her.'

Amy stopped walking. 'Look, Leo, I don't know what's got into you. I thought we were having a good time. Why are you being so funny with me?'

He flicked his finger against the coin hanging around her neck. 'Why did you take it? To have a souvenir of your trip? I can't believe you'd do this to my nonna when she's been so kind to you.'

She stared at him. 'Are you accusing me of stealing this?'

'What do you think? My nonna loses her sister's precious necklace and a few hours later it turns up around your neck.'

'I can't believe this!' Amy marched off in the direction of Fernanda's house as fast as she could, her eyes pricking with angry tears. 'You might as well hurry up. The sooner we see Fernanda, the sooner she can tell you this isn't hers.'

* * *

'I was not expecting you back so early.' Fernanda looked from Amy to Leo and back again.

'Amy has something to show you.'

Amy's hand went to her chest. 'This necklace...'

Fernanda's eyes darkened. 'That is mine. It belonged to Violetta. Why have you taken it?'

'It isn't yours.' Amy tried to keep her voice level. 'Grandpa Lance gave it to me.'

'You have switched the leather for a chain. Did you think I would not recognise it?'

'Maybe your sister had something similar but it's not this. Do you want to look more closely?'

'Let me see the back. Mine has a curve etched onto the reverse side.'

Amy went cold.

Fernanda reached out a bony hand, her old engagement ring glinting under the hall light. She turned the coin, her fingers pressing against Amy's chest. 'It *is* mine! You stole it!'

'No! I swear I didn't.' She tried to prise Fernanda's fingers open but the old woman held the coin too tightly. The only way Amy could loosen Fernanda's grip was to give her an almighty shove. But no matter how unjust the accusations were, Amy wasn't going to have Fernanda's broken bones on her conscience. She jerked backwards to try to get away. The cheap chain snapped. Fernanda's fist balled around her prize.

'It's not what you think.' Amy looked at Leo in despair. He wouldn't meet her eyes, looking down at the floor and shaking his head.

'You'd better go and get your things, the last bus won't have left yet,' Fernanda said. 'Leo will wait while you pack and walk you to the bus stop.'

Amy barged her way out of the hall into her bedroom, her eyes screwed up, desperately fighting her tears. She opened the wardrobe doors, hurling her clothes into her case any old how. She swiped everything from the bathroom shelf into her wash-bag, grabbed her book from the bedside table and yanked out her phone charger. She checked around quickly. Apart from the rumpled quilt there was now no sign she'd ever been there.

She dumped her case in the hall. Fernanda was waiting by the front door.

'I haven't paid for my stay,' Amy said. She undid the catch of her bag.

Fernanda squared her shoulders. She peered down her nose. 'I do not want your money. Just go.'

Amy ignored her. She opened her purse and threw a handful of notes onto the hall table. Leo marched out of the door, and she followed him down the road, dragging her case behind her.

Leo walked with her as far as the bus stop. He leant against the window of the salumeria.

'Why don't you go?' Amy said. 'Why are you waiting here?'

'I just want to understand. Why did you do it, Amy?'

'I didn't. I've told you, that necklace is mine. They must be identical. I'm the one who's been robbed.'

'I can't believe you won't even own up to it. You know some-thing, Amy? I really liked you. I thought... Well, it doesn't matter now.'

'Thought what?' Amy said. She didn't know if it would make her feel better or worse if he admitted to some feelings for her.

'I thought I knew you. I thought you were nice, a good

person... special. I thought there was something between us. Deep down, I knew it was probably too good to last. But now I won't even be able to treasure the memories.' He laughed and shook his head. 'You did a good job, Amy. I even found myself searching the local ads for a second-hand potter's wheel. Someone in Apricale was selling one. I almost went to get it.'

'What for? You really thought I might stay in a boring little village like this? You've got to be kidding! Why would I want to do that?' She dug her nails into her palms, willing him to go away.

He turned around, shoulders slumped, as he set off back towards Fernanda's. The tears she'd fought to hold back began to fall. The bus was due in less than half an hour. If only it would come straight away. Tonight, she'd find a cheap hotel in Sanremo; tomorrow she'd search for a flight back to England.

The sound of the band thrashing out 'Rock Around the Clock' drifted over from the piazza. The villagers would be dancing and singing long into the night.

40

'Coffee?' Gino said.

'Please.' Stella didn't feel like one but it was a safer bet than drinking another glass of wine and saying something she'd come to regret. Like, 'Did you know your family was responsible for the death of my grandfather as well as my papà?'

Gino busied himself at the stove. Stella walked over to the kitchen window. The air was warm, still. There wasn't a wisp of a breeze. Music drifted over from the piazza, several streets away. She was tempted to suggest they abandon Leo's house and join in with the dancing and raucous singing. Immersing themselves in the revelry would be an easy way to avoid conversation.

He set down the coffee.

Stella found it hard to meet his eye. The effort of making small talk with the man with whom she'd wanted to share everything was bringing her close to tears. She faked a yawn.

'Sorry. I really am tired.'

'Looking after the shop and your uncle coming home, it's

been too much for you. It was selfish of me to think you'd have much energy left this evening.'

'I'm sorry I've not been good company.'

'Don't be daft.' He knocked back his coffee in two mouthfuls. 'Finish your drink then I will walk you back.'

'There's no need.'

'Okay.' He looked too defeated to argue.

She tipped back her coffee. 'Thank you for dinner. It was delicious.'

'My pleasure.' He walked her to the door.

'Goodnight, Gino.'

He kissed her on both cheeks. Like a friend.

'You do still want to have dinner with me on Saturday, don't you?' he said. 'I've booked a table at Da Luca; I thought a sixtieth birthday deserved more than a return trip to the pizzeria.'

'Of course I do, that would be lovely.'

She stepped outside; the door closed behind her. She stood in the road, fighting the urge to turn back and bang the knocker. To try and explain. But how could she put into words what she couldn't understand herself? Logically, she knew that nothing Violetta had done was Gino's fault. She needed time to think, to be alone.

She walked aimlessly for a while. She didn't want to go back to her uncle's house and explain why she'd curtailed her evening. And she didn't fancy fighting through the crowds in the piazza; someone was sure to stop her for a chat. Everyone knew she was back with Gino. How would she explain his absence away?

She wandered through the backstreets, the sound of the rock music becoming progressively louder then quieter as she went up and down steps, ducked and dived under arches and through alleyways. Eventually she looped back to the start of the passageway beside Sant' Agata's and out onto the end of the main street. There was no one around, the shops all shuttered hours before. The bar stood deserted, but the tables and chairs were all set out, ready waiting for the revellers to spill in after the last note played. Behind the counter, a bored member of staff played with his phone.

At the top of the street a lone figure stood at the bus stop, a bag slung over her shoulder, a small suitcase by her feet. The last service of the day hadn't yet come through the village but it seemed strange that someone would be leaving so late in the evening.

As Stella's footsteps drew nearer, the traveller turned. Her hair shone golden red under the streetlamp's soft light. Streaks of dark eye makeup were smudged across her cheeks.

'Amy?'

The girl let out a strangled sob.

'What's happened?' Stella said. 'Where on earth are you going?'

'I can't stay.' Amy swiped a hand roughly across her tear-stained face.

'Is it Leo?' Stella asked.

'It's over.' Amy stared down at the case by her feet. A bra strap poked out of the hastily closed zip.

'Are you sure? Gino says the way Leo talks about you...'

'Please don't.' Amy pressed her lips together.

The sound of a car approaching caught Stella's attention, its headlights too bright in the empty street. Behind it came the bus to Sanremo. Amy picked up her case. She put out her other arm. The bus slowed to a halt. The front and middle doors opened. One lone passenger got off.

'Bye, Stella.'

'No.' Stella caught her by the arm. 'You're not going anywhere. Not tonight, not like this.'

'Why do you care where I'm going?' Amy shook her off. She stepped aboard the bus. 'Sanremo, *per favore*.'

Stella stood half in, half out the door. 'I don't know why I care, I just do.'

'Will you either get on or off please, *signora*.' The bus driver looked weary. A murmur rose from the passengers, someone tutted.

'I can't go back to Fernanda's,' Amy said but she made no attempt to move down the bus and sit down.

'*Sbrigati per favore*! Hurry up, please!' someone shouted from the back of the bus.

Stella swiped Amy's case and plonked it down by the kerb. 'You're going to stay with me and my Uncle Domenico. Please, no arguing. It's late. You can't be wandering around looking for somewhere to stay. If you want, you can leave straight after breakfast. What do you think your mum and dad would say?'

'I suppose you're right.' Amy stepped off the bus. Someone gave a sarcastic cheer. The doors closed with a hiss.

'Everything will look better in the morning.'

'No... No, it won't.' Amy chewed her lip. 'But... umm, thanks so much for giving me somewhere to stay.'

'No problem. We'll go home right now and have a nice cup of tea.'

'Okay.' Amy sniffed. She followed Stella in silence.

* * *

Stella had expected her uncle's house to be in darkness but despite the late hour, it looked as though Domenico hadn't gone to bed. He might not be too impressed that she'd turned up with a visitor in tow, but she knew he wouldn't have the heart to turn Amy away.

Stella opened the unlocked door and waved a hand to indicate where Amy might park her case.

'I'm home,' she called. No answer came. She pushed open the door to the little sitting room. The lamp was on but Domenico's chair was unoccupied. Only the squashed cushions and abandoned newspaper signalled that her uncle had recently been sitting there.

'Sit down, make yourself comfortable. I'll make that tea.'

'I don't think...' Amy hovered.

'Sit,' Stella said.

She stepped back into the hall. The sound of running water came from the kitchen.

'Domenico, are you there?'

She turned the handle.

'You're back early.' Her uncle was standing by the kitchen sink, a guilty look on his face.

'I said to leave your washing up for me to do.'

'All done and put away.' He moved one hand behind his back, a gesture that drew attention to whatever he was trying to hide.

Stella crossed the room. 'Show me your hand.' It was the voice she'd used when Lauren was small.

Domenico's eyes shifted sideways. He held out his knobbly hand, the skin painfully pink.

'You've burnt yourself! I wouldn't have left you that *frandura* if I thought you were going to heat it up.'

'Pah! I would not do that. It tastes better at room temperature, it brings all the flavours out.'

'Then how?' Her uncle could make coffee in his sleep and she'd ironed all his shirts.

'That new kettle of yours gives out a lot of steam. I didn't realise it would burn like that, silly old fool that I am.'

Stella was incredulous. 'You were making tea? I've never seen you drink one. Talking of which—' She lifted the offending object off its stand and filled it to the halfway mark. Then she examined Domenico's hand. 'You should hold it under the tap for a while longer.'

'I'm sorry, Stella.'

'Nothing to be sorry for.'

'There is.' He pressed his thin lips together. 'I was trying to surprise you, but I've wrecked that hat.'

'The one I found in the storeroom?'

He tilted his head towards the kitchen table. The hat was still squashed out of shape and now the silk flowers had wilted and some of the colours had run. It looked sorrier than ever.

'Oh dear.'

'I thought if I steamed it like you were planning to do, you'd move it somewhere I wouldn't have to look at it.'

Stella put her hand to her mouth. 'I'm so sorry. I knew Violetta made it, but it was so pretty I just didn't think. To be honest, I hadn't given a moment's thought to what I'd do with it. I suppose I should pass it on to Fernanda.'

'You can't give it to her in that state.'

He looked so serious she wanted to hug him.

'I'll try to revive it in the morning and if it's no better, we'll bin it. It's only a hat.'

'Wait,' Domenico said quietly. 'Did you close the front door? I thought I heard a noise in the hall.'

Stella gasped. 'I almost forgot! We've... umm... I've got a visitor.'

She opened the kitchen door. The hallway was empty. Amy's suitcase had gone.

41

Fernanda's eyes were closing. It was disrespectful to fall asleep whilst studying the words of the Lord; she set aside her bible. She'd neglected the Holy Book these last few days, led astray by her young lodger. Perhaps that should have been a sign that Amy had a wicked streak. But Fernanda still couldn't quite believe it. Amy had seemed so sweet and lovely. And pretty. Fernanda knew it was illogical but somehow she'd always associated evil with ugliness, as if bad deeds showed up on a person's face. She of all people should have known how beauty was only skin deep.

Holding tightly to the banister, she pulled herself up the stairs. Her jewellery box stood proudly in the centre of her dressing table, resting on an embroidered cloth. She lifted the inlaid wooden lid and checked through her meagre collection once more. Her grandmother's amethyst pendant, her mother's wedding ring, the gold bangle Fernanda's husband had bought on their only holiday abroad were all there. Why would Amy ignore these treasures yet steal a worthless old lira coin strung on a leather thong?

The stolen necklace had only sentimental value but it was as precious to Fernanda as baby Gino's first pair of shoes. She'd been left with so few of her sister's things, after the family that took her in sold most of Violetta's possessions to cover the extra mouth they had to feed.

She unpinned her brooch from her dress and unwound the silky scarf that only half disguised her wrinkled neck, sat on the edge of the bed and pulled off her dark stockings. Her shoulder seared with pain as she eased her pintucked blouse over her head. Wincing, she pushed both arms into her long white nightgown and pottered to the bathroom, making preparations for the night, knowing she would get no more than a few hours' sleep.

Teeth brushed, thick, rose-scented cream rubbed into her face, she sat on the small, padded stool, staring at her face in the dressing table mirror. Amy's betrayal had knocked her sideways. But it wasn't almost losing Violetta's necklace that bothered her half as much as Leo's crestfallen face. Her beloved grandson was more hurt by this than he would ever admit.

She suspected Leo would pretend to be okay, to claim Amy was just an inconsequential holiday fling. It would be easy for Fernanda to quote meaningless platitudes and remind him what a very short time he'd known the girl. But she'd seen the look on Leo's face when Amy walked out the door. It was a look she'd seen before. The look on Gino's face when Stella left the village.

First, her darling son Gino, now Leo. Fernanda's love for her sister had led, she realised now, to the pain of those she loved most. Violetta had betrayed the village, causing the death of Arturo and Domenico's papà. And she, Fernanda, in a moment of madness, had dragged Stella by the arm to confess her dalliance with Gino, sending Arturo into the fury that caused his heart attack. She'd killed Stella's papà just as surely as if she'd fired a gun from his doorstep. After that, Stella's departure and Gino's heartbreak had been inevitable. And now, Violetta's necklace had led to Amy's abrupt departure.

Fernanda wound her sister's string of cultured pearls around her fingers. It had been a present to Violetta from her German boyfriend, Franz. Perhaps tonight was a sign that Fernanda should sell it and give the money to the poor. She should have done so long ago. These last eighty years, Fernanda had treasured her sister's memory but now it was as tainted as the pearls from her Nazi lover. Fernanda had to stop sugarcoating the past. Tomorrow she'd make a start.

'I'm sorry, Violetta, I love you but now this must stop,' Fernanda murmured. She buried her face in her pillow.

* * *

Stella stood in the empty hallway. She couldn't believe Amy had gone. The last thing Stella felt like doing was walking the streets searching for her but it had to be done. The poor girl was clearly not thinking straight, Stella couldn't let her wander off on her own.

She fished her housekeys back out of the dish on the console table, glancing in the mirror hanging over it. Her face looked tired, her complexion dull. The strain of Domenico's revelations about Gino's family's role in her nonno's death had etched new lines into her forehead. She looked all of her soon-to-be sixty years.

Slipping the keys into her pocket, she turned to go back into the kitchen to let Domenico know she was popping out for a short while. Above her head, a stair tread creaked. Stella looked up. Amy was coming downstairs, her hand small and pale against the sturdy wooden banister. Stella let out a gasp of relief.

'Sorry,' Amy said. 'I tried to be as quiet as possible. I didn't want to wake your uncle if he's up there sleeping but I desperately needed the bathroom. I left Fernanda's in such a hurry...'

Stella let her keys drop back into the bowl with a clatter. 'That's no problem. Domenico's in the kitchen, the kettle is on. I can't tell you how relieved I am, Amy; I thought you'd gone.'

'Gone? But where would I go?'

'That's exactly what was worrying me. But where's your case?'

'I just moved it out of the way in there.' Amy indicated the sitting room door. 'The hallway's so narrow I didn't think you'd want to keep squeezing past it.'

'That makes sense. Now, please go and sit down. I'll go and explain to Domenico that you're staying here tonight, then we'll have that cup of tea and you can tell me what on earth happened with Leo.'

Amy nodded mutely.

'I'll be right back,' Stella said. Hearing Amy's problems might take her mind off her own. Or, more likely, give Stella twice as many reasons to stare at the ceiling, mulling things over in the small hours when she should be fast asleep.

42

It was no use. Fernanda couldn't reach any further. She shifted position slightly; the chair beneath her wobbled alarmingly. She sucked in her breath sharply. There was no need to panic. She had climbed up, so she must be able to get back down. But how? And now there was someone knocking at the door.

A key rattled in the lock. It had to be Gino or Leo. She hoped it would be her grandson. He was more likely to laugh than give her a ticking off.

'Mamma!'

Fernanda winced. Now she was in trouble. 'In here, Gino!'

Her son thrust open the door. '*Mamma mia*! What are you doing? Are you trying to get yourself killed?'

'I'm only standing on a chair.'

'And you're stuck.'

'Who said I was?'

'Mamma, of course you are! You didn't come to answer the door. Here, let me help you down.' He put his arms around her waist, lifting her as though she were as light as a slice of soft *panarello* sponge cake. It always amazed her how her little boy had grown into such a strong handsome man.

'Thank you. It was much easier to climb up.' She gave him a rueful smile.

'It's a good thing I came past to see how you were. I was worried you'd still be upset about that girl. It's horrible to learn you had a thief in the house. But what on earth were you doing climbing up there? Dusting Violetta's portrait?'

'I've decided to take it down.'

'I don't know what you were thinking, the glass could have broken and cut you if you'd slipped and fallen. Let me do it.' He lifted the picture down easily, without recourse to the chair. 'Where do you want it? Are you moving it somewhere else? If you've got a new hook, I can bring my drill over later.'

'It's going away in a drawer.' She watched his face move as if unsure of what expression to adopt. 'Pietro's remains returning to the village, the plaque Leo is carving... I think it's time I faced the truth about Violetta. To acknowledge what she did.'

'I think you're very brave, Mamma,' Gino said softly. 'I know how much you loved her.'

'I still do.' Fernanda choked back a sob. 'But it's time to take her portrait down.'

'I should stay for coffee.'

'No, you get on. You stopped by to check I was okay after that horrible incident with Amy and I am. You get back to Leo's house, I'm sure there's more left on that DIY list. Or are you seeing Stella?'

Surprise crossed her son's face.

'I can say her name, you know. And Gino, I know you love her. You always did. Will you invite her for dinner tonight? It's about time, don't you think?'

Gino's face lit up. 'Are you sure?'

'Of course. I want to make her welcome. I hope it is not too late.'

'It's never too late, Mamma.' He kissed her cheek. 'I'll see you tonight. I'll let myself out.'

He undid the front door, whistling to himself as he stepped back into the street.

Fernanda picked up the portrait of Violetta. She studied it for a long time.

'I am so sorry, Violetta.' She turned it upside down and slipped it into a drawer. She tied on her apron and gathered up her dustpan and brush, polish and a cloth. Keeping busy would stop her from dwelling on what she'd done.

The morning passed quickly, what hadn't been cleaned would have to stay that way. Fernanda now had a meal to prepare. Luckily, she'd been shopping the day before, planning some of the meals she thought she and Amy might share. The cupboards were groaning.

She chose two large zucchini and began to chop them. One piece bounced off the chopping board, falling onto the floor. Before she had the chance to pick it up, the little so-and-so rolled away beneath the unit. Fernanda tutted. She didn't know if mice were partial to green vegetables but she wasn't willing to leave it there and take the chance.

Her first instinct was to crouch down but she wasn't confident she'd be able to stand back up again. Instead, she fetched the broom. With a wiggle, it would just fit underneath. Careful not to push the zucchino further back, she manoeuvred it out onto the tiles, tutting at the small clump of grey dust she'd also liberated. She turned the broom over to pluck it off. Something metallic sparkled; a coin threaded on a leather thong was tangled up between the bristles.

She eased it out and polished the one-lira piece on her

apron. The hole drilled through it, the flourish scratched onto the back: it was unmistakeable. Fernanda frowned; this made no sense. Violetta's keepsake had been upstairs on her dressing table ever since she'd snatched it back from Amy. She sank down on a kitchen chair, turning the coin over in her hands. Eventually she stood up and made her way over to the stove. She filled the Bialetti. Perhaps a shot of coffee might fire up her slow old brain.

She drank her coffee, savouring the rich taste, but she was still puzzled. She returned to the work surface and started chopping the zucchini again. Snippets from the previous few days floated in and out of her head, vague recollections swirling until they formed a fuzzy picture: Father Filippo calling on her, bringing his sweet little niece; the two of them absorbed in their discussions whilst the child flicked through Gino's old picture book of saints' lives; Fernanda consulting her calendar to mark the date of the church fundraiser; an apologetic Father Filippo jumping up when he realised the little girl had wandered off. Had he found her upstairs? Fernanda tried to remember but she hadn't paid much attention, her thoughts full of brass polishing and hymns. But she did recall the guilty look on the child's face. She'd assumed it was because she'd had a ticking off but had one of her little fists concealed Violetta's necklace? Had a sudden pang of conscience prompted her to slip it out of sight as she played on the kitchen floor whilst Fernanda made more coffee?

Fernanda laid down her knife for a second time. Slipping the necklace into the pocket of her apron, she climbed the stairs to the bedroom. She half expected the other coin to have vanished but it was still exactly where she'd left it. She laid Violetta's necklace next to it. Both coins were identical, minted in the same year, the hole in each perhaps drilled by the same hand.

She turned them over, studying the portraits of the old king on the other side. The same style of curved line was scratched into the reverse of each but they were different ways around, one forming the mirror image of the other. She pushed the coins together so their edges touched. She'd always wondered about the significance of the crude etching, whether it was a hastily executed asymmetrical letter 'U' or a 'J' – a letter that didn't belong in the Italian alphabet but appeared in a few foreign words. It was only when the two coins were united that the drawing made sense. The curved lines weren't initials. Each was one half of a broken heart.

43

The shop doorbell tinkled.

'*Buongiorno,* Gino,' Amy said. Her voice quavered as though she were as old as Fernanda.

Gino looked her up and down. 'What are you doing here? Where's Stella?'

'She's downstairs sorting out stock.'

'You haven't answered my first question.'

'I'm helping out because Stella let me stay with her last night. But you don't need to worry. You won't see me again, I'm leaving on the afternoon bus.'

'Not a moment too soon,' Gino mumbled. He headed for the stairs. 'Stella!'

'Down here!'

He thudded down the stairs, displeasure written all over his face. 'What do you think you're doing? Didn't you hear what happened? You're putting a thief in charge of the till. Do you want Domenico to be robbed?'

Stella put a steadying hand on a shelving unit. 'Amy's no

thief. There's obviously been some misunderstanding. Fernanda must have got muddled up.'

'My mother,' Gino said slowly, 'is in full command of all her faculties. She lost her coin necklace. The very next day, your little friend is wearing it. It's a pretty open and shut case, don't you think? Amy's lucky Mamma didn't go to the police.'

Stella took Domenico's tray of costume jewellery from the shelf and rooted around amongst the gaudy contents. She handed him a slim golden chain.

'The coin, was it strung on something like this?'

He ran it though his fingers. 'The coin was originally on a leather thong but yes, Amy swapped it over for a chain like this one.'

'That was the chain that I put on it. Amy didn't steal that necklace. It was the broken one she brought in here several days ago.'

Gino's brow crinkled. 'That cannot be right. Violetta's necklace only vanished yesterday. It makes no sense.'

'Exactly.' Stella folded her arms. 'Or are you going to accuse me of handling stolen property?'

Gino rubbed his forehead. 'So, you're telling me that Amy and my mother own identical necklaces?'

Stella shrugged. 'I admit it's a strange coincidence.'

'So, where's Mamma's necklace?'

'That I cannot help you with. But perhaps you and Leo can help Fernanda to look for it instead of accusing some innocent girl.'

Stella returned the chain to the tray of costume jewellery and put it back on the shelf.

'Stella, please don't be angry.'

'Really, Gino, I'm not.' It was Violetta and the gang of

German soldiers who deserved her wrath. Not the man she couldn't help but love despite his family.

'Good, because I came here with an invitation from Fernanda. To come to dinner this evening.'

Stella felt her jaw drop. 'You're joking! Really? How did you put her up to that?'

'I didn't. Something's triggered a change in her. Maybe it's all the talk about Pietro's burial or Leo creating the memorial plaque. She's taken down the portrait of Violetta.'

'I never thought I'd see the day. That must have been hard.'

'Yes. I'm proud of Mamma. She wants to make amends, Stella. Will you come tonight?'

She looked into his troubled eyes. 'I will, Gino. Tell her I will. I just need to find someone to stay in with Domenico. I don't want him to spend this evening on his own and have another accident.'

Gino's eyes widened. 'Oh, no, what's happened? Is he okay?'

'Just scorched his hand in the steam from a kettle.'

'A kettle? Don't tell me he's swapped his coffee habit for a cup of tea.'

Stella laughed. 'No, that's less likely than Fernanda taking down her sister's portrait.'

'I'll see you tonight then.' Gino kissed her quickly.

'I'll come upstairs with you and see how Amy's doing. I've finished down here.'

* * *

Amy unboxed another sandwich toaster, hoping Stella wouldn't be downstairs too long. She could manage to exchange the odd word in Italian but her extremely limited vocabulary certainly didn't stretch to 'crimped edges' or 'toasting times'.

Stella and Gino's voices drifted up from the basement. She couldn't understand what they were saying but she could tell from Stella's tone of voice that they weren't having a row, thank goodness. Gino and Leo had treated Amy abominably but she didn't want her presence to cause a rift between Stella and the man she was obviously in love with.

Footsteps clumped up the stairs. Stella's head appeared first, Gino's just behind.

'All okay, Amy? *Buongiorno, Signora Togliatti, come sta?*' Stella smoothly took over, opening the toaster's lid and chatting away until the old lady left.

Amy busied herself with a display of cutlery, conscious of Gino's eyes upon her. She felt, rather than saw, him come nearer.

'Amy, I'm so sorry.'

Her hands stopped sifting the knives and forks, but she didn't turn around.

'I owe you an apology,' he said.

Now she looked at him. His eyes were sincere but still she didn't respond. She wasn't going to make things easy for him.

'It seems,' he continued, 'that the necklace Stella mended looks very like the one my mother lost. But that is no excuse. My family and I accused you of theft. We were terribly wrong.'

His phone rang.

'Take it,' Amy said. She retrieved a rogue teaspoon from amidst the forks.

Gino pulled out his mobile, frowning at the screen. 'Mamma?' His frown deepened as he listened. His mouth opened and closed in a vain attempt to interrupt Fernanda's monologue. At last, he managed to speak. '*Sì, certo! Ciao, Mamma!*'

He stowed his phone. 'I cannot believe this: Mamma has found her sister's necklace.'

'So there really are two of them,' Stella said.

'It seems so. Mamma is so embarrassed. Amy, she wants to apologise to you in person. She is on her way to Sant' Agata's. Would you meet her there? I hope and pray that you will be able to forgive her, forgive all of us.'

'I will meet her but it will have to be during my lunchbreak.'

'Go now,' Stella said. 'That cutlery display can wait.'

Amy hurried towards the church. Despite the upset of the day before, she was glad to have the chance to see Fernanda again. The old lady must be mortified to realise her mistake.

She turned the corner to the church. Outside, Fernanda was waiting. But she wasn't the only one standing there. Fiddling with a button on his dust-covered overalls stood Leo. Her heart leapt.

'Amy, I'm so sorry,' Leo burst out before she had time to say a word. 'I should never have accused you the way I did. Deep down I couldn't believe you'd do something like that. But I told myself I was blinded by the way I feel about you. Can you ever forgive me?'

'No, no, it was all my fault,' Fernanda interrupted. 'Maybe I have been a bad judge of character, defending my sister all my life. But I found nothing but goodness in you, Amy. That was what gave me such a shock. Now I feel so ashamed for doubting you.'

'Come here!' Amy said.

Fernanda stood as stiff as a church pillar but after a moment her body relaxed into Amy's arms. Over Fernanda's shoulder, Amy watched Leo's face soften. His love for his grandmother brought an image of Grandpa Lance to her mind and all that she'd lost. She swallowed hard before she spoke.

'Oh, Fernanda, of course I will forgive you, I'm just so glad you believe me. I was so hurt you'd think I could steal from you. But how could I expect you to deny the evidence? I was wearing the necklace you thought you had lost. Anyone would put two and two together.'

'I can hardly believe there are two such similar necklaces,' Leo said. 'It is the strangest thing.'

'I should have brought your necklace with me, Amy, but I left it in your room for you. I hope you will come back and stay. Tonight, Gino and Stella are coming for dinner and I'd like you two young people to be there. But first perhaps I can treat you both to a coffee at the bar? Unless you need to get back to work, Leo.'

Leo grinned. 'The plaque is finished.'

'That's fantastic!' Amy hugged him.

'*Bravo!*' Fernanda clapped her hands. '*Allora*, let us have our coffee.' She took Leo's arm.

He turned to Amy. 'I'm so relieved. I didn't know if you would ever forgive me.'

'I haven't actually said that I have forgiven you,' Amy said primly. 'There's still one condition.'

'Anything.'

'You treat me to one of those jammy *gobeletti*.'

'I'll buy you one every morning for the rest of your life.'

'The rest of this week will do and we're quits,' Amy said, amused at his flushed cheeks.

'Are you two going to stand there all morning smiling at each other or are we going to have this coffee?' Fernanda said. Her voice was stern but her eyes twinkled.

44

'Stop fussing, Stella!' Domenico tried not to sound too exasperated. 'I've already told you I'm glad you are going out. It's given me a chance to invite Goffredo over this evening.'

'You should have done that before. I can't believe you put him off on my account.'

'You're being an angel, cooking for me and looking after the shop. The least I can do is spare you having to spend your evening listening to two old men talking nonsense in dialect.'

Stella rummaged in her handbag. Was she ever going to go? He'd already had to nod along to a list of dos and don'ts as though she were his mamma. Okay, he'd burnt his hand on the kettle but that didn't mean he was going to set the house on fire or let the sink overflow if he was left to his own devices.

'Now, are you sure I've prepared enough meatballs for two?'

'Stella, just go!'

His niece put her hands up. 'Okay! I get the message. You'll be fine.'

The door shut. He waited in the hallway until he was sure she wouldn't reappear, having forgotten something. Two minutes passed; he was safe. He opened the corner cupboard and retrieved a bottle of Basanotto; that would make an excellent aperitif. There was plenty of the local red wine to hand and a rather nice bottle of white from the Cinque Terre. He set four glasses on the coffee table, chuckling to himself. He'd survived his fall with no broken bones, he had a new assistant starting in just over a week and Stella had even managed to sell that ridiculous Dolce and Gabbana kettle. He deserved to celebrate. No tutting doctors, no bossy daughter, no overattentive niece to stop the fun. His three old mates would be gone by the time Stella got home. She would never know he'd thrown a little party.

* * *

Stella stood on Fernanda's doorstep clutching a bottle of wine. After more than forty years, she had finally been invited in. But her curiosity about the home where her childhood sweetheart had grown up was nothing compared to the intriguing puzzle of Fernanda and Amy's coin necklaces.

It was no longer just Stella, Gino and Fernanda eating together tonight. Both Amy, who had settled back into her old room, and Leo were joining them. If they all put their heads together, they might be able to work out if the existence of the two necklaces was more than one of life's bizarre coincidences. And if they couldn't make head nor tail of it all, the evening still wouldn't be wasted. They'd taken the first step to overcoming the old family feud that threatened to keep her and Gino apart.

Fernanda welcomed her in. She took the wine, her beady eyes scanning the label. 'Vermentino, my favourite. *Grazie mille, molto gentile.* Let us put this in the room where we are eating.'

Stella followed her into the back room where the oval table was set with placemats printed with scenes of Olde Liguria and cut glasses. Above the cupboard on the near wall, a pale rectangle marked the place where Stella imagined Violetta's portrait had hung. It must have pained the old lady to take down the likeness of the sister she'd loved so much and to finally face up to Violetta's part in the war.

The knocking at the front door interrupted Stella's musings. Fernanda went to answer it, Stella following right behind.

'Mamma!' Gino hugged and kissed the old lady, then kissed Stella too. Out of the corner of her eye, Stella could see Fernanda was actually smiling. A moment later, Leo appeared, changed out of his overalls into a clean shirt for the evening. Amy bounded out of the kitchen wearing a striped apron, a corkscrew in her hand. The two youngsters hugged. Stella and Gino exchanged glances.

They all trooped into the small living room, Fernanda and Amy carrying in trays of *antipasti*. There wasn't quite enough seating, so Amy perched on the arm of a chair, glancing sideways at Leo as though she'd rather be sitting on his lap. Fernanda pointedly moved her grandson's glass onto a coaster. Stella suppressed a smile. Fernanda had mellowed these last few days but there were still standards to uphold.

'More *fritelle*, Stella?' Fernanda asked. 'When we've finished these we'll have the rest of the meal in the dining room.'

'The necklaces?' Gino prompted. They were all waiting for Fernanda's big reveal. She'd been playing them like a singer holding back her number one hit to tease her audience.

'*Allora*... You have waited long enough,' Fernanda said, 'but I wanted everyone to have something to eat first. Amy, would you be kind enough to clear away these things?'

Amy leapt up, swiping the plates. Leo took the serving platters. They were back in a trice.

Fernanda laid the two necklaces on the coffee table, side by side, Amy's now shorn of its broken golden chain. The other coin sported its original leather thong. They all craned forward for a closer look. Stella's nose filled with the scent of Fernanda's hairspray and Gino's cologne.

'They really are identical,' Gino said.

'But that's not all. They are a pair. My sister Violetta's necklace and Amy's.'

With a flourish worthy of the Magic Circle, Fernanda flipped over the coins. The reverse of each was etched with a simple curve. She lined them up carefully, sat back and folded her arms.

'It's a heart!' Stella said.

'Only when they're joined together,' Amy added. 'That means my Grandpa Lance and Violetta must have been in love. But how and when?'

Gino rubbed his forehead. He moved the coins apart and pushed them back together again. 'Amy, your grandpa must have been in Liguria during the war, one of the prisoners transported from North Africa to the mainland.'

'But Papà,' Leo interrupted. 'You told me yourself there were no escaped POWs here. The Germans didn't find anyone like that when they swooped on the village.'

'Perhaps they didn't search properly,' Amy said.

Fernanda shook her head. 'No, those men were thorough. If anyone had been hiding here, they would have found them.'

'Except there was one place they wouldn't have looked. In your home, Mamma. Everyone knew Violetta fraternised with the Germans. They wouldn't have searched her house.'

'That's absurd. Where do you think Amy's nonno was? In

our basement, or under the bed? I was an inquisitive little girl, always playing. I was in and out of every nook and cranny in that house, no one could have been hiding there. And my sister was a fascist, through and through.'

'I know it sounds far-fetched but perhaps she met Lance and fell in love with him despite her politics,' Gino said. 'Stranger things have happened. And if she did, there's one place she could have let him hide. Somewhere you never went, Fernanda.'

'Your grandparents' old *rustico*?' Stella said.

'That's what I'm thinking.'

'If my great-aunt was secretly in love with Lance, that must have weakened her commitment to the fascist cause. Surely she wouldn't have betrayed the village by giving a list of names to the Germans?'

'Perhaps it wasn't her,' Amy said.

Fernanda patted her arm. 'That's a sweet thing to say. But it is just wishful thinking. My sister had Mussolini's photo on the wall.'

'What about the necklace?'

'Violetta could have found it. There's no proof Lance gave it to her.'

'Wait!' Amy brought her hands to her face. 'I almost forgot. Grandpa left me two postcards. One a picture of Alassio, where he grew up, the other was this village.'

'And you showed me a message on the back.' Stella felt her heart start to beat a little faster. 'There's no name but Fernanda, you might recognise the handwriting. Have you got it with you, Amy?'

Amy jumped up. 'Yes, yes, I have. It's here in my bag. Here, Fernanda.' Her hand trembled as she handed over the postcard.

Fernanda glanced at the black and white photograph for a mere second, flipped it over and gasped.

'What is it? Is it Violetta's handwriting?' Amy said.

'This is not my sister's beautiful hand, but she wrote it, I know she did.'

'I'm confused,' Stella said. She glanced around at the equally puzzled faces.

'Violetta disguised her writing and crossed through the name of the village, but there's one thing that gives it away, a little touch she couldn't resist.' Fernanda smiled. 'Leo, would you fetch something from the middle drawer over there? A small olive-green leather folder.'

'Of course, Nonna... There you are. What's in here?'

'Just cards and sentimental nonsense.' Fernanda loosened the faded ribbon. She held up a crayon drawing of a space rocket. 'You drew this when you were only three or four, Leo.'

'You've kept it all this time!' Leo shook his head.

'Ah, here is what I am looking for.' Fernanda retrieved what looked like a homemade card decorated with pink and orange flowers. 'We couldn't afford to spend money on birthday cards when I was a child. We always made them ourselves. This was the last one Violetta gave me, a few weeks before she was killed. Look at the way she finished off the letter "I" in her name with a heart on top, a little flourish just for me. And there on your grandpa Lance's card she'd topped the I in *baci* just the same. That postcard is from my sister, I am sure of it.'

An escaped Allied prisoner and the most ardent fascist in the village had fallen in love. It was the strangest thing Stella had ever heard.

45

Stella had expected Domenico's house to be in darkness but lights blazed from both downstairs rooms. Her uncle must be up and about, revitalised by the visit from his pal Goffredo. She stepped into the hallway. The smell that greeted her reminded her of the mornings after Ricky had invited all his mates round. Great rumbling snores rose from the living room. She tiptoed in. Domenico lay in his chair, head back, mouth open, sleeping soundlessly. Lying flat out on the couch, one cushion under his head, lay another fully clothed figure. But this wasn't Goffredo, this was the father of the man who ran the salumeria. What on earth was he doing here?

Now, Stella's eyes swept the room. An empty bottle of Basanotto, two packs of cards strewn across the table and four empty glasses. A snort came from the far corner. Stella whipped around. So that's where Goffredo was, zonked out, Violetta's hat crammed on his head. *Mamma mia!* What had they been doing? It looked as if only the fourth card player had managed to make it home. Stella was not going to deal with this mess now. Quietly she crept upstairs to bed.

* * *

Domenico's hand shook as he lifted the coffee cup to his lips.

'Don't look at me like that, Stella.'

'Just wondering if you'd like a glass of water and a painkiller.' She pursed her lips.

Domenico nodded, eyes closed. He hadn't moved from his chair. 'It feels like Leo's taken his chisel to my skull.'

'At least you haven't got to face your wife like Goffredo has. The way that woman was hammering on the door was enough to waken the dead.'

'I feel like the dead.' Domenico groaned. 'The water – please!'

'Just coming up.' He looked so pitiful she couldn't help chuckling to herself as she fetched them both a glass and carried them back in.

'*Grazie mille*! Sorry, Stella, and sorry about the hat. It's definitely beyond repair.'

'What were you doing with it? Is that stain red wine?'

'We had a bit of an accident with Goffredo's glass. And then we were doing forfeits. Whoever lost their hand of cards had to wear it and recite a limerick.'

'A rude one, I bet.' Stella tried to look stern.

'There was a young lady from Puglia who came over all peculiar...' he croaked.

Stella raised a hand. 'I don't think I'd better hear any more.'

Domenico took a huge swig of water. 'Ah, how I needed that.'

Stella turned Violetta's hat in her hands. 'The state of you! And this! You're right, this is beyond saving, even the lining is coming adrift.' She stroked the silky material. 'This is strange. It feels like there's something tucked in here.'

'It must be the way hats are made,' Domenico said.

'I don't think so, it doesn't feel right.' Stella used her little fingernail to ease the loose stitching. 'I can just see the edge of some paper, that's odd.'

'It probably replaced something Violetta couldn't get hold of. People had to use all sorts during the war.'

'I'm not so sure. Let me get some scissors.' She stood up and headed for the bathroom. Retrieving a pair of nail scissors from the cabinet above the sink, she sat back down and put on her reading glasses. She snipped at the stitching and gave the thread a sharp tug. The lining came away, a piece of folded graph paper with it.

Stella unfolded the paper. It was crisscrossed with dotted lines and spotted with a series of dashes and crosses. 'What on earth? This looks like some sort of little map.'

Domenico rubbed his eyes. 'Let me see... Wait a moment, that dotted line there – it follows the shape of the path that leads through the hills, the one poor Pietro took when he tried to flee the village that day.'

'Would that be Sant' Agata's?' Stella pointed.

'Not if that other line in the top left shows the mountain ridge. If this map is drawn to scale that cross wouldn't indicate the centre of the village, it would mark the location of Fernanda and Violetta's parents' old *rustico*.' Domenico scratched his head. 'But why would Violetta want to hide that in her hat? She must have known those paths like the back of her hand.'

'An English POW on the run wouldn't have.'

'I know my brain isn't as quick as it was, Stella. And with this hangover...' Domenico winced.

'That's because you weren't there last night when Fernanda showed us the two coin necklaces.'

'Two necklaces? Now you really have lost me.'

'Why don't I make us some more coffee and I'll tell you everything,' Stella said. She hurried off to the kitchen, as keen to get back and share her discovery as Domenico was to hear it.

Her uncle stared in astonishment as Stella recounted her tale.

'Don't you see?' Stella said. 'Two pendants forming a heart, the message on the postcard and now this map showing the paths leading from the old *rustico* – it all proves Violetta and Amy's grandfather Lance were in love and she was helping him. And maybe other prisoners on the run.'

'But Violetta was a fascist – that German boyfriend, those parties in Sanremo. Everyone knows that woman betrayed the village.' A vein was jumping in Domenico's forehead.

'Maybe all that was a front. Don't you see? What if Violetta wasn't passing information to the Germans, what if she was spying on them?' Stella's voice came out all in a rush. 'What if Violetta was working for the partisans?'

The cup dropped from Domenico's hand; dark coffee spread across the table.

'My dear, dear friend Fernanda! How I have wronged her.' Tears sprang to the old man's eyes.

'It's okay, Domenico.' Stella dabbed at the coffee with a tissue. 'You can't blame yourself. The whole village had it the wrong way round, Violetta kept up the pretence so well. And you and Papà weren't the only ones to disapprove of the way Fernanda refused to disown her sister.'

'No, no, it is all my fault.' Domenico wrenched at his hair, his eyes wild. 'I shouldn't have tried to conceal the truth. I shouldn't have kept quiet all these years.'

'What do you mean?' Stella asked, trying to play down her concern at her uncle's near hysteria.

Domenico's shoulders sank. He turned his grey face to hers. 'I had an argument with your papà on the morning of the day he died. I told him I'd discovered something about your nonno. Something you should know.'

Stella swallowed. She had a strong suspicion she wasn't going to like what she was about to hear.

'Arturo was so angry that day,' Domenico began.

'Well, that was my fault,' Stella interrupted. If she closed her eyes she could still see Papà grabbing at the bedhead, his face contorted with pain.

'He wasn't pleased with you defying him, of course he wasn't. But it was me he was angry with, and our father and himself. The shop was quiet that morning. I was serving; Arturo decided to go down and check on some stock. The wife of the original owner of the bar came in. I remember my heart sinking, knowing I would be subjected to all the village gossip whether I wanted to hear or not. She had such a loud voice too; she'd set my eardrums ringing.'

'You could hear her over the church bells,' Stella remembered.

'But now I'd happily listen to her twenty-four hours a day if it would turn back the clock. I nodded and smiled as she was talking, not taking much notice, like I always did. And then she dropped her bombshell. She said she'd seen you and Gino on a red moped hightailing it out of the village. Arturo could not help but overhear, he came thudding up the stairs. The look on his face sent her scurrying out of the door so fast she left half her purchases behind.

'Your papà started to rant and rave about Gino and Fernanda, calling them every name under the sun. I told him you were a teenager in love and to keep you and Gino apart would only drive you away. He wouldn't listen, just said he would never have a boy from Violetta's family under his roof. So I told him something... something I will always regret.' Domenico's voice cracked.

Stella sat quietly, hands in her lap, waiting for him to gather himself.

'I told your papà that our family was no better than Gino's. He banged his fist on the shop counter, demanding to know what I meant. Immediately I regretted opening my mouth. I tried to pretend it was a throwaway remark but Arturo wasn't having it. His face was scarlet, the look in his eyes frightened me half to death. I bolted the shop door and tried to calm him down. But there was no going back. I had to tell him the truth.'

Domenico took a swig of water. 'Would you fetch the small wooden box on top of the chest in your room? There's a brass key taped behind the back of the bookshelf on the landing.'

Stella climbed the stairs. Her feet felt heavy, her sense of foreboding increasing with every tread. She found both the box and the key easily enough. She forced herself to resist the impulse to peek inside. This was her uncle's tale to tell. She had to let it unfold.

She paused in the doorway of the living room. Domenico's eyes were closed. For a moment she thought he'd nodded off but then she noticed his clasped hands and the way his mouth moved silently. He was praying. How bad could this be?

The contents of the box rattled as she set it down. His head jerked up.

'Would you open it, Stella, please?'

She fumbled with the lock, the hinge opened with a squeak. Old coins, buttons and even a radiator bleeding key. But amongst the bits and bobs lay a folded sheet of lined paper. She looked at Domenico; he gave her the smallest of nods.

Stella smoothed out the paper. It was a list of names written in a spidery hand. She read the first of them: 'Signor e Signora Pedemonte.'

'They were the couple who concealed the little Jewish boy.'

Stella already knew what she was looking at but she didn't want to believe it. She read the next name: 'Eduardo Pastorino.'

'A quiet fellow, walked with a stick. He'd been a communist agitator in the Fiat factory in Turin.'

'These people were killed in the *rastrellamento*...' Stella looked to Domenico for confirmation.

'Those and others. And this was our papà's handwriting.'

'Are you telling me that my nonno was responsible for what happened here?'

Domenico rubbed his forehead. 'I found this a few months before Arturo died, tucked inside an old book, and I vowed to myself I would not tell a soul. Oh, how I wished I had kept that promise. When I showed it to Arturo he insisted it was a forgery. But he knew, Stella, he knew. I believe I broke his heart that day.'

'But he was so angry when Fernanda found me with Gino and marched me home.'

'He still blamed Fernanda's family for everything. I think he was trying to make excuses for our papà by convincing himself that Violetta used her feminine wiles to suck him into her scheme. Of course, he was angry with you for sneaking off with Gino but that was just a small part of why he worked himself into a frenzy. I think perhaps he was scared that Fernanda knew your nonno had played a part and that one day she might let that slip.'

Stella couldn't speak. One sheet of paper and her whole world had changed. The nonno she'd never known wasn't a tragic victim of the war but a secret fascist who had died in the atrocity he'd unleashed upon the village.

'But you told me they shot Nonno. You told me Papà watched his father die. You told me about the blood on his *zoccoli*.'

Her uncle sighed. He ran his hand through his sparse, white hair. 'Whenever I thought about that day, there was one thing that always struck me as odd. It was how calm your nonno was. He told me and Arturo to run and hide, he obviously did not want us to see what he knew would unfold that day, but for himself and Mamma he showed no fear. I was proud of him for being so brave. But now I realise it was because he believed he was safe. But something went wrong, a trigger-happy soldier perhaps or a case of mistaken identity.'

'Why didn't he cry out and save himself?'

'I've wondered about that for many years. He could have raised his arm in a fascist salute, shouted political slogans, given the name of his contact – that might have saved him. But saved for him for what fate? The villagers would have meted their own form of justice on him and perhaps our family. Everyone realised that when the war was over there would be a day of reckoning.'

Domenico coughed. He shifted awkwardly in his chair. 'I believe our father turned to face the wall in order to protect us. He sacrificed himself to save our mamma from shame and me and Arturo from being scorned and shunned. It was the only decent thing he ever did.'

'But what about Fernanda and Gino? For all these years you've let their family take the blame.' If the truth had come out, the schism between their families might have healed; the decades-old feud set aside in time. Perhaps she and Gino... But what was the use in thinking of those wasted years? Maybe with the tables turned, Fernanda would have been determined to keep her son away from the granddaughter of a traitor.

'Until you told me about Violetta and Lance, I believed Violetta and my father conspired together. I asked myself what good would come from revealing my papà's part, of opening up old wounds again? Your poor widowed mamma needed the support of neighbours rallying around. You and your brother and sister had lost your father. You needed love and friendship, not people turning their backs on you. My revelations had helped cause my brother's heart attack. The least I could do was protect his family. But now, everything we knew about Violetta has been turned inside out. I must go to see Fernanda, to tell the truth to her face.'

46

Fernanda rinsed the tureen under the running tap and set it on the draining rack. Last night she'd gone to bed without washing up. The revelations about Violetta had left her so mentally exhausted she had barely managed to brush her teeth.

The radio was playing, sun streamed through the window highlighting flashes of purple on the bubbles in the sink. Another beautiful morning; a new day in every way. Carefully, she dried the pink and white tureen. It was one of her favourite pieces, oval with a pretty toile de jouy pattern. To think that she had hesitated to use it for her guests because it had belonged to Violetta. Now she planned to search through every drawer and cupboard, pulling out the few things she owned that her sister had once touched and display it all with pride. She wanted to run down the street telling everyone she met they'd got Violetta all wrong – that she'd helped an English soldier on the run, that she was no fascist collaborator. Fernanda wanted to hang a banner from the façade of Sant' Agata's, hire a light aircraft trailing plumes of red, white and green smoke, writing Violetta's name across the sky!

She laughed out loud. How fanciful she was being! All she really wanted was a quiet acknowledgement of her sister's bravery. And a shamefaced apology from those who'd said things behind her back wouldn't go amiss.

There was one dish left to wash up; this one needed the metal scourer despite its overnight soak. She made a face and turned the radio up. It took her a moment or two to realise that the intermittent knocking sound she could hear wasn't part of the beat. She peeled off her rubber gloves and went to open the front door.

Domenico stood on the doorstep holding a potted cyclamen in a vivid shade of pink. In the other hand he clutched a squashed and battered cocktail hat.

'*Buongiorno*,' Fernanda said.

'*Buongiorno*.' Domenico stood awkwardly.

Fernanda stepped backwards into her hallway. 'I suppose you had better come in.'

* * *

Amy climbed into the back of Gino's car and grappled with the seatbelt.

'We will drive most of the way and then we will have to walk,' Gino said. He glanced in the mirror and pulled out of the village car park.

'Did Leo show you the *rustico* before?' Stella asked.

'I walked over there the other day, going the long way round, down past the old water mill. I didn't see a reason to go inside then but now I'm itching to. I know it's not very likely that I'll find any clue that Lance and Violetta were meeting there but you never know.'

'It gives us a good excuse to go back again, doesn't it, Stella?' Gino said, glancing over his shoulder. A car horn tooted. 'Oh, better keep my eye on the road.'

'Please do,' Stella said. She looked happy and relaxed today. Even her short hairstyle seemed to have grown out slightly, giving her a softer look. But Amy knew it wasn't the tan or the hair or even the loose linen dress Stella was wearing that gave her that glow. It was the man driving them and knowing the weight of history was no longer standing in their way.

The car pulled up on a scrubby bit of land. Amy clambered out. She walked beside Stella as Gino led the way.

He turned his head. 'Have you told Amy about our plans?'

'Our very tentative plans? No, I haven't.' A cloud crossed Stella's face.

'I'm planning to sell up in Alassio and move back here,' Gino said. 'I've spoken to my daughter, Isabella, and she's relaxed about it so that's one hurdle out of the way. Stella and I want to buy a place in the village and revitalise my grandparents' land. We will produce our own olive oil, perhaps diversify into some wild herbs and maybe even get a few goats.'

Amy glanced at Stella, wondering why she hadn't mentioned any of this.

'I didn't want to tempt fate by talking about it,' Stella said. 'There's still a lot to sort out and I'm not sure how it will work – in practical terms, I mean. To tell you the truth, Amy, I was hoping to keep some hours at Domenico's shop but he'd already promised a job to Signora Togliatti's grandson.'

'We'll work something out.' Gino took Stella's hand. Amy trotted along behind the two of them until the path narrowed and they all had to walk single file. It was particularly beautiful to approach the *rustico* this way, through the heathery yarrow and the hawthorn trees. She inhaled a great lungful of fresh air. Ahead of them the olive grove stretched away, the *rustico* just visible beyond the trees. This place was glorious, she didn't want to think about leaving.

Gino's stride lengthened; the two women hurried along behind him, neither speaking, both lost in their own thoughts. They stopped on the edge of the olive grove. Gino ran his hand along a twisted branch. His face softened.

'All the years I've lived in Alassio whilst some other family farmed here, I dreamt of coming back to Leto. But there was always something missing from the picture I created in my mind that stopped me. I didn't know what it was until I saw you again.' He reached out and touched Stella's cheek.

Amy looked away. She was happy for them, of course she was, but it made her own inevitable departure feel worse.

'I'm going to walk around here and inspect the trees,' Gino said. 'Why don't you two go inside?'

'Come on, Amy,' Stella said. They walked up the gentle incline to the back of the property. Amy glanced behind her. Gino stood, one hand shielding his eyes, gazing out across his family's land.

Stella unlocked the door, pushing her sunglasses up on top of her head. Amy blinked, the light was dim after the brightness outside. Where the light did get in, dust motes danced in the air.

Stella waved an arm. 'It's quite a mess: old farming equipment, wooden poles and olive nets.'

'And a bed!'

'Fernanda moved some old furniture in here that she

couldn't bear to get rid of,' Stella said, her cheeks strangely flushed.

'So, my grandpa couldn't have slept on that.'

'No, the chest and the bed and the other bits wouldn't have been here then. Lance would have had to make do with some sacking on the floor. But it would have been dry and better than sleeping in the open air.'

'Do you really think he was here?' Amy said.

Stella ran her finger through a trail of dust on the windowsill. 'We can never know for sure but it would make sense. And when he realised something had happened to Violetta and she wasn't coming back, he probably made his way up through the woods and into the hills. I wonder how long he stayed here and how often they met. Gino and I used to come here to escape our families, it was our special place. We carved our initials on a pillar, I'll show you.' Stella paused, the nostalgic look in her eyes vanished; a huge smile split her face. 'I've just had a thought. Some other kids left their marks here too but maybe they weren't the only ones.'

'Do you think...?' Amy's heart beat a little faster.

'Oh, I hope so,' Stella said. 'It's that pillar over there.'

Amy crouched down beside her.

'There,' Stella pointed. '*G +S sempre* – that means "always".'

'How romantic,' Amy said but she wasn't looking at the graffiti Gino had left. Her finger was tracing a tiny heart scratched into the woodgrain, so faint she'd almost missed it. 'Stella, look!'

'I wish I'd brought my reading glasses,' Stella tutted, sitting down cross-legged on the floor.

'Here.' Amy moved Stella's hand.

Stella's fingers traced the faint indentations. '*L + V*. I think we've found the last piece of the puzzle.'

Amy sat down beside her, not caring how filthy her shorts would get. 'You really think it was them?'

'Why? Don't you?'

'Yes, yes, I do.' She could already picture them here: him tired, hungry, unshaven, too thin; her with a pretty smile and a parcel of smuggled food, willing to risk everything.

'I wish he was here.' Amy sighed. 'If only I could speak to him one more time.'

'What would you say?' Stella said softly, absentmindedly drawing a letter G in the dirt.

'I'd ask him if he still thought of Violetta every day, or whether she was just a fond memory. He always seemed so happy with Grandma but now I feel bad for her.'

'Violetta was a beautiful young woman killed before she and Lance could meet again,' Stella said. 'And she almost certainly saved his life. But my guess is that after the war he blocked out those old memories and tidied them away with the postcards he left you and that broken heart necklace. A stiff upper lip you might call it, but that was the way so many people dealt with losing their loved ones in the war. But loving someone once doesn't mean you can't love again. I'm sure that nothing that happened between your grandpa and Violetta diminished the love your grandparents had for each other.'

'You're so wise, Stella.'

'Not me.' Stella laughed. 'It's taken me more than half a lifetime to realise my future is back in this village.'

Amy got up, swiping the dirt from her shorts. She didn't want to think about the future. She'd rather think about Grandpa and Violetta and what happened in the past.

Stella clambered to her feet too, making a huffing sound. 'Let's go and find Gino. Then we'll drive back.'

'Sure.' Amy shot one last glance at the wartime lovers'

initials – proof of Grandpa's Italian adventure, eighty years before. She couldn't wait to tell her family what she'd found. That up in the Ligurian hills, a little of Grandpa Lance lived on.

47

Domenico linked his fingers together. He shifted in Fernanda's upright kitchen chair.

'So, now you know everything,' he said.

'I see,' Fernanda replied. Right now, those were all the words she could manage. Last night's revelations about Violetta had put her on such a high she hadn't given a moment's thought to the obvious question: if Violetta hadn't passed information to the Germans, who had?

'I can't apologise enough for how I've treated you all these years and if Arturo were alive, I know he would say the same. And now I suppose you will have to tell everyone about this list.' Domenico's fingers drummed on the table centimetres from where the piece of paper lay.

'People would say it was the right thing to do.'

He cleared his throat. 'It takes courage to see someone you love for what they really are and I have been a coward. But now I am ready to face the consequences. It is Stella and my daughter I feel sorry for, yet that cannot be helped. They will be innocent victims of people's gossip the way your son Gino was.'

'You are right, it is not their fault.' Fernanda lifted her coffee cup and inspected the contents. 'This has gone cold. I don't suppose you've touched yours either. I will make some more.'

'There's no need. You don't have to spend another second of your time with me.' He scraped back his chair.

Fernanda stood up. She pressed her hands on his shoulders, gently pushing him back down. How strange it felt to touch him after eighty years when once it had been so natural, linking arms as they raced around Sant' Agata's, huddling close together in some nook or cranny exchanging secrets.

'You will stay for some hot coffee,' she said firmly.

'If you insist.' His voice was bleak.

She filled the Bialetti, her eyes on him. He was an old man now, that carefree child long gone. They had all lost their innocence the day the soldiers came.

'Let me see that list again.' She made a show of studying it as she walked towards the stove. She lit the gas and dropped it in the ring of flame. The paper caught immediately, its edges blackening.

Domenico gasped.

'It's over,' Fernanda said. Calmly she placed the coffee pot onto a different ring.

'But why destroy the evidence? After the way we've treated you...' Domenico dropped his eyes.

Fernanda made him wait until the coffee was poured before she spoke, groping for the words that would explain her gut feeling in a way that made sense.

'Amy has Lance's necklace and Violetta's postcard. With those, my sister's reputation will be restored. That is all that matters to me. I am eighty-seven years old. Whether I live another five or ten years or won't make it past Christmas, only the good Lord knows. But I will not let bitterness or division be my legacy.

'You and I lived through a time when this country was tearing itself in two. So much bloodshed, tears, hatred and suffering. But there was also so much good, like the selfless neighbour who took me in after Violetta died. As little children we were such good friends, you, Arturo and me. Your brother is no longer here, God rest his soul. But you and I have the gift of life. Let us use that gift for good.

'Tomorrow Pietro will be laid to rest. Father Filippo will draw the curtain back on the memorial plaque commemorating the victims of the massacre, a plaque my grandson has carved. We will never forget and nor should we, but it is time for the village to come together. People may speculate about what happened all they like but they will not have any family on which to pin the blame. Perhaps they will conclude that it was pure bad luck the Germans came this way.'

Tears swam in Domenico's rheumy old eyes. 'Oh, Fernanda, why did we let our feud drag on?'

'There's no good in looking back. Soon our families' rift will be well and truly healed, if the younger generation have their way.'

'Stella and Gino? Will you give them your blessing?' Domenico said.

'Of course. And I have a good feeling about my Leo and Amy. Wouldn't it be wonderful if Violetta and Lance brought them together?'

'That would be some legacy and well deserved. You've been so generous and kind. You're a wonderful woman, Fernanda.'

Finally, he took a sip of his neglected coffee, lifting the cup with a trembling hand.

'Hush, you will make me vain! But if you feel that way, would you do me one favour? If I hold a dining chair steady, would you be able to stand on it and rehang Violetta's picture?'

'Risking life and limb? Only for you, my dear old friend.'

48

Mario from the pizzeria and his father, officious in their hi-visibility vests, stood ready to halt the traffic.

'I don't fancy that job much,' Amy said.

Stella laughed. 'There's going to be angry drivers backed up halfway to Sanremo by the time this procession has got up the road.'

It seemed that most of the village had assembled in the car park ready to accompany Pietro Parodi's smooth wooden casket to the church. Father Filippo, all robed in white, stood chatting with the mayor and other local dignitaries. The shining instruments of the village brass band, the costumes of the choir and the banners of the local fraternities all added to the colourful spectacle. The return of Pietro's bones was a matter for celebration as well as sombre reflection. All eyes were on Father Filippo, counting the minutes until he gave the signal for the procession to begin.

Amy seemed to be studying the banner of the local communist party portraying a bright yellow hammer and sickle.

'Some people might not approve of politics on a day like today,' Stella said. 'But Pietro's beliefs contributed to his death and his sister wanted to acknowledge that.'

'I think someone wants you,' Gino said.

Stella felt a tap on her shoulder. She swung around to see a strangely familiar woman of about her own age. Stella blinked. The woman's wavy chin-length bob and formal bottle-green dress disappeared, replaced by the long messy plait and a pair of blue jeans belonging to the tuba-playing teenager she'd once known.

Gino's ex-wife smiled. 'Stella! I so hoped I would see you today.'

'Gaia, how long it's been!'

'Don't look so concerned. I know you are seeing Gino and if you can make my grumpy ex-husband happy, you have my admiration. Besides, I have met someone myself recently.'

'Who is he?' Gino butted in. 'And what do you mean by grumpy?'

Gaia laughed. 'Never you mind. And you... you must be Amy. Leo has talked about you. Do you see that young woman in the striped dress with the clarinet over there? That's his sister Isabella. I used to play the tuba but Isabella is the musician in the family now. She usually plays with an orchestra in Alassio but staying with her nonna so often, she sometimes plays with the village band.'

'You heard I was staying with Fernanda?'

'Yes. That must be interesting.' Gaia raised her eyebrows.

'I hope you're not insulting my mother,' Gino said but he had a smile in his voice.

Someone crashed two cymbals together; Stella almost jumped out of her skin. She must have been so distracted by the appearance of Gaia she'd missed Father Filippo giving the signal for the procession to begin.

The religious leaders began to move out of the car park followed by the children of the choir all dressed in white smocks, their faces scrubbed and hair brushed until it shone. One of the four pallbearers laid a spray of red and white flowers on Pietro's casket before they carefully took it upon their shoulders. The liturgical banners swayed. Stella, Gino and Amy joined the straggling band of ordinary folk in their Sunday best bringing up the rear. Four young women wheeling pushchairs were the very last in line. The pizzeria owner stood in the middle of the road, arms akimbo, defying any vehicle to pass. A car hooted. Signora Togliatti, doused in lily-of-the-valley cologne, a boxy handbag dangling from her skinny elbow, adjusted her hat. They set off towards Sant' Agata's.

Stella walked by Gino's side. The procession progressed slowly, hampered by the heat and by smart shoes that were better suited to a short walk from home to church. At last, they turned into the high street, the villagers streaming across the road to assemble by the war memorial and join those who by reason of age or infirmity were only able to follow the procession for its final leg. The traffic that crawled along behind them was waved ahead, receiving a chorus of toots and ironic cheers. Signora Togliatti sank onto a bench to rub her swollen ankles.

Stella searched the crowd for Domenico. He'd been wanting to walk the whole route, stopped only by her threat to stop baking his favourite treats. Eventually she spotted him, smart in a brass-buttoned blazer, standing right by the old memorial, examining a fresh wreath propped against its base. With him were her cousin Luisa, a man in his early sixties and three young children, one clutching a knitted rabbit.

'My husband, Andrea,' Luisa said.

'How lovely to meet you.'

'It is nice to support the village at a time like this, even though the grandchildren may not appreciate it.' He prised a small boy from his trouser leg.

'We are not the only ones to come back...' Luisa hesitated.

Stella glanced at Domenico. His grin was as wide as a slice of watermelon. 'I took the liberty of inviting some relatives.'

'Who is it? Who's here?'

'Over there, by the fountain...'

But Stella wasn't listening any more. She was pushing her way through the crowd with a '*permesso*' here and a '*scusi*' there to where her brother and sister were standing.

'Stella, oh, Stella!' Giovanni pulled her into a bear hug.

'We didn't think we'd ever see you again. We thought you didn't want to know us any more,' Marta sobbed.

All the words, all the apologies and explanations Stella had rehearsed over the years had deserted her. She just clung to them, drinking in their dear familiar faces.

* * *

Stella and Gino took their seats at the back of the church. She could hardly believe she'd followed the rest of the procession arm in arm with Giovanni and Marta. Now her brother and sister sat within touching distance, just in front of Fernanda who had taken a seat nearest to the aisle. Amy sat a little way in front, Leo by her side. He had changed into a long-sleeved shirt and dark trousers but there were traces of stone dust in his hair.

Pietro's elderly sister sat in the front row, sobbing softly. Father Filippo gave the address. The service went on a long time, the way Stella remembered from her childhood when she'd itched to get away. Now, she didn't mind at all. The bible verses had a soothing familiarity, the children in the choir sang prettily and the sermon on love and forgiveness felt as if it had been written just for her.

'Now we have come to the second part of our service,' Father Filippo said. He nodded towards the mayor, who got up from his seat in the second row and walked to the front. He adjusted his tricolour sash and began to speak.

'In a few weeks' time we will be commemorating the eightieth anniversary of a calamity that struck this village, seventeen of our citizens struck down in a cruel and brutal massacre. For years we counted only sixteen victims. It was hoped that Pietro Parodi, who disappeared that day, had somehow managed to escape. But now we know that another family lost a son, grandson, nephew and brother, that Pietro was the seventeenth victim, shot by a coward as he made his way up through the hills.

'With the return of the earthly bones of our beloved Pietro, all of the victims are back where they belong, sleeping their eternal sleep amongst us, their family and friends. Many of you remember the previous monument to those poor, innocent souls. Alas, a road accident led to its destruction when a lorry had to swerve. After too many years we can now unveil a new tribute to those men and women and one thirteen-year-old boy, victims of the senseless violence of war. I am honoured that I was invited to draw back the curtain to reveal our new plaque in this safe and holy space, carved by Leo Perillo, one of our own.'

He paused. It seemed as though the congregation held their breath.

'But I am afraid I must decline our priest's kind invitation.'

Heads turned; mutterings rose from the rows of seats.

'What is he saying?' Marta hissed.

The mayor rose a hand for silence, a smile upon his lips. 'Instead, I would like to bestow the honour of the unveiling on someone who lived through the events this plaque commemorates... a devout lady, a pillar of this church, our very own Fernanda Oliveri-Perillo.'

Fernanda gripped the back of the pew in front. Slowly, she rose from her seat. Gino stood up to help his mother down the aisle.

'No,' Fernanda said. She indicated that he should sit back down.

Shaking his head, he did just that. He looked at Stella. 'So stubborn,' he muttered.

Fernanda advanced slowly across the stone flags, her stick tapping out her progress. Her posture was a little bent, but her white quiff jutted out proudly above her forehead like a figurehead on a stately galleon. She stopped at the end of the row where Uncle Domenico sat with his card-playing chums. She leant down, saying something Stella couldn't catch.

Domenico stood up. He took Fernanda's free arm. Together they walked towards the mayor and Father Filippo.

The mayor indicated the cord that Fernanda should use to draw the velvet curtain back. She handed her stick to Domenico, batting away the mayor's helping hand. Fernanda pulled the cord. Necks craned towards the wall.

'*Brava!*' someone called, prompting a chorus of tut-tutting; they were in church, after all.

'*Grazie*, Fernanda,' Father Filippo said. 'I understand our sculptor, Leo, made a final adjustment to the plaque, one which was not in the sketch submitted for approval but one I feel you will all applaud. Look carefully, Fernanda. Touch it, if you like, I know your hands are clean.'

'What is it? What's changed?' someone in the row in front whispered.

Stella watched the old lady reach out, her shaking fingers tracing the stone. Fernanda turned to face the congregation, her face lit up as though she'd been painted by the same hand as the portrait of Sant' Agata in the side chapel.

'Violets,' Fernanda said, her voice clear and strong. 'Violets to remember my sister, Violetta, and all those others whose quiet acts of bravery and self-sacrifice we will never know.'

Domenico took her arm once more. Slowly, they made their way back down the aisle, each leaning on the other. It was hard to tell who was holding up who.

* * *

The piazza was buzzing. The few who hadn't yet heard about Violetta's bravery were clustered around Fernanda. Father Filippo's face shone with pride and relief. Leo was equally in demand, accepting congratulations from every quarter. Domenico was chatting to Signora Togliatti and the grandson who would become his new assistant in a few days' time.

'It's so good to see Papà up and about. I can't thank you enough for all you've done, Stella,' Luisa said.

'It's nothing. I'm just glad he'll be back behind his beloved shop counter on Tuesday.'

'Thanks to you being willing to carry on part time. He's not strong enough to open five days a week with just that young lad who's still got everything to learn.'

'It's nothing,' Stella said. She was glad to be able to continue in the shop for a few hours a week but it wasn't enough to ease the worry of what came next. Gino would have to invest all his savings into revitalising his grandparents' old olive grove, she couldn't – wouldn't – be the weak link that scuppered his plans. But this evening she wasn't going to waste a precious moment worrying. Pietro's return, the unveiling of the plaque and the rehabilitation of Violetta's reputation were all deserving of a joyous celebration. And as if that wasn't enough reason to drink and eat and dance and sing, she had her brother and sister back. Tomorrow she was turning sixty; she couldn't have wished for a better gift.

Stella scanned the crowd; Marta and Giovanni were standing with Gino. She excused herself and weaved her way towards them. The band was striking up.

'Oh, good, you got away. I trust you wanted wine,' Gino said, handing her a glass.

'And I managed to fight my way to the focaccia.' Her brother laughed. He offered round a paper plate piled with the salty tomato-topped bread.

Stella devoured a piece in just a few bites. She took a sip of her wine and slipped her arm through her sister's.

* * *

Leo was surrounded by a bevy of admirers. Amy couldn't follow much of what was being said but she understood by the tone and hand gestures that even those who had been confident that he'd create a fitting memorial hadn't expected something quite as intricately executed. She'd tried to slip away and leave him to bask in their acclaim but he'd clasped her hand and every so often glanced her way with a look that told her that he wanted her by his side. And not just for this evening.

Amy's phone vibrated in her bag; she ignored it. She didn't want any messages from the outside world intruding on her evening. She couldn't think about England, about going back home, applying for jobs, not seeing Leo again.

The band were playing '*Bocca di rosa*'. She'd heard them rehearsing it earlier in the day.

She drained her wine glass.

Leo smiled at her. 'Would you like to dance?'

'Yes,' Amy said. 'I want to dance all night.'

49

Fernanda settled into her armchair, cradling a glass of amaro. What a day it had been! The unveiling of the plaque had left her feeling quite drained. Gino and Leo had urged her to stay and enjoy the festa but she wanted nothing more than to be left alone with her thoughts.

Violetta's old hat sat on the mantelpiece. It was the last piece of millinery her sister had ever crafted. Fernanda could still remember it sitting on Violetta's workbench. If she closed her eyes, she could travel back there. Back to 1944.

* * *

The hat was so pretty, the prettiest one seven-year-old Fernanda had ever seen. The fabric was a pale leaf green, the silk violets two shades of purple. Each petal was attached with such delicate stitching, Fernanda would have believed the spray of flowers had been sewn by fairies, if she hadn't seen Violetta wield her needle. Fernanda knew she wasn't supposed to touch it. The only hat she was allowed to play with was an old misshapen one, but still her hand reached for her sister's latest creation, her tummy tingling with longing.

Fernanda stole another glance at Violetta; her sister's head was bent over her paperwork. Fernanda's arm stretched as far as it could. Her fingers made contact with the soft felt. The three-legged stool slipped from under her, crashing to the floor. She fell heavily, too shocked even to cry.

Violetta was by her side in an instant. 'Ferdi, *carina*! What happened? How did you fall?'

'I don't know.' Her face heated as though the lie was a flame burning her skin from within.

'Does it hurt?' Violetta bent to examine the big graze on Fernanda's knee.

Fernanda shook her head. It was good to be strong, like one of Mussolini's brave soldiers.

'There.' Violetta planted a kiss by the broken skin, leaving a trace of plum-coloured lipstick. Then she noticed the hat, fallen on the floor. Her eyes flashed. 'Did you touch this? After all I said?'

'I know I shouldn't have.' Fernanda's lip began to tremble.

'Don't ever touch that again.' Her sister's voice was harsh like the men shouting communist slogans outside the butcher's shop.

Fernanda shrank back. She began to sob.

Violetta turned the hat upside down, prodding and peering at the lining. She exhaled loudly. Carefully, she set the hat back down. 'It's okay, Ferdi, don't cry.' Her voice was softer now. 'I'm not going to tell you off again. You've hurt your poor knee, that's enough punishment.'

'It's so nice. Who did you make it for?'

'I've made this one for me.'

'Is that why you put violets on it?'

Violetta didn't reply; she looked as though her mind had wandered somewhere else. She was probably thinking about the hat or the accounts books she'd been poring over before Fernanda had caused such a commotion. Her sister's eyes were tired; she worked so hard to look after them both.

Fernanda searched for a way to cheer her up. 'Shall we sing a song?'

'That's a good idea.' Violetta smiled but her eyes were still sad.

Fernanda launched into '*Giovinezza*', the fascist anthem she knew so well, raising her arm and belting out the first words as if performing for Il Duce himself.

'Not that one,' Violetta interrupted. 'Let's sing "*Chi bella nova*".'

The old folk song wasn't as rousing but Fernanda knew all the words and soon her sister was joining in, their two voices filling the workshop.

'You're a good little singer.' Violetta patted her on the head. 'Now, in a few minutes I want you to run on home and set the table, then you can read your book. I must carry on working here for a little while. Do you remember I'm visiting my friend at the hospital tomorrow? I can't be sure when I will be home, what with the strikers and the roadblocks, but you know that if it gets dark and I'm not back, you can go and knock next door.'

'I won't be scared,' Fernanda lied.

Violetta sat back down behind her workbench. She patted her knee. 'Come here for a minute.'

Fernanda climbed onto her lap, even though she was a big girl of seven and three quarters and far too old for cuddles. She snuggled against Violetta's soft sweater.

'You smell so nice, Letta. You smell like roses.'

Violetta fiddled with the coin that dangled from a thin

leather thong around her neck. Fernanda hadn't seen it before; she wondered where her sister had found it.

'One day this war will be over and everything will be different,' Violetta said.

'Will all the people in the world be friends?' It was something Fernanda often wondered.

'I hope so, darling.' Violetta hugged Fernanda tightly. It made Fernanda's itchy jumper scratch against her skin but she didn't want her to stop. She stroked her big sister's silky locks, giggling as the curls sprang up again. Her fingers caught against something in the back of Violetta's hair.

'Look, an olive leaf.' Fernanda held it up.

'I wonder how that got there.' Violetta took the leaf, turning it over in her hand, a soft smile on her face as though her thoughts were far away again.

'Do you think the trees get really sad when the people come and take all the olives away?'

'Yes,' Violetta said. 'I think they must get sad, when the fruit is gone and the sky is cold and grey. But then they remember that the winter can't last forever. And that spring will come again.'

50

Stella fastened the catch on her bra; she pulled a T-shirt over her head. It was strange to realise she was sixty today. With all that had occurred over the last few days, her so-called landmark birthday seemed quite irrelevant. Still, it was nice to wake up to messages on her phone from Lauren and Carol and to know she would be celebrating over dinner with Gino that night.

Her younger sister stood by the mirror, drying off her hair. Marta showed no signs of remembering what day it was and that didn't matter a jot. It had been decades since Stella had celebrated any birthday with one of her siblings. But now she and Marta and Giovanni were reunited. That was worth any number of birthday wishes and fancy gifts.

'Did you sleep all right?' Stella said.

'Remarkably well. This is way more comfortable than it looks.' Marta indicated the narrow pull-out bed.

'Much better than the couch.' Stella smiled.

'And less noisy than sleeping under Domenico's room! I

don't know who's the worse snorer, him or our brother. They could form their own band!'

'I don't know how the two of them didn't wake up when one of us was showering, the way the pipes clank.' Stella gave her hair a quick comb, feeling rather than seeing what she was doing, as Marta was still hogging the mirror.

Marta drew a pencil line around her lips. She twisted her tube of lipstick, painting on a berry red.

'Very glam! We're only getting our breakfast at the village bar; this isn't Sanremo, you know. I can't believe Joe and I were staying in a hotel just a few roads away from where you're living.'

'I still can't believe you're here.'

'I wouldn't have come back if Joe hadn't booked that trip. I thought everyone despised me, blaming me for causing Papà's death. I thought you and Giovanni and Mamma hated me.'

'Mamma was shocked and upset but she never hated you, I promise you that. And neither did Giovanni and I. We thought you never wanted to see us again because we didn't stand up for you when our parents tried to keep you and Gino apart.'

'All those years...'

Marta frowned. 'Last night Domenico told me he and Papà had argued the morning Papà died.'

'Do you know what about?' Stella trod carefully. Domenico and Fernanda had vowed not to unmask her nonno, not wanting to reopen old wounds. But perhaps a few drinks at the festa had loosened her uncle's tongue.

'He didn't say. Only that it was about something Nonno did when they were kids.'

'It was a long time ago.' Stella kept her eyes down, checking for her purse and sunglasses before fastening her handbag.

'I told Domenico there was no point looking back. Whatever Nonno did or didn't do in the past, none of us will ever know what was going on inside his head. It's too easy to sit here making judgements about the past but none of us will really know what made people act the way they did.'

'I guess you're right. Look at the things people said about Violetta. Now, are we going to the bar for coffee or is your beauty regime going to take all day?'

'You always were impatient.' Marta stashed the lipstick away.

Stella put her finger to her lips. 'We'd better be quiet. We don't want to wake our pair of sleeping beauties.'

Marta picked up her sandals. They crept barefooted down the stairs.

The tables outside the bar were all taken. Amy gave Stella a little wave.

'Hey! Come and sit with me.'

'Thanks! You two met last night, didn't you?' Stella ushered her sister towards one of the spare seats. 'Oh, there's only three chairs, we'll need a fourth.'

'Leo's not coming. He's making an early start on his next project. He's so fired up after the success of the plaque.'

'Is everything okay with Leo?' Stella said. 'Tell me to shut up if I'm out of order but you seemed so happy last night.'

'That's the problem.' Amy sighed.

Marta stood up. 'I'll go inside and order at the bar.'

Amy passed her phone across the table. 'Last night I got this message from my brother Jack.'

JACK

Hope you had fun at the village party. Now where to next? My mates say Prague and Berlin both rock!

'Hmm. Why does he think you want to go there?'

'I told him I was staying here until after the unveiling. Now he assumes I'll go off travelling. He's amazed I've stayed so long in one village. Jack's been travelling all over: Mexico, Thailand, Japan... He's been rafting, bungee jumping, you name it. He's always been fearless...'

'He's visited all these places, done the backpacker trails but you've done something he hasn't. You've been living here. And you don't look to me like you want to leave.'

'I don't, but I don't know how to stay.'

'You and me both,' Stella said.

'Sorry it took so long. The coffee and pastries will be here in a minute. The poor woman is run off her feet,' Marta said. She sat back down.

'Amy's been telling me about her brother Jack's travels.'

Amy chewed the skin around her thumbnail. 'He must think I'm pretty dull, staying here.'

'You didn't look like you were having a dull time last night.' Marta's eyes flashed mischievously. She moved her bag so that the waitress could put down her tray. 'You don't really want to leave, do you?'

'Sometimes the biggest adventure is staying somewhere and not going anywhere,' Stella said.

'But even if you stand still, things change,' Marta said. 'Remember how Mamma used to send us to pick up the goat's cheese and flour from Signora Togliatti? I can hardly believe her old *alimentari* has closed down.'

'Uh!' Stella spluttered. She began to cough.

Marta slapped her on the back. 'Are you okay? Here, have some water.'

Stella chugged back half a glass in one go.

'I forgot all about it!' she exclaimed once she'd recovered.

'What a fool! I walked past it on my first day here but I haven't been back that way... Of course, why didn't I think? The For Sale sign – is it still in the window?'

'It was yesterday.'

'We've got to go there!' Stella pushed back her chair.

'What's the rush? The place has been closed up for years. There's still a poster in the window advertising some festa from 2019.' Marta tore a piece off her *focaccia dolce*, popping the sweetened bread into her mouth.

'But don't you see?' Stella was almost shaking with excitement. 'It's perfect!'

'Stella! What are you wittering on about?' Marta said.

'I know!' Amy said. 'It's where you could sell the olive oil you and Gino will produce, and the herbs and whatever else. It's not too big and it could be a bargain if it's been sitting on the market for years.'

Stella's excitement ebbed away as quickly as it had come. 'It's no use. I've only got a few months' redundancy money and it will need doing up. I won't have nearly enough.'

'You could rent out your house back home or even sell it,' Marta said. 'Come on. We'll go and take a proper look at it.'

'There's no harm in looking, is there?' Amy said.

'Okay, you've convinced me.' Did she really have a chance?

* * *

The smeared windows, broken step and old newspapers strewn across the floor of Signora Togliatti's old shop didn't matter. Stella could visualise a fresh white interior, a shiny counter, a clutch of olives painted on a sign over the door. She stood in the street, heart racing, feeling that she could hardly breathe.

'Dream, Stella. Tell me what you see,' Marta said.

'Rows of bottles of home-grown olive oil. Not just litres and half litres for local customers but small quantities that passing tourists could pop in their bags and take home.'

'What else would they buy?' Marta stretched out her arms, seemingly measuring the width of the window with her hands.

'Olive tapenade to smear on crostini, dried herbs in little bags...'

Marta took out her phone. She started to punch in some numbers. 'I'm ringing them. Let's find out what they want for it.'

Stella opened her mouth to protest.

'You might as well know. What harm can it do?'

Stella's stomach twisted. This was when her dream died. But she said: 'Sure, I may as well know.'

Amy's face was tense. 'I've got my fingers crossed so tightly for you.'

They both lapsed into silence, watching Marta march up and down, the phone clamped to her ear. Finally, she wandered back towards them, still talking. She handed the phone to Stella.

Stella took the phone. 'Sorry. Could you say that again?'

The woman at the end of the line repeated the asking price. A price that made Stella want to squeal and shout and jump and fling her arms up in the air.

'So, are you interested?'

She tried to keep her voice steady. 'Yes. Yes, I am. Very interested.'

The call finished. Stella held the phone, knowing she was staring at it as if she'd never seen one before.

'*Brava! Brava!*' Marta kissed her.

'Oh, Stella, I'm so happy for you.' Amy's voice caught. 'Sorry. I'm feeling a bit emotional. The last few days have been so wonderful. Fernanda's so happy and Leo's got more enquiries about commissions than he could ever deal with. And now you and Gino – well, you're going to make your dreams come true. Ignore me, I'm just feeling sorry for myself.'

'We all feel like that sometimes when a holiday comes to an end,' Stella said.

Amy looked at her as if she couldn't quite believe what she'd said.

'Sorry. I wasn't thinking. My mind was on packaging.'

'For the olive oil? Wouldn't you just put it in glass bottles?'

'Yes, for the litre bottles but for the little souvenirs I was thinking of something quite different. Something special.'

'Like what?' Marta said.

'Decorative pottery jugs for the olive oil; tapenade and pastes in little lidded pots. Nothing factory produced. I'd want all handmade. Of course, I could import but then there's the risk of breakages...'

Stella smiled as the expression on Amy's face changed.

'Handmade pottery?' Amy sounded cautious.

'Of course, but I don't know how you feel about getting involved.'

Amy pulled her into a huge hug. 'I feel like I'm about to start the biggest adventure of my life.'

Marta clapped her hands together. 'I don't care if it's only ten in the morning, this deserves a celebration. Who's coming back to the bar with me?'

'I'll meet you there,' Amy said.

'I think I can guess where you're going.' Stella smiled. 'Go on, run and tell him your news.'

Amy didn't hesitate a moment longer, dashing across the courtyard and running down the winding street as fast as she could on the uneven paving. She was bursting to tell Mum and

Dad her news, not to mention Jack and the friends she hoped she could persuade to come out and visit her. But before she did any of that, she had to find Leo. She couldn't wait to see his face when she told him she was here to stay.

In her haste she almost shot past the entrance to his workshop.

'Leo!' She had to yell above the sound of Oasis blasting from his old CD player.

'Amy?' He removed his goggles. 'I didn't expect to see you until later on.'

'Oh.' A pang of doubt hit her. What if he'd said all his sweet words safe in the knowledge she'd soon be gone? 'I had to see you. I...'

'Don't look so worried. What is it?'

'That second-hand potter's wheel you mentioned. Do you think it's still for sale?'

'You mean...' He sounded as nervous as she did.

'Yes,' she butted in. And then it all came tumbling out: the old *alimentari*, Stella's plans, Amy's part in it all, the pots and jars she planned to make.

'Stop!' Leo said.

'Sorry, I know I'm jabbering on.'

'It's not that. I want to hear everything but I need to leave in a few minutes to meet Nonna. And if you don't stop talking I won't have time to do something I have to do this very moment.'

'Oh, what's that?'

He reached out a hand and traced her upper lip with a rough fingertip, the look in his eyes telling her more than any words could say. And now his mouth was on hers, sending a thrilling shiver right through her. She wrapped her arms around him, holding him tighter, heedless of his dust-covered overalls pressed against her clean cotton dress. 'You're staying,' he murmured between kisses. 'I can hardly believe it.'

Eventually, he let her go. She opened her eyes, almost surprised to see she was still standing on the concrete floor, surrounded by slabs of marble and a tool-strewn workbench. The setting wasn't nearly as romantic as the old archway where they'd shared their first kiss but this moment was another she would never forget.

* * *

Stella watched Amy's departing back. 'Okay, let's get going. It's a bit early for a drink, but who cares?'

'Sure,' Marta said. She set off towards the bar at an ambling pace, pausing to admire an array of pot plants by someone's front steps, stopping to chat to an old man carrying his shopping home and bending to stroke a cat. Stella was surprised by her sister's tardiness, it was almost as though she were waiting for Amy to come back and catch them up. As they got nearer to the bar, Stella could see there was only one empty table outside but that still didn't cause Marta to speed up.

'Let's sit inside,' Marta said. It seemed a strange decision on such a nice day but Stella was on too much of a high to argue.

Marta appeared to hang back as Stella pushed open the door. Her brother Giovanni was standing just inside.

'You decided to get out of bed at last,' Stella quipped.

'It's not every day my big sister turns sixty.' Giovanni grinned.

'You remembered!'

'Of course we did. We all did.' Marta gestured towards the *Buon compleanno* banner strung across the wall behind the bar.

A cork popped loudly. Stella swung around. Gino was holding an open bottle of basurà rosa.

'Happy birthday, my darling!'

Stella accepted a glass. 'To old friends and new ones! Talking of which...' She looked towards a rather pink-faced Amy, who'd just flown through the door.

'Ah, there you are, Amy, I thought you'd got lost,' Marta joked. She held up her glass. 'Happy birthday to Stella! And a toast to all of us, to adventures, near or far.'

Amy's hand reached for the coin nestling at the base of her throat. 'And to Grandpa Lance and Violetta, for changing all our lives.'

'And now we have cake,' Leo said, appearing from the door leading to the kitchen. 'Papà wanted to try and make you a *torta sacripantina*.'

Stella thought of the fancy tiered liqueur-soaked sponges. 'That would be impressive.'

'But sadly too ambitious,' Gino said. 'So, I was persuaded to leave your cake to the experts.'

'You can come out now, Nonna,' Leo called.

And out of the kitchen stepped Fernanda, her arm through Domenico's. He was carrying a pale-yellow sponge cake on a round tray crowned with six lit candles. A *panarello*: the soft almond birthday cake beloved by every Ligurian child.

'I didn't think we could fit sixty candles on,' Domenico said.

'You made this?' Stella said.

He laughed. 'Don't be daft, Fernanda did.'

'I hope you like it,' Fernanda said.

Tears filled Stella's eyes, blurring the diamond pattern Fernanda had so carefully stencilled on the top. 'I haven't had one of these for years. Too many years.'

'Blow out the candles, Stella, make a wish,' Marta urged.

'Go on, Stella!' Amy said.

'What are you going to wish for?' Gino asked.

'I can't say. You know it's bad luck to tell.'

In truth, Stella had nothing left to wish for. She closed her eyes and blew softly on the flames.

* * *

MORE FROM VICTORIA SPRINGFIELD

Another book from Victoria Springfield, is available to order now here:

https://mybook.to/NewVictoriaBackAd

ACKNOWLEDGEMENTS

Firstly, a thank you to all at Boldwood for putting a third book of mine out into the world. Special thanks to my editor, Francesca Best, who always comes up with the perfect tweaks.

Thank you to my agent Camilla Shestopal of Shesto Literary for representing me for more than five years and calmly dealing with all the ups and downs along the way.

The village of Leto is a fictional one but the inspiration, as always, comes from real life. Whilst planning this book I visited the village of Ceriana which like Leto is a bus ride north of Sanremo. This gorgeous little place gave me masses of ideas for the look of 'my' village and some of its layout. I also spent a few days in Sanremo where Stella and Joe start their ill-fated holiday. A day trip to Alassio turned into two more visits, the second of which included a look inside the town's tennis club where Amy meets Stella's old love Gino.

The backstory of Gino's aunt Violetta might seem fanciful but Italian women played a key role in the Italian resistance, carrying maps rolled up in the handles of their bicycles and hiding heavy guns in baskets of laundry. If my story has sparked your interest I recommend Caroline Moorehead's fascinating *A House in the Mountains – The Women who Liberated Italy from Fascism*. Grandpa Lance's past adventures were inspired by travel writer Eric Newby's classic *Love and War in the Apennines* and *From Liguria with Love* by Michael Ross both of which provide first-hand accounts of the derring-do of the escaped prisoners of war and the bravery of the ordinary Italian folk and resistance fighters who risked everything to help those strangers in hiding.

Finally, thank you to all the encouraging writers I have met along the way especially the members of the marvellous Romantic Novelists' Association and members of Anita Faulkner's fantastic Chick Lit and Prosecco Facebook group.

You can find me on:

Facebook: https://www.facebook.com/VictoriaSpringfield Author

Instagram: @VictoriaSWrites

X: @VictoriaSWrites

ABOUT THE AUTHOR

Victoria Springfield writes contemporary 'wish you were here' evocative women's fiction set in Italy. Her feel-good books follow unforgettable characters of all ages as they deal with love, loss, friendship and family secrets. Readers can feel the sunshine!

Download your exclusive bonus content from Victoria Springfield here:

Follow Victoria on social media here:

facebook.com/VictoriaSpringfieldAuthor
x.com/victoriaswrites
instagram.com/victoriaswrites
bookbub.com/authors/victoria-springfield

ALSO BY VICTORIA SPRINGFIELD

An Italian Island Secret

One Summer in Italy

The Italian Village in the Hills

Boldwod

Boldwood Books is an award-winning fiction publishing company seeking out the best stories from around the world.

Find out more at www.boldwoodbooks.com

Join our reader community for brilliant books, competitions and offers!

Follow us
@BoldwoodBooks
@TheBoldBookClub

Sign up to our weekly deals newsletter

https://bit.ly/BoldwoodBNewsletter